monsoonbooks

THE ENGLISH CONCUBINE

Dawn Farnham is the author of *The Red Thread*, *The Shallow Seas*, *The Hills of Singapore* and *The English Concubine* (which comprise The Straits Quartet, a bestselling series of historical romance set in 19th-century Singapore), *A Crowd of Twisted Things*, a novel set in 1950 Singapore, as well as numerous short stories, plays and children's books. A former longterm resident of Singapore, Dawn now calls Perth, Australia, home. Learn more about Dawn at *www.dawnfarnham.com*.

The English Concubine is the fourth and final volume in The Straits Quartet.

Praise for *The Straits Quartet*

'Immaculately researched' *The Daily Telegraph*, UK

'Multiple protagonists and perspectives, both Eastern and Western, and elaborate description transport the reader to a fascinating time and place brimming with mystical and poetic flourishes' *Booklist*, USA

'Exceptionally well-written ... A beautiful story to relish on every page' *Review of the Historical Novels Society*

'Rollicking saga ... a brilliant evocation of the settlement in its early days, both in its physical details and socio-cultural nuances' *Expat Living*, Singapore

'Thoroughly enjoyable historical romance' *Lifestyle*, Singapore

BOOKS BY DAWN FARNHAM

A Crowd of Twisted Things

The Straits Quartet
The Red Thread (VOL.1)
The Shallow Seas (VOL.2)
The Hills of Singapore (VOL.3)
The English Concubine (VOL.4)

ANTHOLOGIES FEATURING SHORT STORIES
BY DAWN FARNHAM

Crime Scene Singapore
Crime Scene Asia (VOL.1)
Love and Lust in Singapore
The Best of Southeast Asian Erotica

The English Concubine

Passion and Power in 1860s Singapore

DAWN FARNHAM

monsoonbooks

First published in 2013
by Monsoon Books Pte Ltd
71 Ayer Rajah Crescent #01-01, Singapore 139951
www.monsoonbooks.com.sg

ISBN (print): 978-981-4423-62-5
ISBN (ebook): 978-981-4423-23-6
ISBN (box set): 978-981-4423-63-2

This second (updated) edition published in 2014

Copyright©Dawn Farnham, 2014

The moral right of the author has been asserted. All rights reserved. No part of this publication may be reproduced, stored in a retrieval system, or transmitted, in any form or by any means without the prior written permission of the publisher, nor be otherwise circulated in any form of binding or cover other than that in which it is published and without a similar condition being imposed on the subsequent purchaser.

Cover design by Cover Kitchen.

National Library Board, Singapore Cataloguing-in-Publication Data
Farnham, Dawn, 1949-
The English concubine : passion and power in 1860s Singapore / Dawn Farnham. – Second (updated) edition. – Singapore : Monsoon Books Pte Ltd, 2014.
pages cm. – (The Straits quartet ; vol. 4)
ISBN : 978-981-4423-62-5 (paperback)

1. Scandals – Fiction. 2. Triads (Gangs) – Singapore – History – 19th century – Fiction. 3. Singapore – History – 19th century – Fiction. I. Title. II. Series: Straits quartet ; vol. 4.

PR6106
823.92 -- dc23   OCN859514278

Printed in Singapore
17 16 15 14   2 3 4 5

This book is dedicated to all those who strive to keep alive the rich historical heritage of Singapore.
In particular, Geraldine Lowe-Ismael who has been an advocate for and dedicated guide to the stories and memories of Singapore's past for over forty years.
Also to the Friends of the Museums of Singapore, an organisation of passionate volunteers who support heritage in Singapore. There is no doubt that my time as a docent in the Peranakan Museum inspired this series.

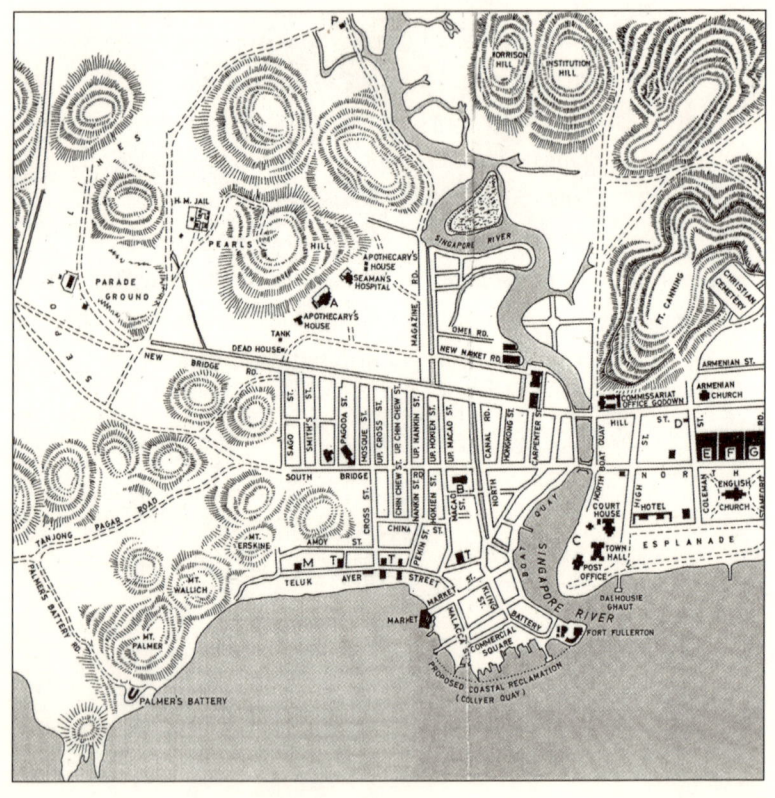

Singapore Town in 1862

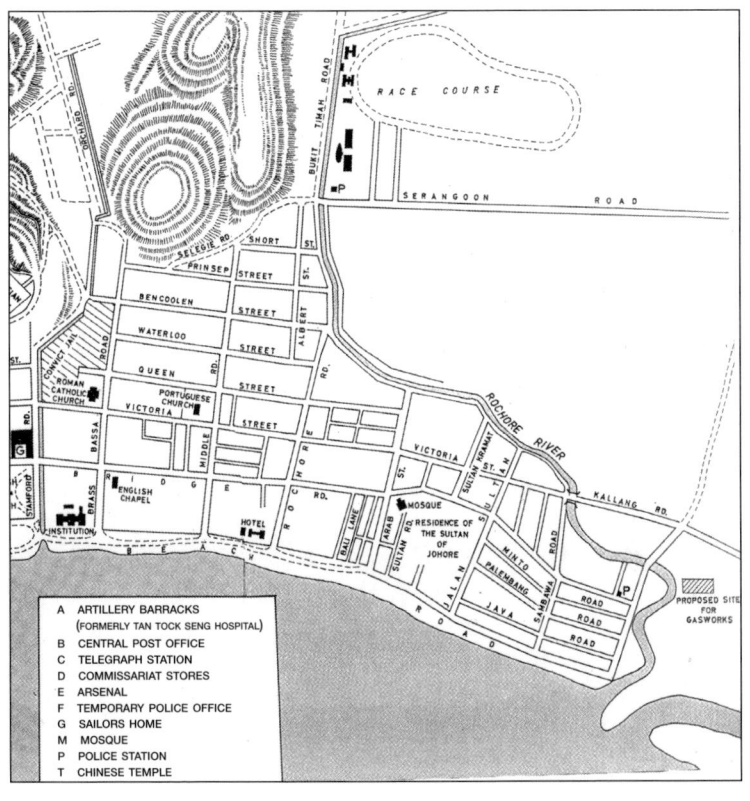

Based on a map of Singapore and environs by J.M. Moniot,
Surveyor General Straits Settlements, 1862

Glossary

Ah ku: Chinese prostitute.

Ang moh: A racial epithet to describe caucasians. Literally means red hair.

Chandu: Refined opium for retail sale.

Chintengs: Revenue police. The opium and spirit farmer controlled a private police force and a small army of informers in order to prevent illegal production and sale of chandu over which the legitimate opium farmer had a monopoly.

Chukang: Headquarters of the Kangchu, see below. The legacy of the pepper and gambier agriculture lives on in Singapore in place names like Choa Chu Kang and Yio Chu Kang.

Kajang: Palm leaf in Malay

Kang Chu: 'Lord of the River'. Name given to the Chinese headman of river settlements and plantations.

Kapitan: Kapitan Cina was originally a Portuguese title for the leader of a Chinese enclave which provided colonial authorities with a method of indirect rule. The Dutch and British adopted it though the British abolished the title in 1825.

Kongsi: "Company", a generic Chinese term for a range of social and economic configurations that includes everything from business partnerships to clan and regional associations to secret triad societies. The kongsi emerged in Southeast Asia in the 18th century and, although they soon absorbed the ideas, rituals and oath-taking of the triad, their origins are, first and foremost, an economic brotherhood which sprang up round the mining, agricultural and commercial interests of the overseas Chinese as they spread throughout the region.

For the single male migrant Chinese in 'barbarian' lands, where family and Confucian relationships had been left behind, what filled the gap was the kongsi, the 'government' of the Chinese, who were always left by local rulers to take care of their own internal affairs. The kongsi were sometimes organised on dialect and clan lines, sometimes not, depending on individual situations. This could change over time. The triad organisation gathered different kongsi under its umbrella of common Chinese brotherhood and in the nineteenth century the triad was inextricably bound up in kongsi affairs.

The Shan Chu, Lord of the Kongsi, was always leader of the triad and always the richest merchant who had access to capital and had the greatest control over the labouring masses of coolies. He was the 'head of the corporation' with access to many thousands of 'brother' foot soldiers to do his bidding. In 19th century Singapore the colonial authorities knew nothing about the membership, authority, activities or internal workings of the kongsi.

Nyai: The native mistress or concubine of a foreign male.

Revenue farmer: Colonial governments of Southeast Asia 'farmed' out annual rights to run opium, spirit, gambling, sireh and other monopolies in return for a monthly payment.

Samseng: Gangster.

Surat Sungei: 'River document'. A permit given by a Malay leader to a Chinese headman which allowed him to establish plantations along the river banks. In return, the headman paid taxes on any profits. The lease had to be renewed after a specific period of time.

Towkay: Wealthy merchant.

Triad: The Heaven and Earth Society (Tiandihui) emerged in the 1760s as a brotherhood of disaffected young men aimed at the overthrowing of the Manchu Qing dynasty and the restoration of the Ming, gathered round the worship of Guan Yu, a legendary third century BC general, the epitome of loyalty and righteousness. The Tiandihui finaced itself with robbery and violence. As it spread throughout China it branched into different groups with different names, many of which adopted the number three – Three Dots Society; Three Harmonies Society. The term 'triad' in English was applied first in a study of the secret socities in 1821 by Dr. William Milne, principal of the Anglo Chinese College at Malacca, in recognition of the prevalence of the number three in societies' names. The Chinese call it the Tiandihui or more commonly the Hongmen, the Vast Gate.

Excise farm: The practice of colonial governments to 'farm' out to the highest bidder, the licence to manufacture and sell profitable commodities like opium or spirits. In a free port like Singapore, this was often the only source of income the colonial authorities could rely on.

Sangkek Um/Pak Chindek: The wedding mistress and master of ceremony, they were the specialists required to advise on and conduct the lengthy, complex and elaborate Peranakan wedding ceremony.

1

'The whole of Singapore is going to the dogs.'

As if to lend credence to these words, half a dozen rib-caged mongrels on the riverside set about each other, growling and snarling over some slops hurled onto the fetid bank of low tide.

For the thousands of inhabitants of the squat kajang-roofed boats, the river served every daily purpose. When the river water dragged away to its rendezvous with the ocean, the wind carried the stench of the muddy sludge over the government offices, which lay mere feet away, and a choice had to be made between cloacal odour and sweltering heat. The newspapers said it killed the Chinese and Klings who lived on and along it even though scores of Indian convicts laboured up to their knees on every low tide, bucketing out the foul mud and filth that built up against the quay walls.

The press raised fears of the noxious gases rising from the rubbish-dumped upper river which endangered the town. Dr. Cowper, the military surgeon, said the gangrenous bodies of sick Chinese and the improper disposal of corpses was to blame for the cholera epidemic in Chinatown and Kampong Glam. Heated debate went back and forth in the newspaper regarding the controversial theory that the disease was spread by polluted water and not foul air with neither side winning the argument. In the meantime the bodies of the dying continued to litter the streets and the riverside, and ten funerals in the Chinese and native cemeteries took place every day.

The Chinese didn't read the newspapers and held firecracker-popping processions with drums and gongs, carrying palanquins of deities and great smoking tubs of joss. Only in this way could they exorcise the power of *huoluan*, the sudden chaos, which they knew perfectly well was caused by the malign forces of demons serving the Wangye, the Kings of Pestilence.

Robert Macleod, Commissioner of Police, rubbed his shoulder, a dark mood hanging on him like the river smell. An old wound had begun to give him trouble but this was not the cause of his bad temper.

The editor of *The Straits Times* blamed the police for not ensuring more sanitary conditions to dispel the noxious odours in their districts and accused them of misreporting deaths. The proliferation of half-starved men and dogs was a bane on his life. The crazed man in China who thought he was the brother of Jesus Christ had ignited a vast uprising and brought thousands of criminals and desperate men on every junk to Singapore. Piracy was carried out within sight of the shore. The *Free Press* reported that there were more whores in Singapore than respectable women and that two-thirds of the Chinese male population were opium addicts.

But despite this formidable litany of ills, none of these was the cause of his bad temper.

He transferred his attention to the men atop Government Hill. From the river's edge they looked like scurrying ants. The house, which had been the Governor of Singapore's home since Raffles' time, had been demolished and hundreds of Chinese coolies and Indian convicts were building up and flattening the top of the hill, rock by rock.

'A fort,' he spluttered. 'Ridiculous to set a fort miles from the shore all for the sake of a mutiny which took place a thousand miles away. Just because it scared the damned Indian government to death. What has that to do with us? Who will attack us and how, with a fort on this hill, out of range of enemy ships, overlooking the very town it should defend, will we avoid blowing the place to bits? The cannon are trained on Chinatown, for God's sake. And it is to be named for that stupendous idiot Charles Canning, the man virtually responsible for the mutiny in the first place. It's intolerable. And all these new names for perfectly good streets. I hardly know what anyone is talking about. Did you know that Tavern Street is now Bonham and Commercial Square renamed Raffles Place. Why ...'

Charlotte Manouk placed a hand on her brother's arm.

'Robbie, for heaven's sake, I know, but I want to talk to you of Alexander.'

In truth Charlotte, too, like all of the town, was aghast at the works into which poor Singapore had been thrown because of the rebellion in India two years ago. The British government had got a terrible fright. In consequence the Crown had gathered the government of India into the Colonial Office, ending a hundred years of East India Company rule. At this news, the Straits Settlements pricked up their ears and sought to extricate themselves from their own indifferent Company authority and petitioned to be made a Crown Colony with direct appeal to London. But that was not to be. She was to continue to be governed from Calcutta who cared not a whit for the island of Singapore or its interests, yet, like all of Her Majesty's colonies, must be fortified whether she needed it or not.

Robert ignored his sister.

'We need more police. Crime is rampant because the coolies have no means of livelihood. Moving Tock Seng's hospital from Pearl's Hill to the swamps of Balestier Plain means a death warrant and no-one dare go there and wail if they are dragged away. I have fourteen police officers in a town of over fifty thousand. Yet funds are found for useless forts which will never fire a shot and Collyer runs around building batteries and redoubts, barracks and magazines, walls and fortifications as if his life depended ...'

'Robbie!'

Robert threw an annoyed glance at his sister though these considerations were also not the cause of his bad temper.

'Well, don't bother me with Alexander. You have spoiled him rotten, indulged his every whim and financed his appalling habits. You have known this for the past two years. And now he has gone too far. What is it? A married woman, the Dean's wife no less. No, sister. It is your fault and you must find a way out.'

Charlotte looked downcast.

'Rob, don't be angry. I know you're right. But I have no idea how to tell him about, well, about, any of this.'

Robert sighed and folded Charlotte's arm into his. They walked slowly back towards the Court House.

'I know. You are scarce less scandalous than him. Worse, actually.'

His laugh was tinged with irony.

'Did you hear the new pastor has fulminated from the pulpit about fornicators etcetera? That means you. And me. And the whole town.'

'Yes, yes,' Charlotte sighed. 'We will not inherit the Kingdom of God. At least this one has not mentioned me by name and put the mark of Cain on me. And he seems a little more concerned about the drug addictions of virtually the entire town. But I was talking of Alex.'

He patted her hand. 'You have spoiled him because of guilt. Because there are secrets and lies between you. Tell him the truth.'

He stopped and turned Charlotte to face him.

'Tell him all the truth.'

Charlotte shook her head. 'Not all. I dare not.'

Robert dropped his sister's arm.

'Then you will pay the price. He is coming back from Scotland under a cloud, but older, eighteen, a young man with all his wits. He will find out. Be warned.'

Robert's tone was severe. He was fed up with Charlotte's nonsense with the boy who needed a good slap. But this was most certainly not the cause of his bad temper.

'Well, I'm in a terrible mood and not worth the talking to. I must sort out this divorce business by hook or by crook.'

Charlotte turned away, now as annoyed as her brother.

'For heaven's sake Robbie, Teresa will never divorce you and you cannot find grounds to divorce her. You might as well get used to it.'

Robert glowered at her and strode away.

Charlotte was sick to the back teeth of the question of Robert's blessed divorce. If he wasn't moaning about the state of the town and lack of money he was going on and on about this divorce until he drove all his acquaintance distracted. Really he had become grumpy and self-centred.

Ever since Shilah, his Anglo-Indian mistress, and mother of his eldest daughter Amber, had become pregnant he talked of nothing else. He had become a bore on the subject of the new Matrimonial Causes Act, which he knew by heart, and now so did

19

Charlotte and all his long-suffering friends.

The Act made marriage a contract rather than a sacrament and made allowance for divorce in a civil court. To rid himself of a wife a man had only to prove his wife's adultery which, since Teresa lived an exemplary life with their son Andrew amidst the copious numbers of aunts and uncles of the enormous da Souza family, there was nothing he could do. Not an ounce of scandal attached itself to Teresa and it drove Robert mad.

He had married Teresa because she was upright and respectable and he had been too ambitious and too scared to risk condemnation by marrying a half-blood woman, the illegitimate child of convicts. But Charlotte was sure that he had loved Teresa too, as she still loved him, and he had been happy and contented with his wife for many years. Yet somehow this passion for Shilah had been re-ignited and he had found the courage to leave Teresa, even after the birth of Andrew; had risked losing his position, risked his reputation. He had survived it all, to his credit, because he was invaluable to the town, and recently had risen to the official position of Commissioner. Now, with a new child on the way, he had become obsessed with marrying Shilah.

'Guilt, guilt. He is right, perhaps. We are all driven by guilt,' Charlotte said to herself.

She turned, raising her parasol against the sun and the inevitable stares of passers-by and gazed over the river to Boat Quay and the godown of Baba Tan, now the commerce and property of Zhen, the man she had shared her life with for the past three years and by whom she had a daughter.

A year ago some visiting wag had laughingly dubbed her the English concubine over a dinner full of drunken revellers and it had found its way into the column of 'Delta', the town's self-appointed wit and purveyor of gossip. It had stuck. The fact that she was Scottish was hardly the point. She tried to laugh it off but increasingly she felt the power of the endless tittle-tattle. It wore away at you. Drip, drip, drip. A rebuff here, a whispering there, a row of open stares, even public denunciation. She was never free of it, on either side of the river, and it took its toll.

This was the veiled life she had kept from both Alexander and her younger son, Adam. But deeper than this was the dark secret of Alexander's real paternity. The terrifying fact that he was not, as he believed, the son of Tigran Manouk, one of the great Dutch Armenian merchants of the East Indies. This father was his pride and in such a lineage lay Alexander's deepest feelings of belonging. To deny it would, she feared, shatter him utterly and destroy his affection for her as Tigran's widow. Children cared so little for the truth in such matters and she knew he would blame her, judge her, condemn her and wish she had never told him. So she did not.

She felt the ache creep into her neck. It would crawl up into her head and grip her like a vice. She turned her steps to home and some quiet rest. Soon he would be here and, for the first time, she admitted to herself the unpalatable truth that she was not looking forward to seeing her elder son.

2

'We come together to honour the yishi of the Ming, patriotic guardsmen of our Chinese legacy and renew our pledge to overthrow the foreign Qing dynasty and restore the Ming.'

Three hundred men shouted *fanqing fuming*, with more or less enthusiasm, to the funerary tablets lining the walls of the Five Tiger Shrine which stood in the courtyard of the great lodge of the Ghee Hin Kongsi in Rochor.

The Deputy Mountain Lord, Fu Shan Chu Teo, rose and the formal part of the evening ended. The Mountain Lord, Shan Chu Wei Sun Wei, was in China.

Zhen and Qian rose too with the others, all important and, above all, wealthy members of the Hongmen, the triad society which, since the violent eruptions between the Teochew and Hokkien sects four years ago, had united all the different dialect groups in Singapore in relative peace. They made their way to the banqueting room.

'Restore the Ming,' Zhen said and shook his head. 'Restore their youth more like. We're the only ones under fifty.'

Naturally he attended, like all the towkay, the annual tribute to the spiritual ancestors of the kongsi. The kongsi was in effect the government of the Chinese in Singapore and no-one who wished to have any influence here could ignore it. It provided welfare and employment for the thousands of coolies pouring into the Straits at every tide. It controlled the labour force, regulated affairs in its own courts of law, its leaders had muscle and capital and much business was conducted in its shadow. But these old-fashioned oaths meant nothing, at least to him.

Hong Boon Tek sidled, slug-like, over to Zhen, mopping his forehead.

'There is a rumour the Mountain Lord is dead,' he whispered. 'What do you hear?'

This rumour had circulated for the last week or so and some sort of announcement had been expected. This had not come. Hong was so fat his eyes got lost inside the pockets of his cheeks. His breath smelled and he was always slick with sweat. All this would not have mattered had he been an agreeable man but he was mean, vindictive and venal. It was said he kept slave women on his plantation.

'Why ask me? Why don't you ask the Deputy Lord and see if he likes the question?'

Hong threw a glance around him, simpered and oozed away. Hong disliked him, but Hong disliked everyone and Zhen did not care.

'The leases come up in three months,' Qian said. 'He is not content with the spirit farm, he wants the opium lease too. If the leader is dead then the old syndicate will fall apart. It's Wei's money that bankrolls it.'

Zhen watched the men milling and whispering. Qian was merely stating the obvious.

'Who inherits? The son died.'

'I'm not sure. He had several daughters, didn't he? One married the Kapitan in Perak or someone like that? I can't

23

remember.'

'No, nor me.'

'Have you thought of what I asked?'

The two men joined the crowd in the banqueting hall. Rice wine began to circulate. The noise level rose.

'Qian, I told you. They won't have you.'

Qian pulled a face, poured a cup of wine and tossed it back.

'They would if you asked. I could sell two of the ah ku houses to you.'

Zhen glanced at Qian. This man was his closest friend. They had been through poverty and hunger together, endured the long and dangerous journey here to Singapore, faced tigers and misery in the jungle and the new adventures of marriage to strange men's daughters. In a moment of drunken brotherhood they had betrothed their children to each other.

But within the last two years Qian's fortunes had declined greatly. His wife, to whom, despite his own sexual proclivities, he had been surprisingly devoted, had died. Qian's father-in-law, Sang Che Sang, had been leader of the kongsi and had extensive plantations of gambier and pepper with which he financed the leases of the opium farm and the spirit farm, easily the two most lucrative pursuits in the region. Out of respect for the living relative of the former Lord of the Kongsi, Zhen suspected, creditors had bided their time.

The business had declined slowly. Qian did not have Sang's stature or control over the labour force which only a kongsi official could exert, nor his ruthless commercial acumen. When he lost the lease on the opium farm, he had no idea how to recover. Eventually, the gambier and pepper plantation was lost to him too, for without the opium farm and its sales to the tens of thousand of coolies on the island, there was little profit in it.

The land in Singapore had been stripped, ruined and abandoned, bled dry by the heavy demands of the cultivation. When the roads had been made out into the once impenetrable countryside, the colonial government had sent their surveyor to assess and tax the plantations.

Wei Sun Wei had instantly ceased all agriculture and ordered 4,000 labourers to leave Singapore and go to Johor where he was Kang Chu, the head of the river, with ten concessions along the entire east bank of the Johor River, as well as numerous others, employing thirty thousand coolies. He was Kapitan Cina and the most trusted ally of the new Temmengong Abu Bakar who had hegemony over the lands of Johor. The syndicate which Wei headed had had control of the Johor/Singapore joint opium farm for the last five years. Wei's rise from humble cloth pedlar to such wealth and power was legendary and on the lips and in the minds of every penniless coolie who set foot on the island.

When Qian's wife died, the creditors had swarmed out of the woodwork. The great Sang compound on High Street was sold. All that was left to Qian were his four brothels on Hong Kong Street and the small shophouse he lived in. Prostitution was a high-profit business, but even this could not keep up with his too-lavish lifestyle with the Malay boy who ruled him with bonds of lust.

'No. I forbid you to sell the ah ku houses. They are your only means of income. The problem is that greedy boy. Get rid of him and some sense would return to your life.'

Qian shrugged. He could no more do without Hafiz than stop breathing. The boy was as beautiful and sleek as a young god and knew how to make a man's body do things which made your blood ignite. He had found him in the brothel in Malacca and brought him here.

'Since my wife died, I have been alone. You don't understand.'

Zhen shrugged. Qian was besotted, head over heels for this spoilt boy upon whom he lavished money and gifts, diamond earpins, golden bracelets, silken clothes. He pranced through Chinatown dressed like a sultan with his pet monkey on his shoulder, turning heads wherever he passed. No speech would change anything.

'Anyway, the syndicate is for the big money boys.'

'You have money,' Qian said and threw him an acid look, 'and plenty of it.'

'I don't get involved in prostitution or the opium syndicate. And the consortium for the Klang tin mines will not have you.'

Zhen was part of a group of Chinese and European merchants bidding to lease the rich vein of tin in the Klang river basin from the current Sultan. But there was a dispute. There was always a dispute between the sultans. When the old fellow died the succession was always a mess, and each claimant sought British and Chinese aid to settle the disputes.

'In any case it is held up by the fighting between the brothers. Until that's fixed, well.'

'But by that time, we will be related, eh Zhen? Can we not advance the marriage of Lian and Ah Soon? Why wait? She is of marriageable age. Then the English merchants will see I am allied to you and will give me credit. Enough to get into your consortium or into the opium syndicate.'

Zhen felt immense exasperation. Qian just didn't listen to sense. He wanted his boy and his opium and the rest was ignored. He found Qian more and more tiresome. He had caused the problem with his son, Ah Soon, by taking him out of school where he was a clever scholar, fluent in English and Chinese, skilled at mathematics. Now Ah Soon was supposed to help manage the ah ku houses and Zhen knew he resented it. The English school with its Christian teachers installed lofty aims in its pupils. It was dangerous to put sons in them and then expect them to be you or fling them thoughtlessly back to earth. The friend Zhen had loved had somehow disappeared and this greedy, selfish, lustful man had taken his place.

'Qian, you must regulate your finances. As for Ah Soon, you were foolish to take him out of school. I told you. I'll pay the tuition if you allow him to go back.'

Qian shrugged.

'Ah Soon had better learn his business. He has no more need of Shakespeare or Jesus Christ. I came from nothing and he should know what that's like. Get his soft hands a little dirty.'

Zhen had no answer. This little speech was utter hypocrisy. Qian had inherited great wealth and squandered it. He was entirely to blame for the ruin of his family. He wanted the marriage to Lian so that Ah Soon would, in effect, become Zhen's issue as well. Ah Soon's increasingly problematic opium habit was another worrying issue. Zhen knew that sooner or later he would have to step in and sort the boy out. Qian was incapable of it.

The noise in the banqueting room rose another level as food was brought in. Three hundred men enjoying the convivial atmosphere meant a buzz heavier than a meeting of bees. The rice wine circulated and some men had moved away to the opium room for some pipes.

'Why won't you help me?' Qian whined and Zhen shook his head.

A large shape loomed over Zhen's shoulder.

Zhen turned and recognised Wang Chu Wei, head of the Red Rods. Zhen had been an enforcer himself in China years ago and he and Wang often drank together in the town where Wang controlled the gangs of samseng, the men who guarded the ah ku and coolie houses, the illegal gambling dens and the arrack taverns, and carried out any other activity which required them. He rose and clapped a hand on the shoulder of Wang.

'Ironfist Wang, how are you?'

Wang smiled. Two of his front teeth were missing. It just made him look even more frightening than his muscular build and the long scar down his cheek managed to.

'A little trouble with my teeth but otherwise well.'

'I told you to go to my shop. My apothecary will see to you.'

Wang bowed. He was terrified of all apothecaries.

'The Deputy Lord wishes to speak with you.'

'Yes, of course.'

Zhen followed Wang into a smaller room, dominated by the altar to Guan Yu, the spiritual head of all the brotherhoods. Four men were present. Wang closed the door. Before the altar, at a low table, sat the Deputy Mountain Lord, the Incense Master, head of ritual and ceremony, and the Vanguard, in charge of administration and recruitment. These officials were all merchants who occupied the highest positions in the kongsi. The fourth man, seated to one side, Zhen did not know. He bowed low and waited. Something was up.

'This is Master Zhen of the Tan Clan,' the Deputy Mountain Lord said, addressing the man seated to one side. 'He has a trading company and the biggest Chinese-owned fleet in Singapore. He has kinship links in Manila, Siam and Batavia. He is a filial son. His father-in-law's funeral is still talked about today. He also does much charitable work with the Tan Clan temple school, is benefactor of the Chinese hospital and the Thian Hock Keng temple. He is also advisor to the English governor.'

Zhen bowed in acknowledgement of this flattering account.

'From time to time only,' he said.

'This is Cheng Sam Teo, he is the Shan Chu's son-in-law, Kapitan Cina of Riau.'

Zhen bowed to the man. He was thin-lipped and sharp-eyed.

'Please sit.'

Zhen complied.

'What we have to say to you is private, you understand. We should like to ask you to keep this in confidence and to grant a favour.'

Zhen nodded. Whatever was going on, the kongsi leaders controlled the coolie labour force which loaded and unloaded his ships. They could be called out to strike at any moment. No merchant in his right mind would refuse them a favour.

'It is already granted, sir,' he said.

'The Shan Chu, Wei Sun Wei, has died in China.'

Zhen's face showed nothing. He had expected this, especially in the presence of the son-in-law.

'I am sorry. It is very regrettable,' he said.

He turned to Cheng. 'My deepest condolences to your family, sir.'

Cheng gave a nod of acknowledgement.

'The death of the Shan Chu is unfortunate,' the Deputy went on. 'But worse is that it coincides with the bid for the opium farm, which is currently being run by Wei Sun Wei's's deputy, Tay Ong Siang. He will certainly bid for the farm when it comes up. The bad blood between Tay and Hong Boon Tek has been on hold for five peaceful years but now we fear it will re-emerge. Both Tay and Hong want to be leader of the kongsi.'

This was bad news. Tay was a Teochew with his power base in Johor, the second biggest merchant after Wei Sun Wei. Hong was a Hokkien with the only remaining plantations in Singapore, as well as in Johor and Riau. He was the chief coolie broker in Singapore, the main supplier of girls to the brothels and held the spirit farm. The business of the plantations of gambier and pepper and their coolies, the business of the kongsi and the business of the excise farms were inextricably bound. Any power struggle spelled trouble for everyone.

'But how can either displace you,' he said, looking at the Deputy.

'I am too old and have not enough power to hold. I do not control labour.'

'Hong is wealthy and vindictive,' Cheng interjected. 'I am Kapitan at Riau, with the opium farm, but Hong has a network of smugglers who unload tons of chandu from his illegal farms and drive the price into the ground. I have my own chintengs, who police as best they are able but there are a thousand islands and the Dutch Resident sympathises but has little interest once he has the excise revenue.'

'I'm not sure how I can help,' Zhen said.

'You have no interest in the syndicate. Yet you have great wealth through your fleet of ships and your domination of the rice and hardwood trade.'

'Perhaps,' Zhen said cautiously, 'but I have no power to control the labour force.'

'I inherit my late father-in-law's Johor plantations.'

'I see,' Zhen said, though he was still not absolutely sure what was going on.

'I would bid to become the Shan Chu but, though I am heir to Wei Sun Wei, I am, at this time, unknown in Singapore or Johor. At this precarious time, the Grand Triad needs a man who can hold it together, has no interests in the syndicate rivalries. A man respected for his good works in the kongsi, and for his diplomacy.'

Cheng leant forward and gazed at Zhen intensely.

'It needs you.'

Zhen was astounded. 'Me?'

'We have spoken to the Temenggong, of course. He agrees with us. You have an amicable relationship with him and the agent Kerr and lawyer Napier.'

Zhen could only nod. They had thought this out carefully.

'If we back you, it is possible to block both Tay and Hong until the opium farm has been leased again for another year, through a new syndicate.'

'Your syndicate,' Zhen said, seeing where this was going.

'It is for the good of the kongsi,' Cheng said.

Zheng looked back to the Deputy. Clearly they wanted a puppet to hold on to things until they could put their syndicate together. In the meantime, he would be caught in the middle of the in-fighting which would take place. He would spend all his time doing nothing but placating a lot of greedy men intent on ruining each other.

The Incense Master looked down and the Vanguard searched in his ear with his long fingernail for some morsel. The Deputy merely gazed at Zhen and sucked his tea.

This was not a request. These men didn't make requests to a bondsman. How can I wriggle out of this, Zhen thought.

'I am perhaps too close to the Europeans.'

'On the contrary,' Cheng said, 'you are trusted by all members of the community. A good relationship with the English government benefits the kongsi. I hope you will do everything you can to introduce me to the ruling elite. To be known to the governor and the high officials will help with my bid for the farms.'

'You speak their language fluently. You are the acceptable

face of China for the ang moh,' the Deputy said.

Zhen was beginning to understand why he had been chosen.

'But there is perhaps one other problem. I have a close relationship with the police chief and his sister.'

Cheng's face remained impassive. 'Yes, of course. All the more reason for your recommendation to the government on matters Chinese to carry weight.'

Cheng turned away to pick up a tea cup.

'Though for the duration of your stewardship, that particular closeness might be misread by the general populace. Trust in you must be infinite and unquestionable to people with limited imaginations. Coolies are the most ignorant and superstitious of men, attributing their own actions or natural disaster to bad luck and malefic influences. The influence of a blue-eyed ghost woman over the head of the kongsi for example. You understand. Ignorance, but that is how they think.'

Zhen listened but he didn't like it. The man was ordering him to stay away from Xia Lou. The vanguard and the incense master were nodding. They all thought that way, not just the coolies. Zhen knew it.

'Mrs. Manouk is a Scottish woman, not a blue-eyed ghost. You allow yourself to talk most freely about my personal life.'

'Forgive me. It is regrettable I agree but these are the facts. She does not live under your roof and thus is seen not under your control, able to spread her malign influence more freely. No, I think it is safer, for the short time, to distance yourself from the personal nature of that relationship.'

Zhen stood and glared at Cheng.

'Please, I apologise. I am simply stating some facts as they are seen by others.'

Silence fell between the two men. Zhen thought furiously.

'We have more connections than you think.'

Cheng placed his cup carefully on its stand and looked at Zhen.

'My first daughter is the third wife of the Kapitan Cina of Batavia. Your eldest daughter is principal wife to his eldest son. My sister is the principal wife of the Shan Chu of the Semarang Kongsi, son of the Goei family.'

Zhen nodded. The Goei were the oldest and richest family of Straits Chinese in Semarang. Semarang was a great port in central Java. Much timber was shipped through it. Whoever controlled the kongsi there controlled the labour force which brought the logs to the mill and thence to the port. Cheng was telling him that he had influential tentacles in many levels of the Chinese society of the Dutch East Indies. This may have been the reason Wei Sun Wei had married his daughter to Cheng in the first place.

In one breath Cheng had threatened both Charlotte's business interests and his own, for the Manouk House had sugar lands and factories in Semarang. His commercial interests needed the Semarang labour force, but Zhen knew, too, that there was trouble in the Manouk House with debts linked to the sugar lands. Any such trouble now could cause her great financial distress.

Cheng rose and bowed to Zhen. 'I would be most obliged and would attempt to grant you any favours you might ask. We can be friends. It is only for a short time.'

The iron fist in the silken glove. All things considered, Zhen saw he had little choice.

'For the kongsi,' Zhen said.

3

'They say his leg was shot away and he has no use of one arm. What a sight he must be.' Sarah Blundell giggled and put her hand in front of her mouth, somewhat ashamed.

'How must it be for his poor wife? How on earth do they, well, *you know*.'

The two girls shared a look and giggled even harder.

'Do you think he has a wooden leg? Gosh, it must clonk on the floor and drive everyone distracted.'

The girls began to limp woodenly around the room, their legs becoming entangled in their skirts until they collapsed on the sofa in laughter.

Sarah arranged her blue and white voile dress more decorously over her silk petticoat. Amber too, took a moment to straighten her yellow figured organza over her hoop petticoat, making sure Sarah got a good look at this new item of apparel. Sarah chose to ignore it. The fashion for hoops and layers of petticoats, whalebone ribbing and vast flounces had recently arrived in Singapore but her father forbade it on grounds of extravagance and health.

'She must love him, mustn't she, with all that clanking,' Sarah said. 'I shall only marry for love. My cousin, Victoria, married some rich old stinker in Calcutta. For his money.'

'Gosh, I'll only marry for love too. Imagine, some old rich stinker with a big fat belly. Horrid.'

The girls giggled and picked up their teacups. Amber Macleod looked at her friend.

'But how shall it be for you, Sarah, when your father leaves? You shall miss him terribly.'

Sarah Blundell, last child of the eleven children of Governor Edmund Augustus Blundell, smiled at Amber.

'Oh not in the least bit. We girls have so little to do with him, after all; and he is so unpopular, you know, since he tried to sell off the land before the Beach Road houses and asked for a harbour tax. Everyone complains of him and he has probably had enough. I shall stay with Ann until I marry. Ann's husband, James, is popular with the other officers and I shall be thrown amongst them. And I am happy to be with Mother.'

Amber sipped her tea. Of course. Sarah's mother would not be returning to England with her father. She was Burmese and not actually the Governor's wife at all, but his nyai. She was a slightly built, shy woman who, naturally, never attended official functions and kept very much to herself. She had a small coterie of Burmese friends and family with whom she spent most of her time.

'It seems hard for your mother,' Amber said.

'It's hard to say. She says so little. But Father has made sure she is well cared for. He has bought her the new house at Kampong Glam, she has her friends and my widowed sister Mary with her children who will live with her. And of course they are both now so old, so perhaps she shall not miss him so much.'

Amber nodded. Of course, the Governor was decrepit, almost sixty. But still, his Burmese mistress had been by his side for more than thirty years and borne him eleven children. Can it truly be said that she would not be distressed at his departure? This was a subject which Amber thought on often, for the idea of her own father deserting her mother and sailing away to the other side of the world was one which she found most distressing. She was glad he was seeking to marry her. It was only right. She gave no thought to Teresa, her father's legitimate wife. She cared for her half-brother Andrew, of course, who was sweet, but she wished, with no more thought than a moment, that Teresa would stop being so stubborn.

Since she had been old enough to understand such things, she found this habit of English men living almost the whole of their lives with an Asian mistress then simply returning home to marry some so-called respectable matron in their doting years extremely distasteful. Of course they took care of their offspring. Sarah's sisters, like Sarah herself, had all been educated at the girls' school at the Institution. Her brothers were schooled in Calcutta. One had joined Jardines in Hong Kong and another was at university in Oxford. But still.

But go he chose to do, resigning his position, and he was to be replaced by the new governor, William Orfeur Cavenagh, and his wife Elizabeth. This was exciting news for Colonel Cavenagh was a war hero, a saviour of the Indian Mutiny when he had held Fort William from the savage and ungodly hordes.

'I have heard that Colonel Cavenagh has two good-looking sons. They are at school in Calcutta with my third brother. Perhaps I shall marry one of them.'

'Not likely,' retorted Amber. 'His snooty sons will not be doing with half-blood creatures like us. They must have white horse-faces with pedigrees like Emily Blackwood.'

Both girls fell into a fit of giggles.

'Alexander is returning. My aunt is all of a dither.'

Sarah looked at her friend. 'The English concubine, your scandalous aunt.'

Amber smiled. 'Yes, my scandalous aunt.'

'And now the scandalous Alexander. Are you still madly in love with him?'

Amber blushed. 'Silly girl. I grew up with him. He's my cousin.'

Sarah nodded and threw a knowing look at her friend. The sound of conversation began in the hall and she rose.

'Here is Ann with little Thomas to visit Mother and finish sorting out all her things. We shall be moving out tomorrow.'

Amber rose and kissed her friend. 'I shall see you at the ball next Friday. We shall see how the new governor dances with his peg leg.'

Both girls went off in peals of merry laughter.

Amber left the ramshackle mansion on Leonie Hill which had become the residence of the Governor of Singapore since the demolition of the house on Government Hill. It was so far from the town and so unsuitable for large functions that the governor held all such events at the Court House. So it was to be for his official farewell and the welcome of Colonel Cavenagh. There would be the officers from the Royal Navy on their way to China and, too, the Rajah Brook of Sarawak who was passing through on his way to London. He was said to be old and ailing and his face was a positive horror of pox marks. With such pleasures in store she could hardly wait.

Amber's thoughts turned to Alexander with a tremor of anticipation. She had been in love with him since childhood though he barely took any notice of her at all. She longed to see him again. This scandalous business of some woman in Scotland meant nothing to her. In her heart she forgave him everything and hoped against hope that, when he saw her again, now she had grown so pretty, that he would fall madly in love with her.

She directed the Indian syce to take her to the house of her friend Lian, the daughter of her aunt's Chinese lover. It always made her giggle and quickened her blood to think of him this way. Zhen was an object of intense interest to all the girls at school. He was handsome and spoke excellent English. He was tall and well-made and exuded an exotic excitement. Lian was her school friend and lived with her crazy aunt who Lian said still lusted after her brother-in-law. She, Lian and Sarah chattered endlessly about all this.

She waved her fan to catch the air. It was so hot and these petticoats and flounces were the very devil in the climate. She had no intention, however, of returning to the soft voiles and cool cottons of her youth. She was no longer a girl and the most hated garment in her wardrobe was the plain blue dress and white cotton apron all the girls were forced to wear at school. She longed to wear the French lace corset she had seen in Little's Store on Raffles Place but her father would not allow it.

Amber dismissed the syce at Thomson's Bridge. He hated to go into the Chinese town because of the cholera but she didn't care. No European had caught it and she certainly wouldn't. Her Malay maid trailed along behind her. Unlike most girls her age, she never went about with an older chaperone. Her mother had not thought it necessary and her father paid no attention. Aunt Charlotte had spoken to her about the impropriety of walking alone and everyone had agreed the maid would be sufficient.

She examined all the wares spilling out of the shops along Circular Road, silks and nankeens from China, muslins and shawls from India, exquisite beaded slippers, silver and ivory jewellery, bangles of jade and amber. She purchased a Chinese silk purse and, lifting her petticoat from the dusty street, turned into North Canal Street and into the verandah of the house of her friend. The door was opened by the housekeeper, a Javanese Chinese woman. The usually quiet house was filled with noise and bustle.

'Hello, Ah Ma,' she said to the housekeeper. This woman had been with Lian's family for years. She told the maid to go to the kitchen.

Lian rushed out to greet Amber, her hands covered in rice flour. Both girls hugged and Lian glanced upstairs.

'Mother Lilin is sleeping,' she said, glancing at Ah Ma, who nodded. Lian put her finger to her lips, smudging her cheek with white rice flour.

Amber smiled at Lian's mocking reference to the woman upstairs who was not her mother but her aunt. Everyone at school knew that Lian's aunt was as crazy as a wild monkey and poor Lian had to put up with all sorts of nonsense. Amber brushed away the flour from her friend's face. She was the prettiest girl in school, with her long black hair and beautiful eyes. At home Lian wore the nonya dress with its tight dark sarong and shapeless white cotton kebaya, barely distinguishable from her school clothes. Amber thought these garments the devil's handwork they were so ugly, but had to admit Lian and her slenderness would have been lost in petticoats.

'Oh you look so cool in your sarong. I'm so terribly warm in this petticoat and flounces.' Amber twirled for effect and Lian smiled.

'Take them off then,' she said, wiping her hands on her apron.

Amber made a face and ignored her.

'We are making rice dumplings for Cheng Beng. Can't do that in flounces, which I know you love.'

Amber giggled.

'Come into the parlour. I want to see you sit in that thing.'

Amber followed Lian and sat with the ease of two hours of practice. It was impossible to actually sit. One could only perch, but it was worth it.

'Actually it's much cooler than all those stiff petticoats.'

'But you can't sit comfortably.'

Amber shook her head. 'Oh pooh, never mind. Look.'

She took out her purchase.

'How do you like my new silk purse?'

Lian took it and turned it over.

'Nice enough,' she said. 'Do you not have at least a hundred?'

'One cannot have too many silk purses.'

Lian laughed. 'No, nor Indian shawls.'

'Alexander is coming home,' Amber said. Lian put the purse on the table.

Everyone at school knew that Amber was mad about Alex. Lian remembered him well enough. It had been at her twelfth birthday party and he was fourteen, almost fifteen. Mother Lilin had thrown them together somewhat before he departed for Scotland. She had never understood why. But then she never understood anything her aunt did. The woman had become more and more distracted and depressed over the past three years. All Lian knew was that it had something to do with her father, Zhen, for whom her aunt harboured some lingering passions. She was a perceptive girl. Growing up in the precarious sanity of the home of Mother Lilin had taught her useful lessons in self-preservation, her lack of parental guidance had made her independent and worldly-wise and her English education had made her clever and ambitious.

Alexander had kissed her. Well, hardly a kiss, when she

thought about it now, a touch of the lips. But extraordinary nevertheless, for in a good and decent Straits Chinese family touching in public between the sexes was, if not actually taboo, certainly unacceptable. As for boys and girls, well, now she could hardly imagine what had possessed her aunt to allow it. She would never tell Amber about this of course and, doubtless, Alex had forgotten it himself. He was probably dreadful now, red-faced, fat, bluff and Scottish, filled with his own importance like the English officers she saw about town.

Besides, her emotions had recently been engaged by the incredibly handsome Jemadar Kumar of the contingent of the Madras Regiment, who guarded the jail. She had met him on the several occasions when she shopped with Ah Fu, her maid, for wicker baskets and woven rattans, goods which the prisoners made and sold at the prison. He was as forbidden to her as she to him but that did not stop their eyes meeting. He had wide, dark limpid eyes and a moustache to quell the masses and stop the hearts of maidens. She felt a welling up inside herself, a rising tide of anticipation. She wanted her life to begin. Not with Kumar, he was merely a titillating pastime. Not with marriage to Ah Soon which was ridiculous. But something. Someone.

'What is the scandal about?' she said.

Amber shrugged. 'Some woman chasing him, no doubt. I hear that Scottish matrons are forward and bold.'

'It cannot be Alexander's fault, eh?' Lian smiled at her friend. Amber regretted mentioning him and changed the subject.

'You wanted to tell me something.'

'My father says I must stop school and prepare for my marriage.'

Amber put her hand to her mouth. 'No. You are not yet sixteen.'

'My birthday is in six months. I am to prepare shoes for the bridegroom. Can you imagine? Look.'

Lian took up a basket on a nearby table and opened it. She brought out a piece of cloth.

'For the past two weeks I have been tutored in beadwork. It is entirely ridiculous and backward.'

Amber took up the cloth. 'It is extremely poor.'

Lian snatched it, flung it into the basket and closed the lid.

'Of course it is. Why on earth must I know beadwork? Are there not beaders or seamstresses or whatever they are called in the town who know about such things?'

Lian's lips tightened. Amber put her hand to her friend's and gripped it. The subject of this marriage to Ah Soon, the son of her father's friend, was well known in school.

'Oh Amber,' Lian said. 'To be married and to have hardly lived. I shall be forced to become a housewife, obey a man I don't love and who is a fool, have ten babies and get fat and stupid. And do beadwork from morning to night. I can't bear it.'

The two girls fell into each other's arms.

'You are so lucky. Should you choose it, you may not marry. Your father would not force you. He is a kind man.'

Amber clutched her friend. To be forced to lie with a man you hated. It was abominable. They both knew how a baby was made, for Sarah's many sisters had been completely frank on the subject. In addition, Lian had one day found a stash of scandalous Chinese prints in Mother Lilin's room which she must have somehow purchased in the town, and had shown them to Amber. The duties of marriage didn't seem such a bane, thought Amber, recalling the erect male member and the looks of swooning abandonment of the women in those pictures, and she secretly thrilled at the thought of such activities with Alexander.

'Ah Soon is skinny and debauched. I hate my father,' Lian whispered, 'I won't do it.'

Amber was shocked. 'But what can you do?'

'I don't know.'

The girls stared at each other.

4

'She is fifteen. A young, obedient girl of great beauty.'

This was the hundredth girl, some as young as fourteen, who had been presented to him since his wife, Noan, had died ten years ago. He had no idea what they thought he would do with a fourteen-year-old girl. His mother-in-law was behind it all. The widow Tan was not only bored but had, since the death of her husband, become obsessed with the idea of more grandchildren, particularly grandsons. Noan had died giving birth to Kai. This death had affected his parents-in-law profoundly and, he believed, precipitated Tan's own decline.

His last daughter, Lian, was the same age as these girls. Her marriage would take place when she turned sixteen. Lian had been given, since the death of her mother, to her aunt Lilin, Tan's second daughter. Zhen had never liked this arrangement, which Tan had insisted on after the death of Noan. Lilin was a woman of uncertain temperament who had lusted after he himself for years, had a wild and uncontrollable nature, and, after the death of her infant son, had become half-crazed. Tan had hoped that the raising of Lian would settle her and to some extent that had been true. Lilin, for some reason, had sought to give Lian an English education and, in order to remove her as far as possible from what Zhen saw as Lilin's pernicious influence, Zhen had agreed.

So Lian had been enrolled in the girl's school of the Singapore Institution. She had received the Christian and English education that neither of her sisters was permitted. His first two daughters and his son Kai had been raised in the country by his mother-in-law. Presently Kai attended Saint Joseph's Institution for his education. In this respect all of Tan's wishes, as patriarch of the house, had been respected. Only in the matter of his own remarriage had he been obliged to ignore his father-in-law.

But they had been close, he and Tan, for Tan had had no sons and Zhen, the son of a mere third concubine, had hated his distant and cruel father. When Tan had died, Zhen had truly mourned him and paid this man all the respect that he was due. His funeral had been the finest that money could buy and Zhen tried to listen to Tan's widow on most things. On this business of remarriage however, he had gently but firmly insisted on doing nothing and relations with the old woman had soured.

Zhen contemplated the matchmaker, an old lean man whose wispy beard grew thinner and thinner with each passing year and now floated like spun sugar around his chin.

'Lao Liu, how many does this make? I have told you that I am not interested in marrying again.'

Lao Liu contemplated Zhen. He was fully aware of this man's relationship with this concubine of his, this English woman. But it would not do.

'Honourable sir, let me be frank. This is not just a matter of sex or sons. Women are about status. The more you have the greater your status in other men's eyes. Wives are about your heredity. Concubines are for your pleasure.'

Lao Liu bowed.

'Naturally, the pleasures of a foreign concubine are the envy of all powerful men everywhere and this brings you enormous prestige. Especially one from the ruling elite class who has wealth and beauty, for such a thing is as rare as an honest pawnbroker.'

Zhen raised an eyebrow but said nothing.

'But, sir, it will not do. For a man like you, with your wealth, not to have many women about him is a great loss of face. It is stubbornly wilful and wrong.'

Lao Liu's voice took on a beseeching tone.

'Even if you do not wish to pleasure yourself with them, sir. Just to have them around enhances your eminence. Can you not consider taking one or two?'

He waited but there was no response. He sighed. 'It is a subject of much talk. I am being frank.'

Lao Liu stood, silent now. He had had his say. It was only fair to point out what, apparently, this man couldn't see.

Zhen rose. 'I thank you, Lao Liu, for the graciousness of your advice. I would be obliged if you would let me reflect on it.'

Lao Liu bowed courteously. Clearly his little speech had had no effect.

Lao Liu melted away and Zhen's thoughts turned to Charlotte. This little foreign concubine who gave him such 'pleasure and prestige' was forbidden him for months. He recognised that, whether it should or not, it made her suddenly doubly desirable. He had to comply. But not until tomorrow. He took up a slip of paper and sent a note away with the boy.

* * *

'Lian, a nice surprise. And Amber. Sit.'

Charlotte rose from the table nestled in the arms of the rain tree and kissed both girls on the cheek.

Lian and Amber had clearly come straight from school for they were both in their school uniforms. It must be important, otherwise Amber would have rushed straight home to fit herself up in her petticoats and crinolines. Their maids, who doubled as chaperones, would be installed in the kitchen eating English cakes.

'Tea,' she said to Malik, her Indian majordomo, as he came quietly to her side.

She caught the glance, a flick of his eyes, which Malik directed at Lian. He disapproved of Zhen and by extension, his Chinese daughter, but usually he concealed it well. She should dismiss him, but he had been with her for years. A good majordomo was incredibly hard to find and her house ran like clockwork.

She contemplated the two of them. So young and fresh. Amber was brown-haired, brown-eyed and looked like Robert. She was pretty, certainly, but she paled in comparison to the girl by her side. Lian was utterly beautiful, almost magnetically so. She had perfect skin and the blackest hair, full pink lips and her almond eyes had a small tilt to them which gave her an air of mystery. She had an inner beauty too, which glowed out of her, like a calm strength, and imparted a depth to her external appearance. Amber could be all bounce and go like a puppy, but Lian was as graceful as a princess.

She was the only child of Zhen's Chinese family that she could ever know and she liked this, knowing this child, who was half sister to Lily. Kai, his son, she saw from time to time, but he was forbidden to speak to her by his grandmother and, rather shufflingly, ran away if he saw her. To this grandmother she was an abomination, the reason there were no more grandsons.

Lian was scarcely better, an abomination of a different kind and Charlotte felt a kinship of the damned with her.

After some desultory conversation about school, Amber suddenly turned to Charlotte.

'Aunt, can you help Lian?'

'In what way?'

'Miss Charlotte, I am obliged to bead.'

'To bead?'

'Yes, shoes. Beading for shoes. It is unbelievable.'

The tea tray arrived and conversation ended. As the servant moved away, Amber turned again urgently to Charlotte.

'Lian must bead because she must be domesticated and marry this Ah Soon. At the end of this term she must quit school. Aunt, you must help her.'

Charlotte frowned.

'I understand. The time has come, has it?'

'Yes, and I am so desperately unhappy.'

'He is an opium fiend, Aunt. He smokes and smokes and why on earth doesn't he just die?'

'Amber!' Charlotte looked severely at her niece. Lian put her hand to Amber's.

'Of course we do not wish such a wicked thing. I ask only that you speak to my father. Try to persuade him away from this marriage.'

Charlotte poured the tea and handed the cups. The two girls drank and looked at her over the rims. She never spoke to Zhen about his Chinese family. They discussed everything else but on this issue he was silent. How would he take her interference? Not well, she imagined. On the matter of Alexander he had agreed to her wishes, though he did not like it. On the matter of Lily they both agreed that she would be raised as both a Chinese and English girl. Of course they knew that, in this manner, Lily, with an English education, would be more English than Chinese but

Zhen seemed to have accepted that as well. But this was different.

Something in Charlotte felt repulsed suddenly. Lian's quiet beauty, why was this to be given away to an opium addict? She would be miserable until the end of her days.

'I will speak to Zhen,' she said and Amber squealed.

'Thank you,' Lian said, and tears welled in her eyes.

'There, there. No promises,' she said and now was not sure of what she had started.

There was a sudden flurry of activity as Lily's Chinese maid brought her from her nap. Charlotte held her sleepy child, her face so much that of Alex as a baby. When she had woken fully, Amber and Lian kissed her and began to run around chasing her playfully. Lian caught her and held her over her head, making Lily giggle. Lily was a lovely child, so quiet and peaceful. She was so very pretty and almost never cried or fussed. After sons, Charlotte had not expected the pleasure of this daughter.

The rattan ball was produced and Lian and Amber began to throw it around, showing Lily how to catch.

Malik arrived with a tray and Charlotte picked up the note and consulted her watch.

'Girls, you must think of going. Lian, your father will here within the hour.'

The two girls kissed Lily again and bobbed a curtsy to Charlotte then raced across the lawn and into the house. Charlotte took Lily on her knee and opened the picture book to the story of Cinderella.

5

She gazed into the mirror, running the tip of her finger over the fine lines at the corner of her eyes, and glanced at her hands which betrayed the laxity of time.

'Charlotte Macleod, where did the years go?'

Her skin was good but the sun, no matter how hard one tried, was harsh. Her waist had coarsened a little after the birth of Lily, despite all the efforts of her Javanese maids with their balsams and bindings, but her bosom was firm. Her eyes were clear and she knew the violet depths still attracted Zhen.

He had suddenly decided to come to her in the middle of the afternoon. She knew what he wanted and now she thought of nothing else. She had felt distanced from him. The news of Alex had caused her anxiety. Adam had written that there were debts, that Aunt Jeanne's health had been affected. Now too, this morning, she had received news of even greater trouble in Batavia with the business of Manouk & Son, from which she drew a good portion of her fortune. Something was very wrong in Semarang and she hardly understood what it was.

She pulled a grey strand from the thick black hair which framed her face. She was slightly depressed. And now the slide into middle age. When would it start to make a difference to him?

The door opened and she turned.

'I'm glad you came,' she said.

Zhen flung off his coat. His undershirt was wet with sweat and clung to his upper body. He was aroused. The room pulsated with his sexual excitement and she caught it and flew into his arms.

His lips met hers in urgency and she responded, crushing her mouth to his, encircling his head in her arms. He pulled her closer to him so hard she let out a small cry. He took her hand and put it to the bulge between his legs and let slip a small groan of pleasure. This intense need of her made her mad for him.

* * *

She rose from the bed and poured water into the bowl. She wet the sponge and came back to him, squeezing the water on his chest and around his neck. He put his hand to her breast and his lips to her neck.

'Lovemaking in the afternoon is folly in this climate. You have half killed me. And we took no precautions and you were less, well, controlled than usual.' She kissed his lips gently. 'Which I love, but if I get pregnant …'

'Not what you said only a short time ago,' he said and grinned, '"Oh Zhen. Don't stop. Don't …"'

She pulled away and threw the wet sponge at him.

'What has happened? I don't attribute your intense arousal to just missing me, especially when I've been so distracted.'

Zhen contemplated her, wild-looking, with her black hair a riot around her face and streaming down her back. She was as lovely as when he had seen her for the first time, even more when she was flushed from loving him. It bruised his heart.

'You are beautiful,' he murmured but her words came over his.

'I have ice. An ice shipment came in as ballast yesterday from America and I took half.'

She rang the bell and when the maid knocked went to the door.

'Ice,' she said through it, 'and more water.'

She went into his arms and felt him, slippery under her fingers. She traced the line of his body. He didn't seem to age; his body was as sleek as twenty years ago. She lay her cheek on his hard abdomen and played with him. She loved him like this. He felt vulnerable, not rampant.

'Do you remember our first time?' she said.

'Everything.'

'Is it the same for you?'

'Not the same. Nothing can be like the first time. But if you mean do I still like to pleasure you with the same passion, then it is the same.'

'You might have just said yes,' she said, and he smiled.

They had met and fallen dangerously in love and they had been alive and then they had been apart and it had been like death. Pregnant with his child, she had fled to Batavia and married rich and safe Tigran. She had given birth to Alexander, his son, longing for him, lonely years spent longing for him. And it was the same for him. He had married and made children and gone through the days as one is forced to do for there is no other choice, and when she had come back, years later, again pregnant but this time with Tigran's child, nothing had changed. They had come together as if the years between had not existed. And then she had been pulled away again, back to Batavia, to misery, and more time had passed and then he had come to her and she had made a choice, because he was married and it was all too impossible. She had stayed with Tigran and found contentment until he had died, thrown from his horse. And, for a long time, she had not wanted anything at all. It all seemed like a tale of another life. But perhaps that was what the past was. A fairytale.

He caressed her hair as she caressed him.

'I love you,' she said.

She felt him twitch and she laughed. But it was always a small disappointment. He never said the words. She understood it was not in his nature to express such things in this way. He sent her poetry, full of flowery expressions of adoration and longing, pearls and the sea, jade and phoenixes, smoke and misty mountains. It was lovely. But just once, Charlotte thought, I would just once like to hear the words.

The maid knocked. Charlotte rose, threw on a robe and took the ice and water.

'In an hour bring Lily,' she said and turned her head to Zhen. He nodded.

She opened the container packed around with watery saltpetre to keep it cold and slipped a chip between his lips. She took all the jagged blocks and poured the water and the ice into the bowl.

'Quick, it melts so fast.'

She let slip the robe and he rose and they plunged their hands in the water, the blocks crashing against each other, splashing their faces and bodies, laughing with the invigorating pleasure of it. She took the sponge dripping with the icy water and squeezed it over his head. He pulled her against him, wet and cool, and kissed her, the melted ice from his mouth on her lips.

'I will stay here tonight,' he said.

'Yes,' she murmured against his mouth. 'Cook will make your favourite dishes.'

'Malik will not approve.'

She smiled. 'No.'

She took the sponge, saturated and heavy, and began to sponge his body, watching the water drip from his arms, over the muscles of his chest , then to his back, the water coursing into his lustrous queue, and spilling onto the skin of his buttocks, so hard, so silken, this silent passage of the sponge and its coursing water over every part of his perfect body so pleasurable she could never have put it into words.

It was always a thing of wonder, the way he abandoned himself so easily to his own sensuality. He made this natural, this unconscious enjoyment of sensation and the compulsions it inspired. He had neither shame nor guilt for any aspect of their sexual life. On the contrary, as a Taoist he had explained that the principle of sexual pleasure was built into its beliefs and essential for health. The guilt-laden European concepts about love and sex were so alien to him that he hardly understood when she tried to explain.

He wound his fingers into her hair, gripping her hard and moved close to her, dominating her. She knew his emotions had spilled over into darker desires. She felt them too, intense and disturbing. His body was tense, coiled. She shuddered and he pulled her head back and gazed into her eyes, a straight dark look.

'Trust me,' he said and her pulse went wild.

'Zhen,' she said, hot with embarrassment, sliding her eyes away.

He didn't move, waiting, judging if she really wanted him to stop. Sometimes, not often, this mood came over them like a dark cloak but she always resisted.

'I know you want it and I know how to do it, a little pain adds to pleasure, just enough. Sometimes I need this too.'

He gripped her hair harder, put his hand to her neck, squeezing lightly and took her mouth in his. She moaned, her breath became short. She began to tremble and her hands came against his chest pushing him.

'Trust me,' he murmured against her mouth but her struggles against him intensified. It was arousing but he recognised her fear and that was not what he wanted.

He dropped his hands and took her in his arms to calm her tremblings.

'You have to trust me completely. It takes time.'

'I trust you,' she whispered, 'but something ... I can't let go.'

'I know. It's all right.'

She lay against him, recovering her breath. The thoughts of this kind of sex with him came often, but she hadn't, despite all the sexual play they enjoyed, yet found the courage to go down that road.

She put on her robe and took up a brush to make sense of the tangle of her hair. He settled back on the bed and closed his eyes.

Sometimes he wanted this, he said. She had never considered this before, that he had desires of which he did not speak, which she did not fulfil. Does he go elsewhere to quench these dark wants? To women who refuse him nothing. To the prostitutes in the town? I wouldn't know, she thought. She gazed at him lying quietly, his brown skin against the white sheets.

'What do you know of this new governor?' he said.

She frowned.

'Since we were on the subject.' He smiled and sat up cross-legged. She dismissed these wormlike and corrosive thoughts gladly.

'Well, he has one good leg and is a hero. Robert says he knows even less than most about the affairs of the Straits. Being an Indian civil servant he cannot speak Malay or Chinese nor knows anything about the peoples and cultures of the south seas. He is a soldier so has no idea about commerce and apparently is said to love Lord Canning, the Governor of India, more than his wife.'

Zhen smiled.

'He knows nothing and doubtless is arrogant and proud of the fact and therefore perfect for his position. Robert is hoping that, being a darling of the said Canning, he will get some money out of him for his police force to fight the crime and disturbances in your part of the town.'

She turned and looked pointedly at him.

'You Chinese are the problem.'

'Ah, yes. Well, if the British lion wishes to rule Malaya, he must ride the Chinese dragon.'

She thought about this. 'That is true and well put.'

'Thank you. We are sixty thousand more than you. That is most of the problem. And just more money from India will not solve it. It's more complicated than that.'

'Is it? You should tell Robert.'

'I cannot do that. Xia Lou, come here.'

She rose and went into his arms and rested her head against his shoulder.

'Listen to me carefully. After tonight I cannot come to you again for three months.'

She attempted to rise but he held her tight against him.

'There is something I must do for the kongsi. I must distance myself from you for this time.'

Charlotte digested this information. What little she understood about these brotherhood organisations was that they were like the freemasons. They swore oaths and had rituals. She knew they helped the poor Chinese coolies who swamped the town. She knew Zhen gave money to the boys' schools at the temples and to the Chinese hospital, that he was important in his clan association. But what all this truly meant she had no idea.

'I don't understand.'

'I am a bondsman. I swore an oath of obedience. I have no choice.'

She ran her finger over the tattoo of Guan Yu, the god of these brotherhoods, whose stern red face adorned Zhen's chest. He had been a sort of policeman for them in China and had needed them when he came to Singapore. Robert said they were dangerous, but the government did nothing to stop them or regulate them. Indeed the governor entertained them for they were the mechanism of control over the entire Chinese community. Were they vital social organisations for the Chinese, or gangs of thugs? Whampoa and other Chinese merchants she had come to know well were members so it was slightly beyond her but she understood the kongsi was the bewhiskered head of the Chinese dragon Zhen spoke of.

Zhen waited.

'And this thing means you cannot be with me? Do you want this?' she said.

'No.'

She raised her face to his. 'If you don't do it what will happen?'

'Trouble. More trouble. Financial ruin. Violence.'

Charlotte let out a gasp.

He pulled her to him, into the circle of his arms and put his lips to her ear.

'It's all right. It will be all right, but you must understand why I cannot be with you and not blame me.'

Charlotte held him, crushing herself against him, burying her face into his neck. She understood so little of this other life of his and it terrified her.

'It's all right. I will take care of it.'

He held her tightly against him, waiting for her tension to subside.

'Tonight we will take out the old pillow books. There is one position which needs a rope but I believe you are still perhaps supple enough …'

She laughed and pushed away from him. 'Perhaps with Alex coming it is a good thing. A little time to sort things out. Eh, xiao baobei?'

He took her face between his hands and kissed her.

'Let's get Lily.'

6

'Who is the dashing man enthralling all the ladies?' Charlotte asked.

Her companion was Isabella Kemp, formerly da Souza. She and her twin sister had formed a close friendship with Charlotte when she had first arrived in Singapore. Isabella was half sister to Teresa, Charlotte's sister-in-law, and the subject of the divorce was never far from her lips. As protocol decreed it, Teresa was present in the company of her husband to greet the new governor and it caused a great strain for everyone concerned.

To deflect Isabella from further conversation on the matter, Charlotte had turned her attention across the crowded room to the dark-haired man surrounded by a throng of young women. The new governor had not yet arrived but was awaited with eager anticipation. His injuries and his bravery were on everyone's lips.

'I understand that is Commodore Mallory. He was of the company of naval officers who dined with Joseph and all those silly men at the Masonic Lodge last night. He is on his way to Hong Kong. Something about treaties, I do not fully understand.'

Charlotte looked more intensely but all she could see was a tallish figure with a broad back and dark wavy hair surrounded by the women. Mallory, Commodore Mallory, could it be … ?

Was this Edmund Mallory?

Edmund Mallory had been First Lieutenant aboard the Madras, the East Indiaman that had carried her from England to Calcutta. Of formidable courage and ability, he had been her guardian during the interminable voyage and she had been immensely grateful, for his eyes were of steel and no man dared to cross him. That his feelings had been much greater than hers was proved on the night they dropped anchor in the harbour at Calcutta. He had proposed marriage, professed with a painful hesitancy his deep feelings for her. But she had been terrified at the depth of his emotion and had refused him, grateful to go ashore and escape the anguish which she had clearly caused him.

He had been made a captain she knew but, now, could this be the same man, Commodore Mallory, a royal navy position?

'Is it Edmund Mallory you speak of?' Charlotte asked her companion.

'I believe so. But Charlotte, you must speak to Robert. Teresa is terribly upset. The mere idea of divorce, why …'

Charlotte began to move away. 'Of course, Isabella, it is distressing, but it is between Robert and Teresa, you see.'

Isabella put out a hand to restrain her but Charlotte escaped.

Edmund Mallory? Could it be the same man? She walked slowly through the crush. The governor and Colonel Cavenagh were expected within the next minutes. In the meantime all the European, Chinese and Arab merchants, the Temmengong and his entourage, the government officials, chaplains, army and naval officers, the entire upper echelons of Singapore society had begun gathering.

Charlotte had been looking out for Zhen. She would miss him but twelve weeks was not so very long. And it would be even a little exciting to see each other when they could not be together, like the heady days of their first kisses. She had a little space to get Alexander back on the straight and narrow. And then when Zhen came back to her ... The thought was arrested by the sight of Edmund.

The slow movement through the crowd, greeting various acquaintances here and there, meant that she approached at a pace which enabled her to take in the figure of the man she believed to be her close companion of years ago. The fashion just now for new arrivals from England was for great caged crinolines, which jutted out yards from their body in vast swathes of cloth.

How did these women survive in these hot, cumbersome cages, she thought as she edged by. She was reminded of Carlyle's pronouncement of the first purpose of Clothes being not for warmth or decency but ornament. Man might warm himself from the toils of the chase or amid dried leaves in his tree or bark shed, but for Decoration he must have Clothes.

Her own choice of Decoration was far simpler and of an older time. The petticoats were silk and soft and the outer dress of organza for lightness. She deliberately wore pale shades to these events, though always with a touch of colour. Tonight she was in white with ruby earrings and necklace.

Several women turned away from her or talked behind their fans and she chose, as she always had, to ignore this.

She was greeted by the St. Joseph's contingent, Father Beurel, Evangeline, his housekeeper and Joseph Lee, the Chinese priest. She had known them almost twenty years and they spoke briefly. It was people like these and others like the da Souza family, Reverend Keaseberry and his wife, old, old friends, and new ones who felt no imperative to take a moral stance. These came from unlikely quarters. Miss Cooke, to whose school Charlotte made donations, and many of the German and

French merchant families.

Thus, stopping to greet friends, and ignore enemies, knowing she left a frothy wake of gossip in her passage, she made her way towards the man she believed to be Edmund. The band began a lively tune which signalled the arrival of the Governor's carriage and the crowd ebbed suddenly. The dark-haired man turned and, with a sharp intake of breath, she recognised him.

His attention was momentarily taken with the throng at the door and the insistent conversation of the woman at his elbow, a woman Charlotte recognised as Emily Blackwood, the pretty young daughter of the new Resident Counsellor.

His head was inclined to Miss Blackwood's in an attitude of gentlemanly attention when a further jostling of the crowd occasioned him to look up and their eyes met.

That he recognised her was not in doubt. They stood, both of them, a moment, then he inclined his head in a bow in her direction and she dropped into a small curtsy.

Emily Blackwood, attentive to his every move, removed her gaze from him to Charlotte and the glance she threw was a blade. Emily's father appeared, gathered up his daughter and bundled her towards the hall to greet the Governor.

The Chinese merchants moved as one through the throng. Zhen sought Charlotte but the crush was too great. Tonight he was accompanied by the Fu Shan Chu and other important members of the kongsi. Hong had been invited but had refused. Zhen knew that Hong was uncomfortable with the men of the government. He spoke no English at all, had no social graces, was as ignorant as a peasant with a peasant's mentality. His entire being was concentrated on money and power. Cheng Sam Teo was in attendance but hung back. This place was new to him. Here he was at the very centre of British power in the Far East.

It was overwhelming when one had spent most of one's life in a small town in Riau. He looked around at the great room with its elegance, the lines of red-coated soldiers, the European women in the silk gowns and exposed bosoms and felt entirely intimidated.

Zhen seemed totally in his element. Cheng looked at the man they had selected. He was to be merely a momentary and useful filler until Cheng could get his bearings and bid for the leases and understand the extent of his father-in-law's power in Johor.

But he did not look like that. His height made him stand out. With his silk robes and the mandarin hat with the diamond, he looked like an emperor. He moved with ease in the throng. He spoke fluent English and bowed and talked to the government men. Everyone knew him. Cheng felt at once that he had been an inspired choice. His mind began to entertain other more interesting possibilities. Ones of a more permanent nature. Where was his English concubine? Cheng searched the crowd for this black-haired woman.

The young Temenggong arrived in the midst of his retinue, resplendent in his rakish turban, tight gold trousers and green silk coat embroidered with gold thread and diamonds. Cheng, Zhen and the Deputy went forward to greet him.

Edmund took three strides and was at her side. She felt short of breath. He was so very unexpected.

'Hello, Charlotte.'

Charlotte had forgotten his voice, the deep, modulated tones. She remembered, in a rush, the calmness of his voice under pressure, when waves were pouring over the ship or when they had, terrifyingly, lost sight of the fleet. Remembered his courage, his unflagging strength which gave strength to others. He was a born naval commander. She had forgotten, though, his physical appearance. He had been only twenty-one when they had met and now he was fully a mature man of forty. His shoulders had broadened, the litheness of his body had changed into the hard sinew and muscle of a seaman, used to hardship. His face was tanned, furrowed from the sea life, his chestnut hair thick and wavy. All these things she could not recall. But his eyes she did remember, brown eyes, filled with intelligence and quickness. These had not changed. He was dressed in the dark blue, white and pale gold uniform of a high-ranking royal naval officer. It suited him very well.

'Edmund, how incredible that you are here.'

Edmund smiled. She had forgotten his smile too, the warmth of it. Edmund was stoical and careful of his emotions, but not guarded with those he trusted.

'You look well, Charlotte, as lovely as I remember you.'

Something in the way he said these words spoke of a constant remembrance, as if he had thought of her often. She could hardly believe that was true but it left her nonplussed. She looked down and a silence fell upon them.

He broke this little moment by taking her hand and putting it to his lips.

Zhen's gaze found Charlotte at that moment with her hand in that of another man, the lips of that man upon her hand, her eyes gazing at him, her body so quiet and attentive to that man, in an attitude of total rapture, or so it seemed. The merchants around him followed his gaze. She was always of interest to these men. A beautiful white woman beyond their own reach, who slept with a Chinese man. Human natured demanded curiosity and envy.

The Deputy whispered to Cheng, who moved to Zhen's side. 'I am sorry to keep you from such beauty,' he said, 'it will not be for long.'

Zhen felt his face grow hot.

'I am so very glad to see you again,' Edmund said, holding on to her hand.

Charlotte smiled and gazed into the warmth of his smile.

'Oh Edmund, and I am so very glad to see you.'

The band struck up God Save the Queen. Edmund released her hand and turned to the door.

Charlotte, too, looked to the door and there saw Zhen, surrounded by the entire Chinese merchant population of the town, all gazing at her. She started, surprised and suddenly guilty. Zhen threw her a deep look of unfathomable meaning and moved away.

Now Edmund too was claimed by duty and his naval colleagues and left, with a small backward look at her, to form the line for the new governor.

Robert came to her side, sliding his arm into hers.

'Come on, time to take our places. Teresa is looking for you.'

She shook him off. 'Why on earth can't you sort out your business, Robbie? Do you really want to spend your life with Shilah when Teresa is your wife and loves you so much?'

Robert's mouth dropped open, staring at his sister. By the time he closed it again, she had moved away, the anthem had finished and Colonel Cavenagh had made his entrance to the room between the serried rows of officers and civilians. He was short and stocky with mutton-chop whiskers and a bald head.

'You can hardly see his false leg.'

Charlotte felt her arm taken and, startled, looked at her niece.

'Amber, it's you. Thank heaven. I thought it might be … never mind.'

They both watched as the new governor approached with Governor Blundell. Behind him, with Mrs. Blackwood, was Mrs. Cavenagh, a slim woman of some elegance but less than compelling beauty.

'She has the face of a horse,' whispered Amber.

Charlotte tapped her niece's hand lightly. 'Stop it. You girls spend all your time in horrid gossip. Now hush.'

Both Charlotte and Amber curtsied gracefully to Colonel Cavenagh as he passed and finally the official arrival ceremony was over. The band began a gay tune and the noise level rose as each and every one found their acquaintance and discussed the new Governor and his lady. Champagne was passed and Charlotte allowed Amber a glass.

'He hardly limps at all. It's marvellous, don't you think? But shall he dance? With only one arm he might attempt a gavotte, perhaps, but I rather think not the waltz.'

Amber laughed gaily and Charlotte smiled. She, Zhen's daughter, Lian, and Sarah Blundell were impossibly high spirited. But she did not begrudge them it for, Charlotte knew their lives would change in some way or other irrevocably all too soon.

As for Lian, despite the shock of Zhen's announcement she had argued the girl's case. Zhen had listened politely and then said he would look into it. She could not go further on the matter and had no desire to spoil their last evening together.

Sarah Blundell had no greater ambition than to be married to some English officer and become a regimental wife. Perhaps, she, of the three, might actually find happiness.

Amber, surprisingly, paid little attention to the young men who had come courting. She was not of the highest birth, of course, being the daughter of a white man and an Indian nyai, and, in consequence, the young men had not been of the highest calibre either, but none of that seemed to matter, in any case, to Amber. She was simply not interested in them. She showed an aptitude for languages and spoke excellent Malay and passably good French.

Charlotte felt it might be time to speak to Amber of her future. She was sixteen and in a short time her days at school would be over. Robert had no time or inclination to concern himself with Amber, though he loved her dearly. Shilah was somewhat out of her depth with her educated daughter and now was entirely involved with her doting love of Robert and the birth, in her late thirties, of a new child. Charlotte and Amber had always been close but Charlotte recognised that, over the last three years, she too, had been taken up with her own life, with her oblivious passion for Zhen and the delight of their love for their daughter.

She patted Amber's hand. She would invite her to luncheon and they would speak of this. Before she could utter a word however, Amber spoke rather breathlessly.

'Aunty Kitt, what news of Alex?'

Charlotte turned and looked Amber in the eye. She had known for some time that Amber had feelings for Alex but, in that instant, it came to her that, actually, Amber might be the kind of young woman that could settle Alexander's wild ways. If they could care for each other and marry quickly, Charlotte would send Alex to Batavia to pick up the reins of the affairs at Brieswijk and discover what was happening in the company. The money which she should have received for the quarter had not arrived. It was a great sum and she had become intensely worried.

'He comes home under a cloud. I have not the faintest idea what to expect.'

Amber looked down and twisted her lace handkerchief. Robert came up, his face set, and took Amber by the arm. 'Sarah's asking for you.'

Amber made to open her mouth but Robert looked severe.

'Off you go. You girls should find plenty to gossip about.'

Amber threw a long glance at Charlotte who nodded to her. As she departed Robert turned to Charlotte.

'Teresa is …'

'No, Robbie.' Charlotte put up her hand. 'Not this evening. I don't care. You must sort this matter out between you. I have my own concerns.'

She turned away abruptly meaning to look for Zhen and found herself gazing again into the eyes of Edmund Mallory.

He glanced over her head at Robert. 'May I take Charlotte away for a few moments?'

Robert stared at Edmund.

'It's all right, Robbie. Edmund and I are old friends.'

Robert threw a look of total incomprehension at his sister and before he could agree or disagree, was joined by his sister's Chinese companion. He was rather relieved. He had no idea who this other fellow was.

'Ah, Zhen, so good to see you.'

Zhen bowed to Robert and turned his gaze to Edmund.

'Charlotte,' he said and Charlotte, who knew him so well, felt the control he was exerting on a situation he did not fully understand. 'Will you introduce us?'

Robert, too, stared at his sister. 'Yes, Kitt, do introduce us.'

'Allow me,' Edmund said, looking at the two men. 'Edmund Mallory. Naval commander in Her Majesty's service.'

He put out his hand to Robert and the men shook. Edmund turned to Zhen.

'Your servant, sir,' he said and once again put out his hand.

Zhen stared at it for a moment. The tension between the two men was palpable. Then Zhen bowed and Edmund dropped his hand.

'Yes, of course. Forgive me. The customs of your country are somewhat new to me.'

'That is surprising since you naval officers spend your time battering China to bits.'

Edmund, if surprised by this riposte, did not show it and looked coolly at Zhen. 'It is regrettable that the Chinese government cannot abide by the treaties it signs.'

'It is regrettable that the Chinese government is forced at the point of a gun to sign such treaties.'

That Edmund was not in the least used to arguments of this kind from stray Chinese merchants who spoke excellent English was blatantly obvious. His eyes narrowed but before he could speak Zhen transferred his gaze to Charlotte.

'Mrs. Manouk. I see you are enjoying yourself. Goodbye.'

He bowed, turned on his heel and left her.

Charlotte felt a blush spread from her neck to her cheeks. She gazed at his back and felt close to tears.

She put her handkerchief to her mouth and moved away from the men towards the terrace.

Edmund looked to Robert. 'What an odd fellow. Is your sister all right?'

Robert frowned.

'I have no idea. I shall go to her,' he said and Edmund bowed slightly. He saw something was amiss and, with a sensitivity not often found among sailoring men, realised his presence, just then, would not help her.

'Yes, please go to her,' he said and Robert departed.

7

'Who is this upstart sultan, cheeky blighter?'

Colonel Cavenagh whacked his artificial leg with a crack against the floorboards. Robert realised that when the new governor was displeased, this was his mode of expression, much the way a judge might use a gavel to get attention.

'Young fool, sir,' said Randolph Blackwood, the Resident Counsellor. 'Needs putting back in line.'

'Flying the British flag on his boats, attacking states in our name. Good God! What's that place again?'

Blackwood put on his pince-nez and consulted his paper. 'Pahang. Large state in central Malaya, timber, possibly tin. Succession dispute between two brothers.'

'These damn princes. Just like India, always fighting some petty wars.'

'If I may, sir,' Robert said and Cavenagh looked over at him.

'Yes, Commissioner, what is it?'

'A little more complicated than that.'

'What, what,' Cavenagh said gruffly. 'Well?'

'Sir, Temenggong Abu Bakar's late father signed an agreement with Tengku Ali, son of the late Sultan of Singapore, in which Ali agreed to give up Johor in exchange for a pension and his recognition as Sultan here, which had been in abeyance for many years. This agreement was put in place by Governor Butterworth. But other Malay sultans were not in agreement and Abu Bakar is facing a threat from Sultan Mahmud Shah, who was deposed at Riau by the Dutch, and now claims suzerainty over both Pahang and Johor through blood lines and marriage. In this pursuit he aims to overthrow the Sultan Umar of Terengganu, his neighbour, with the backing of the Siamese and take both states by force. We have already warned Sultan Umar to resist any such efforts. Now Mahmud Shah has an alliance with Pahang's Prince Wan Ahmad against the interests of his own brother Tun Mahatir. Abu Bakar feels that the fall of Pahang would bring his own position in Johor under threat. Consequently he backs Tun Mahatir and has sent weapons and gunboats.'

Cavenagh stared at Robert as if he were confronted with Isaac Newton asking him to solve the riddle of the spheres. His mouth opened but nothing emerged and he closed it again.

'The Temenggong's wife,' Robert went on, 'is the sister of Tun Mahatir.'

A silence fell on the room and Robert and McNair exchanged a glance. Blackwood, too, had fallen, as if stunned, into a stupor.

Finally the governor, as if released from some hypnotic spell, roused himself.

'Good God, man. Who can make sense of all these sultans? Well, well, what to do,' said Cavenagh and thumped his leg against the floor. 'We don't want Siamese influence down here. What do you say, McNair?'

The governor's ADC stood up and threw a glance at Robert.

'No, sir. We support Abu Bakar. His acquisition of Johor was quite legal. I have looked into the paperwork. He is wealthy through a monopoly on the gutta percha trade and has licensed the

Chinese to set up gambier and pepper plantations on the southern rivers of Johor. In addition, since the establishment of New Harbour, his land at Telok Blangah has become very valuable. But he does need pulling into line, sir. I have it on good authority he has been going around saying that the British governor is his personal tax collector.'

'What!' Cavenagh threw his leg this time against the leg of the table, shaking the pens and inkpots into a minor convulsion.

'What do you mean?' Blackwood said, his pince-nez dropping from his nose.

'The excise farms, sir,' McNair ventured. 'The Johor and Singapore opium farm leases are offered as one and Abu Bakar is boasting that, since his share of the revenue is paid from our Treasury we are, in effect, his tax collectors.'

Robert thought Cavenagh might have a stroke.

'Youthful nonsense,' said McNair in an effort to defuse the situation, 'of course. He aims to impress the other Malay princes with the extent of our Imperial backing.'

'Not entirely,' Blackwood said, '*The Straits Times* claims that the Temenggong receives from our Treasury upwards of $5,000 per month more than the gross sale of excisable articles in Johor amounts to. They claim he is overpaid and is using this surplus to finance his war in Pahang.'

Cavenagh seemed to consider this a moment, then rose in his peculiar way. Having an amputated left lower leg and a corresponding useless left arm, the governor was forced to resort to a series of strange flexions and movements merely to rise with some dignity. Having done so, his wooden foot made a thump as he paced. Robert could not prevent his eyes dropping to this appendage. Cavenagh noticed.

'Pott's leg,' he said. 'Works marvellously well.'

He hitched up his trouser leg.

'Wooden shaft and socket, steel knee joint, articulated with catgut tendons that connect the knee with the foot. Means that the hip has no extraordinary motions and reduces pain.'

All the men examined this marvel. McNair thought Cavenagh the bravest man he knew. He made nothing of these awful injuries and was exceedingly modest about his considerable military achievements.

Cavenagh dropped his trouser leg.

'Actually, Dr. Cowper has suggested the use of gutta percha to ease the attachment to the leg. Splendid idea.'

Cavenagh beamed at the faces around him. 'Now, where were we. Yes. Opium.'

The discussion of his leg seemed to have calmed him and he was in a sunny mood. He returned to his desk and sat.

'McNair, explain the situation to me here in Malaya. I have had no dealings with such things in India.'

'Yes, Governor.'

'Sit, sit, gentlemen. Doubtless you have no idea either, Blackwood. Do you good to listen.'

Blackwood looked slightly miffed but did as he was told.

'The raw opium, as you know, sir, is grown in India and sold at the factory market there, in chests or balls, to the Jewish and Armenian dealers and shipped by them to Singapore where it is purchased by the Chinese holder of the opium farm at the prevailing price. Eighty percent of the production goes to China but the rest lands in Singapore. Currently, with the crisis in India, it is somewhat high. One thousand rupees a chest. The lease on the monopoly to refine and sell the chandu is put up for the highest bidder.

McNair paused and glanced at the governor. Cavenagh sat,

hands steepled.

'Yes, yes, I see. Go on.'

'Ideally there are several syndicates who bid against each other, increasing the revenue of the government. The opium farmer's labourers of course boil and refine the opium into chandu and it is sold, through the farmers' shops in town and on the plantations, to the hundred thousand coolies working in this area. It is, for the opium farmer, a lucrative business as the mark-up can be up to three hundred percent and, as the labourers are the consumers, their wages can be recaptured through opium sales. If the residue from the pipe is sold several times over, the profits are commensurately greater.'

Cavenagh nodded.

'I see. The plantation owners are the syndicate, is that right?'

'Yes, sir. That is almost always true. At least the main money man of the syndicate is always the biggest gambier and pepper plantation owner, always a Chinese merchant, for they understand their people and their business better than us. And it is not advisable for the government to be directly involved in this business.'

'How much was the opium farm leased for last year?'

'Quite low, sir.'

McNair consulted his documents.

'The syndicate has been held these five consecutive years by Wei Sun Wei at fifteen thousand Spanish dollars per month. Of this one third goes to the Temenggong.'

'I see. Yet this is claimed to be excessive.'

'He has some 20,000 coolies working on the plantations in Johor. It was deemed suitable by Governor Blundell.'

'And the farm lease has not risen over five years.'

'No, sir.'

'This is because there is a lack of competition, clearly,' said Blackwood suddenly entering the conversation.

Cavenagh considered this. 'These excise farms are the only revenue which the town may draw upon. Is that correct?'

'Not entirely, sir,' McNair said. 'There are town property taxes, quit rents on country properties but these are small. Then there are judicial fines, fees on land transfers, that sort of thing, but, again, these are minor. The spirit farm excise is quite good, and we lease the sireh farm as well. But the opium farm alone is over half of the town's revenue.'

'And what of duties, port duties, cargo levees, that sort of thing?'

McNair threw a glance at Robert who grimaced.

'Governor Butterworth and Governor Blundell tried to impose port duties, sir, to raise funds for the lighthouses and other port improvements, but the town will not have it. The Chinese and European merchants come together like glue in hysterical protest at any nibbling of what they conceive of as their rights, and throw Raffles and free trade at us like cannonballs. Calcutta sees only losses and refuses to raise its share on what it considers to be an intransigent and untaxed mercantile population. In effect we are dependent on the opium farm.'

'You have had little contact with the Chinese, sir, I understand. But they are a peaceful and industrious people, Governor,' McNair added.

Cavenagh looked at Robert.

'Are they, Commissioner?'

'On the whole. Their secret societies are called "hoeys" or "kongsi". They can occasionally cause the most terrible trouble but for the last years there has been a reasonable level of peace. In the absence of a large enough police force and a proper judiciary we must adopt a laissez-faire attitude.'

'These "hoeys". Tell me about them. Are they like the dacoits in India?'

'Not at all, Governor. They are more like our freemasons, except they have a propensity to violence and their so-called brothers are foot soldiers and can be called upon to do the bidding of their leaders. Occasionally there are territory wars when dialect groups clash. Such violence is never, however, aimed at the colonial government to whom the Chinese leaders are remarkably loyal.'

Cavenagh seemed to consider this.

'However, Governor, they are powerful. Three years ago a misunderstanding occurred between the government and the Chinese population regarding the new Indian Police Act. The Governor found it absolutely impossible to translate into the Chinese hieroglyphics the technicalities of an English document of law and exaggerated rumours circulated like wildfire about the magnitude of fines, the number and gravity of punishable offences and the arbitrary powers of the police.'

'Translators. Do we have any now?'

Robert felt a moment of exasperation. The governor's mind did hop about so.

'One, Governor, and it is not sufficient. Currently we must send documents to Hong Kong for translation.'

Cavenagh frowned.

'As I was saying, sir. The level of discontent was such that the leader of the secret society called a strike. Believe me, Governor, if I tell you that within one hour of the issuance of that order the town of Singapore was hermetically sealed to trade. There was not a door or window open or a man at work at his business in the town. The Klings and others ceased work too for fear of this power, issued they knew not from where, but the effect of which was so obvious. For three days the town and port were utterly deserted. It came to an end only when the government managed to reassure the leading merchants.'

'Good God. Who leads them?'

'Sir, it is a very secret organisation. In general, the wealthiest merchant is their leader but I cannot say that with any absolute certainty. But my example goes to show how closely they control the labouring masses. Without the hoeys we should not be able to police our colonies at all, nor conduct any business. The Chinese are everything, sir, they are skilled in every trade and manufacture, grow the food and commercial crops and labour on the farms and in the town.'

McNair, who had spent several years in Penang, nodded his agreement.

'They are the best and most peaceable colonists in the world. I concur, sir. Their towkays, the wealthy merchants, are our go-betweens, in particular several of those you met at your reception. Whampoa, Seah and Zhen speak excellent English.'

Cavenagh gave this some thought.

'Sir,' Robert said into the silence, 'may I make a request for a return to the gambling farm licenses? It is an enormous source of revenue which the town denies itself.'

'Well, well, explain.'

'Abolished legally in 1829, Governor, but it has not put an end to its practice. It goes on unabated and gives rise to bribery of my policemen who, being so poorly paid, succumb to such corruption. The vice is not checked, but being clandestine it is pursued with even greater ardour. As it stands, sir, the interdict on gambling makes a good police force impossible and the moral mischief might be better dealt with were it not concealed. If we tax opium, surely gambling is no greater an evil.'

'Well, well. All this is most interesting.'

Robert waited for further illuminating words to issue from the governor's mouth but he seemed to be ruminating on an entirely different matter.

'Well, well. So this young Temenggong calls us his tax collectors does he? Perhaps the competition might be raised if we split the farms. We would no longer be his personal tax collectors then, eh, what, what.'

Cavenagh looked at the men around the room.

Robert frowned. The governor's mind seemed to hop about more often than his leg.

'Sir, that might not be wise.'

'And why, sirra?' said Cavenagh, rubbing his left thigh.

'It is likely that both the farmers would aim at smuggling in chandu to the others' domains in order to undermine their rivals. It has happened before. Sir, I have a police force of fourteen officers and three hundred and eighty men in a town of over fifty thousand Chinese.'

'Well, that is another matter,' said Blackwood and smiled at the governor. 'We lease the farm, and the farmer organises himself and his security. With the extra revenue, in any case, there may be money to increase the police force by a jemadar and a couple of peons, enough for more country stations.'

'Yes, indeed,' Cavenagh said. 'And we shall take this prince down a peg or two. Let him gather his own revenues. We shall see what throwing open the bidding can do. We will take offers for the Singapore farm and this young sultan must offer his farm for what he might get and pay us thirty percent.'

'He'll not agree, Governor,' said Robert.

'Then he will have to settle for what we give him, won't he. Perhaps it will deter him from war mongering.'

The governor rose, rubbing his thigh. His face had shut down. It was clear he was in pain.

'This meeting is at an end, sirs. Send Abu Bakar a letter and we shall see.'

8

The ship loomed large as the boatman drew near. HMS Valiant was a man-of-war, bristling with cannon. Admiral Hope had arrived and soon the fleet would depart for Hong Kong.

A week ago she would not, out of respect for Zhen, have thought to come to this ship no matter what her own wishes might have been. But his dismissive attitude had been followed by total silence. She had written once but had received no reply. For that week she had turned around her house and garden, played with Lily and fretted about him.

The only person she had permitted to visit was Teresa for she deserved a friend, and Andrew came to play with Lily. As much as Charlotte tried to stay out of this dispute between her brother and his wife, she was not permitted to do so. She could offer little in the way of advice or guidance but Teresa had talked and she had listened. Sometimes, between women, a sympathetic and sensible ear is sufficient to offer a transitory relief from care.

On the seventh day, she felt a slow anger burn inside her. He had said they may not come together for months, but this silence, this was hurtful. He had not written to her nor attempted to see Lily. It felt like he was punishing her for nothing when his absence was punishment enough.

A wicker armchair was winched over the side and in this rather ungainly but quite enjoyable manner she was brought aboard.

Edmund was waiting. She was piped into his company and the crew, lined up in formation, saluted her. It was all rather wonderful and she felt a thrill. Edmund had arranged the most military and rousing welcome for her. He knew the effect of such compliments and excitements on the susceptible nature of women, even this one. And it raised him to something more than a man, more invincible warrior. At least he hoped it did.

'Come,' Edmund said and led her to his cabin where a luncheon was laid out with white cloth and silver cutlery. He poured champagne and she looked around. The cabin was not large but well appointed, everything a naval man could need carefully in its place. A map of China was spread out on his desk. She went to it.

'Where you go, it will be very dangerous?'

'Yes, perhaps not so much for myself, as for the soldiers I carry.'

She knew instinctively that wasn't true. She felt his eyes on her and turned.

'It is good to see you again.'

He said nothing and she looked away under the intensity of his gaze. An awkward silence lengthened.

He broke it finally. 'You were married, I understand, and widowed. I am sorry.'

Charlotte looked up, wondering how he knew.

'Thank you Edmund, yes, my husband died many years ago. I have two boys and,' she hesitated the space of a breath, 'and, a daughter. One son is returning from Scotland and the other still there. Did you marry, Edmund?'

"I married, yes, a few years ago. My wife gave me one daughter. She died in childbirth with our second child who did not survive.'

Charlotte frowned and felt an anguish.

'Oh Edmund, I am so very sorry.' Charlotte put out her hand to his, but he did not take it and she dropped it back to her side.

'I have found active service has been of benefit in this case. My daughter lives with my parents in Leicestershire.'

Charlotte recalled, instantly, that the Mallorys were a noble Leicestershire family. She remembered vaguely that they lived in a place called Kirkby, or was it Kirby. Edmund made nothing of it, had told her only once, yet she remembered it now.

A servant arrived silently, bringing a tray with a pie and steaming vegetables. Edmund pulled out the chair for Charlotte and she sat.

'Do you recall the food on board the *Madras*? Apart from a few dinners you obligingly managed to get me, the food was appalling.'

'I recall everything on board the *Madras*,' he said.

Charlotte looked down. 'Edmund, I am sorry …'

Edmund raised his hand. 'No, no. I didn't mean to embarrass you.'

Edmund cut the pie and the aroma of beef filled the room. They both smiled.

'Do you like life here, Charlotte?"

Charlotte took a sip of champagne and contemplated her reply. Somehow, she wanted everything to be clear with this man. She knew the heart of him, perhaps better than any other man, even Zhen. He was a man of unflagging courage and honour. She looked into his eyes.

'What have you heard about me, Edmund?'

Edmund looked at her steadily. 'Nothing that means anything to me, if you are happy.'

In an instant, it seemed, they were back on terms of intimacy, as if the intervening years had disappeared; the intimacy of the shipboard companionship they had shared when they had talked of everything, her life, his own, his ambitions, her fears, poetry, music, beauty. They had passed five months in each other's company, on a voyage of dread, monotony, danger and hardship. They had shared the long evenings together when he was not on duty and when he was, she was often by his side.

One evening, he had thrilled her to her core. He had let her steer the ship guided by his hands. She had never forgotten that moment, the almost overpowering emotion of holding the wheel, feeling the hands of the seas holding this ship to its bosom, the arms of the wind rushing around them, the sails gusting and roaring, towering above them like a great forest filled with vast white clouds as they steered towards the moon.

She loved to watch him, calmly ordering the men to positions, taking charge, as if he *was* the ship; so long as he stood solid the ship was secure. She had been vulnerable but he had not once taken advantage of her vulnerability. He had watched over and protected her from the savagery of the ocean, the dangers of the deep and the eyes of the men which followed her every day and every night. Every man aboard the ship knew she was Lieutenant Mallory's woman but she had been too young and naive then to realise that he had been falling in love with her.

Edmund Mallory remembered, too, those days and nights on board the *Madras*. A feeling of the utmost tenderness had entered him almost the moment he had seen her come aboard. So slight, so pale, with her perfect features, her blue eyes, her long black hair. But smart and resourceful too, educated, intelligent, clever about the sea, which she understood. He would have killed any man who touched her and he had made it known on a ship full of lustful men. His control in her presence was wrought with the greatest of difficulty. Had she but known the number of times he wanted simply to forget all decorum, to find a dark place on this dark ship and feel her body against his, his lips on hers, possess her, she would not have thought him quite so gentlemanly.

Now, even now, after so many years, she still had this power. When he passed here for service in China, he had sought her, for he knew Robert was her brother. Then she had been not been in Singapore but in Batavia and he had been disappointed. When he had seen her at the reception he could hardly believe his eyes. After the incident with the Chinese man he had made inquiries. He had been told of her reputation. She was the most notorious woman in Singapore, the English concubine was what she was called. She lived with a Chinese man, had a Chinese child. It was beyond everything but some older families still welcomed her for they had known her a long time. So he had been told. Wealthy too, he had learned, and he knew this also led to jealousies. He wondered what on earth had led her to share her life with a Chinese man. It seemed extraordinary, outlandish, unwise, but it spoke of something deep which he understood. Passion.

After Charlotte had rejected his proposal, he had lost himself in the sea. The long voyage back from Calcutta to England was wretched, a minute and hideous torture, the memory of her everywhere on the *Madras*, and once home, he had sought a different ship, a different life, one full of even more danger than this. He had joined the Royal Navy and his experience on board armed Company vessels had led to rapid advancement. He had served in the suppression of slavery in the Atlantic, captained many hydrographic expeditions to map the seas and seen active service in the Crimea.

He forgot Charlotte, sometimes for a long time. But when the ship was on calm waters and the moon floated its silver rays on the ocean, he remembered her and missed her to his soul. For almost ten years he had settled for the uncertain pleasures of casual liaisons in ports all over the world and the camaraderie of the sea. Then in Hong Kong he had met Lucy, the daughter of an English merchant and his Chinese female companion. The father, as many before him had done, had departed back to his home and an English wife. But he had done a decent thing and left funds for his daughter to be raised properly, and this had come to pass. She had been raised by her mother, who sought a husband for her amongst the English naval officers. Edmund had been perceptive enough to see that Lucy reminded him of Charlotte with her willow figure, the beauty of her eyes, and her long black hair, but he had chosen to embrace it and pour the pent-up well of love he had guarded for so long onto her. She had been just seventeen when they married and he had loved her as tenderly and as passionately as any man could. She had died only two years ago, barely twenty-one years old.

He told Charlotte some, but not all, of this. The servant brought coffee.

'You have had an extraordinary life.'

'These are extraordinary times. No more than any other. No more than you. You became the wealthiest woman in the Indies. Imagine my surprise.'

'I did little to deserve it. Women do not make their own lives.'

'You deserve everything. And you seem to have made a life for yourself.'

She smiled at his kindness. He poured the coffee and handed

her a cup. The aroma was delicious and she inhaled it.

'You didn't answer my question, Kitt. Are you happy?'

She sipped the coffee and put down the cup. 'Happy? Yes, I believe I am happy. My children are healthy though of course there are always worries of some sort or other. I have security and wealth, and … '

Charlotte hesitated and he waited, wanting to know this more than any other thing. The servant lingered, clearing the table and a silence fell.

Happy? Was she happy? She had thought herself so, certainly. Life with Zhen was not in any degree conventional and provoked public censure. Could she imagine herself without him? The weeks ahead loomed and she hardly knew how to answer Edmund.

She felt his gaze and looked over at him.

He had feelings for her still, she could see it and she was moved. She had feelings for him too, stronger than she could have imagined. But what could she do about them? They felt disloyal to Zhen. Yet she could not answer him.

'I …' she began.

He frowned and she felt her heart beat very fast. What am I doing, she thought.

'I …'

A knock came to the door and the First Officer entered.

'Sir, the Admiral has sent for you instantly.'

Edmund turned, annoyed, to the First Officer. 'A moment, James.'

Charlotte rose. 'I must go. Your duty calls.' She felt an immense relief, as if she had stepped away from an abyss.

As the boat pulled away he watched her and she looked back at him, once, and waved her hand. What had she meant to say to him? Damn James for coming in like that. But he would write to her. She had not told him absolutely. Hope long extinguished in his heart sprang forth. He had to leave for battle, but he went no longer quite so indifferent to death.

9

Cheng watched from the edges of the room as Zhen was declared Mountain Lord of the Singapore Ghee Hin Kongsi and of the Grand Triad. It was midnight and the flickering candles threw shapes against the faces of the gods which adorned the walls.

The Incense Master put the ceremonial objects around him and Zhen bowed low to Guan Di, Emperor Guan, the Taoist god of war, a giant, nine-feet tall, with a two-foot long beard, a scarlet face, the eyes of a phoenix and eyebrows of silkworms. He sat on his throne in full armour brandishing his halberd. He gave the kongsi its spiritual tenor and its martial spirit. On either side images of his blood brothers, Liu Bei and Zheng Fei who symbolized undying loyalty and courage.

The ceremony was intimate, only the officers and some important brothers, including Ironfist Wang, were present. In this way was the mystery of the society maintained. A proclamation would be issued tomorrow and all the hundred thousand members in Johor and Singapore would know whom their new leader was. Usually this would be followed, at a propitious time, with a great gathering of the brotherhood, far away, in the jungle, when all the brothers would swear allegiance to Zhen. But this, they had all agreed, would be unnecessary since Zhen's leadership would be of short duration.

Cheng went forward as the others had done and bowed to Zhen, repeating the oath of loyalty. Cheng had his spies and knew that Zhen had stayed away from the English concubine. After the experience of their meeting at the governor's ball, Cheng knew he had felt humiliation. To his credit, he had not shown it. This was how it was, Cheng felt, when one did not have control of one's women. They made a fool of you. Cheng also knew the woman had gone to the ship of the very man who had humiliated Zhen. He was not sure what to do with this information at the moment.

Cheng stepped away and Wang, solid, hard and serious, stepped forward, took his sword and laid it at Zhen's feet. Wang viewed Zhen with awe. One of them, a Red Rod, had risen from lowliness, so young, to this exalted position. Wang fell to his knees and put his head to the floor, kowtowing to his master and repeating the oath of fealty with intensity. The Incense Master exchanged a glance with the Vanguard.

The cock was brought out. Its throat was slit and the blood mixed with the wine. All present drank, raising their cups to Zhen.

A small repast had been placed at the table before the altar and the men sat.

Zhen remained silent and did not take up his chopsticks.

'Zhen,' Cheng began.

Zhen shot his head up throwing a sharp glance at Cheng.

'Shan Chu, do you mean?' he said and kept his eyes on Chang's. 'In this place.'

'Well,' Cheng began.

The door opened and four Red Rods entered and stood menacingly in each of the corners. Cheng and the others stared at them, their chopsticks in mid air. Wang signalled to them and they bowed to Zhen.

'Be careful,' Wang said. 'Those who control the Little Brothers are the Big Brothers, the Red Rods. They are its swift power and they do my bidding. I obey only the Lord of the Kongsi. This is how it is written and always has been so.'

The Incense Master, the Deputy and the Vanguard instantly put down their chopsticks and bowed low to Zhen.

'Shan Chu,' they said.

Zhen turned his gaze onto Cheng. For the first time Cheng felt the great power of the oath he had made. He had sworn fealty to this man, loyalty or death, and suddenly realised what he had done. The instruments of swift justice for any deviation from the oath stood before him. Things like this did not happen in Riau.

Wang's eyes drilled into Cheng.

Cheng bowed his head, suddenly fearful.

'Shan Chu,' he said.

The meal came to a rapid end. No-one was hungry. Zhen picked up his cup of rice wine and tossed it back.

'I am the Lord. You have willed it. Do we understand each other?'

Zhen sent a piercing gaze onto Cheng. The Red Rods gathered behind their Lord. Wang rose and stood next to them, all of their eyes on Cheng.

'I have sacrificed much for you,' he said. 'I know what you want. But be wise how you act or you will know the consequences.'

Zhen walked out of the room followed by his soldiers, leaving the others to gaze at each other uneasily.

Zhen ordered his driver to take the carriage not to his home on Bukit Jagoh or his mansion on Market Street. Instead, he went to the shophouse on Circular Road which was the place of his medicine shop and above which he kept, still, the old apartments where he had first lived in Singapore. Baba Tan had installed him here to prepare for his wedding to his daughter, Noan. He dismissed the guard. As Shan Chu he was entitled to a guard at all times but this was the last thing he wanted.

He climbed the stairs to the upper rooms. Little had changed in many years. The same furniture, including the canopied iron bed. This was a place of significance. When he was able he had bought it outright, and as he walked around he felt Xia Lou here as in no other place. He went to the bathroom and stripped, pouring streams of water over his head and body. He lay half-damp on the bed and looked up at the iron circle which formed its centre.

The man, the naval officer, had shocked him. Her attitude to this man had shocked him. He had never seen Xia Lou look at any other man like that. Everyone knew his relations with her. In front of the entire Chinese community as well as the Europeans, he had been utterly humiliated. The letter she had written was of shock and apology. The man was an old, old friend. He meant nothing. She loved him alone. But he had not replied, too angry.

He turned to sleep, willing sleep to come and put his hand to the sheet, feeling her there. His anger had evaporated. Here in this bed he could not be cold with her. But the loss of face and damage to his authority felt tremendous and he hardly knew what to do about it. He knew what Wang would say and that worried him too. Wang was loyal and obedient, tough and hard. He had come from China only two or three years ago. He didn't understand the world here, his head was back there, in the way they did things there. A place where women did not go out and make fools of their men or, if they did, received swift justice.

He tossed. He had to speak to Wang about this.

10

'Sit down, gentlemen.'

Temenggong Abu Bakar walked slowly into the room and looked around at his assembled guests. He was slender and handsome, with a small dark moustache. His clothes were simple and brilliantly white.

'I have come from the mosque,' he said. 'I am purified and think fondly of my friend Wei Sun Wei, who was beloved of us.'

He sat on the green velvet throne all set about with gold and precious stones.

'I knew him all of my life. He sold cloth here, a humble man of such integrity and honesty that he won my father's heart. He spoke excellent Malay, you know, which was rare for a Chinese man. When we needed his aid, he raised an army to pacify the rebellion in Maur. I mourn him very much.'

Mohammed Salleh, the minister of the new town being build at Tanjong Puteri in Johor, stepped forward. He put his hands to the air, in an attitude of Muslim prayer.

'Allah is well acquainted with what we do,' he said.

William Kerr rose.

'On behalf of your European friends here present, please

accept our deepest condolences, your highness,' he said.

The European friends, William Napier, his lawyer, and David Paterson, his trade agent, murmured in agreement.

Zhen rose next.

'On behalf of your Chinese friends, accept our condolences, highness. Wei Sun Wei died in China and rests in the bosom of his ancestral home.'

'Yes,' Abu Bakar said, looking at Zhen and smiling. 'That is a comfort. Thank you.'

Cheng, who could not understand a word, turned to Zhen. Abu Bakar looked at Cheng indulgently.

'Please explain to Wei Sun Wei's son-in-law, that we are saddened at his loss.'

Zhen translated quickly and Cheng bowed. He had never learned to speak the correct form of Malay in this sort of company and dared not use inappropriate language. In any case, the discussion was being held in English of which he understood not one word.

Abu Bakar clapped his hands and three servants appeared instantly.

'Some refreshment. English tea, what do you say?'

Zhen smiled. Abu Bakar was born and raised here in Telok Blangah. He had attended the Malay Boys' School of Benjamin Keaseberry with all his brothers. He spoke excellent English and had adopted many of the habits of the English gentlemen.

He was young, charming, ambitious and politically astute. When his father's health had begun to fail he had taken the reins of state without the slightest hesitation.

Once tea, impeccably served in the finest English bone china, had been poured and distributed, Abu Bakar turned to Kerr.

'William,' he said, 'what do you make of this letter from the governor?'

'He has decided to split the farms, sir. The papers have railed at you for waging war under the Union Jack, claim that the British government loses prestige in the eyes of the Malays by supporting you, and insist you have too much revenue from the Treasury.'

'Yes, that is what I understand too.'

Zhen expressed no surprise but he felt it. Cheng, sensing something, turned to Zhen.

'The governor has split the farms,' he whispered. Cheng looked shocked.

'What does it mean for us, William?'

'The governor means to drive competition. He sees this as a way to force syndicates to outbid each other and raise the revenue. If you accept less, perhaps a quarter of the bid, he might reconsider but I doubt it. He has been stung by the paper's editorial. As a new governor, he feels he needs to stamp his mark.'

'Yes, I see that. I too am very new in my position.'

Abu Bakar looked at Zhen and Cheng.

'Please translate, Master Zhen. Wei's son-in-law is heir to his chukangs. I understand he wishes to bid for the opium farm.'

Cheng listened to Zhen's translation.

'Yes, sir, I do, but I had understood it would be the two farms combined.'

'The governor has ruled that that is no longer possible. I can attempt to dissuade him but William seems to think the governor will not be obliging for this year at least. Will you bid for Johor or Singapore in that case?'

Cheng felt utterly on the spot. The Singapore farm was, by far, the most lucrative of the two.

'I would need time to consider, Highness,' he said.

The Temenggong nodded and set his teacup on the saucer.

'Well, this is most interesting. Perhaps the governor is right. Perhaps new syndicates with better offers will emerge on both sides of the Straits.'

Zhen sensed Cheng's mistake. He had not immediately offered, as Wei Sun Wei would have done, to take the Johor farm, even at a reduced amount. Wei's loyalty and trust in the Temenggong, both the father and the son, had been absolute and mutual and Wei had profited by it. He had become the Kang Chu of all the best river properties and built great wealth and position as a direct result. He would have backed him no matter what. Cheng had missed his chance to prove that kind of loyalty. He was an outsider and could not read the situation. Abu Bakar knew that Cheng had inherited his plantations from the goodwill the Johor leaders had shown Wei, yet he had not given back what was needed from him.

This was a dangerous situation for Cheng, for the Surat Sungei, the 'river documents' which gave him the monopoly to exploit these lands, were renewable every few years. Cheng could find himself quickly dispossessed of the Johor properties. His inexperience here was so obvious, Zhen almost felt sorry for him.

Doubtless, Tay Ong Siang, the deputy, would make a bid for the Johor farm and the Temenggong would look favourably on it for he knew Tay well. Cheng must now outbid Hong Boon Tek for the Singapore farm and that would not be easy. But if Tay got Johor and Hong got Singapore there would be a turf war and that was not in anyone's interest, although the government would be quite happy at getting a great deal more revenue than they had expected and the rest be damned.

When the meeting came to an end, the men walked to their carriages.

'I don't understand what is happening here,' Cheng said. 'It is much more complicated than I expected.'

Zhen contemplated Cheng. He was a decent man, it seemed. Certainly not as foul as Hong who dealt in the shipment of girls for prostitution and packed the coolie junks so tight that the men hardly had air to breathe. Zhen remembered his own voyage to Singapore very well. It had been difficult but not like now. The demand for berths out of China because of the civil war was vast. But how much should he be telling this man his business?

He was resentful, he knew, of the threats the man had made, being put in this difficult position. But Cheng was at least sixty-five years old and Zhen quite liked him. He was vulnerable and out of his depth here in Singapore.

'You should have bid for Johor. You must tread carefully there. How much money can you put together? Hong certainly wants the farm in Singapore. He runs the traffic of the girls for the whorehouses and the coolie trade, both extremely lucrative. He has a lot of capital and will offer high. He wants to be the Shan Chu and will know you have thwarted him by backing me.'

Cheng listened carefully, grateful for this advice.

'The joint farms were rented for $15,000 a month to Wei. The rent has not shifted for five years, but the price of opium has increased. I can continue to offer $15,000 for the Singapore farm, but more would return a poor profit until the price of raw opium comes down.'

'If you can come to some agreement with Tay Ong Siang in Johor, that would be the best course. He hates Hong and Hong hates him. There's bad blood between them. A woman. A young ah ku whom Tay wanted and Hong refused him. Something like that.'

'Do you know Tay?'

Zhen got into his carriage.

'I know them both.'

'Will you speak to Tay? Persuade him to work with me if I get the farm?'

Zhen took up the reins but made no answer.

'Please. You are the leader, he will listen to you.'

It went against the grain to be disrespectful to Cheng for he was a much older man. And Cheng's voice had adopted a pleading tone.

'If you get the farm I will speak to Tay. But first you have to get the farm. And I'm not sure that will be enough money.' Zhen shook the reins and the horse moved forward.

Cheng mounted his carriage and the syce clicked the horse into movement. Zhen had been a good choice. He wondered now, with all the complications of the Singapore and Johor syndicates, the situation with the Temenggong, the English government and the complex relations between the Chinese, whether he would even be able to cope, at his age, with being the leader of the Kongsi.

He had Wei's wealth, his plantations in Johor, his shops in Singapore, his mansion on Mosque Street. Alongside his own land and influence in Riau, he had a great deal. The position of Shan Chu fit Zhen and he wore the mantle of the Lord well. He was respected and knew everything about the town, knew all the right people.

He could do worse than have him as a son-in-law. It would kill two birds with one stone. His only unmarried daughter was eighteen. He had not married her away young because he loved her too much and he wished to have her at his side. But he was now a resident in Singapore and marriage to this man was an idea which he liked very much. Through marriage he would have the closest alliance to the Lord of the Kongsi who was also a wealthy man and who understood all this world which he found so difficult.

The last thing he wanted now was for Zhen to resign his post and return to this English concubine. He needed to speak to Wang. He settled back and watched the lush countryside go by. Life in Singapore was infinitely more interesting than Riau.

11

The incense swirled through the branches and long aerial roots of the banyan tree like the spirits of the wood. The cemetery overflowed with colours of gold and red and the odour of sandalwood.

It had been three years since Tan had died. Zhen and his family, alongside his mother-in-law, were at his gravesite for the 'picking of the bones' ceremony. The grave had been dug out by the two officers of the dead, and three Buddhist priests were chanting sutras. Overhead, yellow silk umbrellas shielded the gravesite from the sun.

Soon the coffin would be opened and the bones extracted and wrapped in a white cloth. From here, they would go to the temple where they would be picked clean of all remaining skin and dirt. The teeth would be removed from the skull for a legend said that, if the teeth are left in the body, then the spirit would consume its offspring. Red realgar wine cleanses the bones, then each bone is wrapped in tan paper and red string is tied to give the appearance of veins. Red translucent material is wrapped around the skull.

The bones duly prepared would then be placed from the feet upwards to the skull in an urn and reinterred with due ceremony in the ancestral gravesite. All this had been done two years ago for Noan. Zhen had found it unpleasant but this was the belief of his mother-in-law and the ritual had been carried out as required. The pyjamas of white which both she and he had worn for their vowing ceremony was black and rotten. Traditionally he would be buried himself in his own pyjamas and the cloth from which they were made would unite them again in death.

Zhen stared down at the heavy wooden coffin of his father-in-law but his mind was on the conversation he had had yesterday with Ironfist Wang. He had not been able, at first, to comprehend what Wang was saying, why he was even talking about Xia Lou. Then he understood. She had been to the ship of the English captain. She had spent several hours on board alone with this man.

'Are you sure,' he'd asked and Wang had nodded. He had taken the information from Cheng and checked with the boatmen on the harbour. They had told him. Wang had felt the shame and humiliation of such actions towards this man, his sworn liege, very acutely. He hated any woman who could do such a thing.

'Shall I follow her, Master?' Wang had said.

'No, no. Leave her alone.'

Wang had bowed but he was not sure the Master knew what he was saying.

The priest intoned the prayers over the coffin as the men set about removing its heavy lid. Lian gazed quietly at the tomb of her mother nearby. She had hardly known this woman. A vague recollection of sweetness before she had been snatched away from life and her children, and Lian had been given to her aunt.

From that moment she had been separated from her sisters and brother. She barely knew the sisters at all. Their upbringing had been so completely different and they had been married away so very young. Lian thought it was terribly wrong to marry girls aged thirteen away to men twice their age. It horrified her. As for Kai, he was ten and the most self-centred, spoiled and pampered boy in creation, ruined by their doting grandmother. She felt utterly disconnected from this living family and closer to those lying dead in the ground. She had loved her grandfather who had visited often and played with her whereas, other than family occasions, she had rarely seen her grandmother at all for all her attentions were focused on her grandson.

Her eyes swivelled to her aunt. She looked quite reasonable today, her hair neat and stuck with the diamond pins she loved. She had been a beautiful woman, it was clear to see, but misery and gall had made her face bitter and stiff. Zhen stood to one side with the other men of the family and Lian saw the gaze Lilin shot at him. A gaze at once passionate and malevolent. Lian felt sorry for her aunt whose life seemed to have been one long tale of misery. The fate of her sisters and her aunt, the lot of Chinese women which she saw as so crimped and confined, had settled iron into Lian's soul and she was determined she would not go the way of all these women. She took her example from Miss Sophia Cooke, the head of the Chinese Girl's School, a woman filled with the spirit of freedom and education and from Charlotte, her father's mistress, whose own life was of her choosing.

A great gasp went up from the womenfolk and a high pitched scream from her grandmother. Zhen awoke from his reverie and Lian swivelled her eyes to the coffin.

Her grandmother and old aunts began keening, their wails seemingly echoing off the great trunks of the banyan trees like canyon walls.

Baba Tan, instead of being in a state of advanced decomposition, was instead, reasonably well preserved. The clothes had rotted somewhat and the hands were skeletal but the flesh on the face was taught, stretched and somewhat sunken, but otherwise intact.

Zhen knew that it was because the heavy coffin had been prepared with seven coats of tung oil to preserve it and keep the water out. It was, consequently, dry. In its present state it would take years for seepage to occur and rot the flesh away. Zhen had a keen interest in English science and read the books from the Institution library but this was mere common sense.

But, for his superstitious mother-in-law, this was interpreted in a very different way. She saw at is as a condemnation of the original burial, a way of blaming the living for some misdeeds and of course immense bad luck.

The Buddhist priests took all this in their stride. They reassured the old woman and praised Zhen for the quality of the wood. She, nevertheless, threw venomous looks at her son-in-law. The head priest knelt beside the coffin and made a blessing. Then realgar wine was liberally sprinkled on the corpse from head to toe and poured around the body.

Lian turned away. She had been taught to understand that such rituals were pagan. Lilin stared at her dead father, unwaveringly, then suddenly began to laugh. It was so shocking that her mother turned and slapped her. Lilin stopped instantly.

The coffin lid was fitted into place and the gravediggers began refilling the grave. Three more years would go by before they came again by which time the wine would have done its job.

Offerings of food were made, candles and incense lit at all the graves, and bundles of hell's notes and paper ingots thrown into the fire in the great urn. Lian lit the joss in her turn and bowed low to her ancestors' tombs. She placed the tight bud of the lotus she had brought for her mother on her grave.

Lilin came up to Zhen to pay her respects and Lian watched,

curious. Zhen acknowledged her but his body stiffened. That he could not bear to be near her was obvious. What had gone on between these two? She had loved her father with whom she had an easy and pleasant relationship but, since the business of marriage had been announced, she found him overbearing.

As they went down the hill, Zhen signalled to her and she went to him, bowing. Lilin followed them with her eyes.

'Mrs. Manouk spoke to me of you as you asked her.'

Lian turned her eyes to her father's, a bright flare of hope springing into her heart.

'She has argued that a girl of your education and upbringing will not settle into the life of a traditional Chinese wife. She was eloquent but she understands nothing of the Chinese and our culture.'

Lian felt the flame die a little.

'What did you answer her, Father?'

'That I understood her desire to be helpful but that this business was my business.'

Actually Zhen had been appalled at Lian's boldness. Xia Lou had raised the subject at the last dinner they would eat together for many weeks. She had asked him to reconsider, but what was there to reconsider. He had given way on Alex and Lily. This daughter was his alone. Now he was so angry at Xia Lou he was unreachable on this subject.

Lian's heart sank.

'Father, I want to obey you but Ah Soon is an opium addict.'

'Many men are. Should they not have wives?'

Lian felt a coldness enter her. He was determined. She saw his implacability. Nothing she could say would change his mind. He was heartless and she hated him. What difference did it make what she said now?

'You are a hypocrite. You do not marry. You live with the woman you love, a beautiful, intelligent woman who has her own independence. You do not take a wife you do not care for.'

Zhen pulled up abruptly and took her by the arm roughly. 'How dare you?'

Lian looked at him boldly, unflinching. She had rather die or be beaten than go down this path.

'What is not true? You love Miss Charlotte and do not marry another.'

Zhen felt a dagger blow to his heart. To speak of Xia Lou, now, when things had so rapidly become strained. He thought constantly of her eyes turned to this man, her hand in his and now the visit to this sailor, this Commodore Mallory. What had she said, what had she done aboard his ship? He turned to Lian in fury.

'Silence. Am I not free to take another wife if I choose? If my children are so disobedient and wilful I had better have some different ones.'

Lian fell silent. Could this be true? Could it? When she knew he cared so much for Charlotte. She had always secretly admired his unwavering faithfulness to this English woman which was the Christian ideal, and despised the Chinese men who took wives and concubines willy-nilly.

His mother-in-law turned, darting a look of venomous disapproval over them both as if they and their unorthodox lives were the fault of everything. Zhen bowed to her with exaggerated deference and for an instant Lian felt their solidarity. She and her father always found common ground in their feelings of general annoyance at her grandmother. But his tone was icy.

'You will not shame me,' he said severely. 'You will do as you are told. You will prepare yourself for marriage. You are fortunate even to know it or who will be your husband. Resolve yourself. You will marry Ah Soon. Now go and join your grandmother.'

Lian felt that her heart would break. She wanted to shout at him, scream and scream and scream. She hated him, hated them all.

But she knew it was useless and her grandmother would take her in and lock her up and everything would be worse. She turned away from him and walked down the hill.

12

Cheng watched from the upper windows as Zhen arrived.

This house, with its carved wooden shutters, its porcelain tiles, its graceful fountain courtyard, its opulent elegance was a far cry from the attap-roofed compound he had grown up in. Even now, his compound in Tanjong Pinang, whilst spacious and well-made, was nothing compared to this mansion.

His great grandfather, a poor peasant, had come from China to Senggarang and farmed there, marrying a local woman and raising twelve children. All of them, boys and girls, had married into the local Chinese Baba community of merchants for there was a great shortage of their own kind. His grandfather had married fortuitously the daughter of the Chinese interpreter to the Sultan at Tanjong Pinang, who had risen to a position of some importance and that marriage had brought forth seven daughters and six sons. The family fortunes had risen very quickly as his grandfather had found great influence with the Sultan when one of his daughters had married the Sultan's fourth son. Cheng's father had married the daughter of a wealthy Baba plantation owner and inherited his business and status.

Cheng had married as first wife, the daughter of the Sultan's second wife, a nonya who had great influence over the Sultan.

He had benefited, receiving land, honours and riches, including being made Kapitan Cina of Riau. He had met Wei on a visit to Singapore in the company of the Sultan many years ago when Wei was not as rich as he would become and, because Cheng's great grandfather had come from Chenghai, the same small region of Chaozhou as Wei, he had become sentimental and then impressed with Cheng's business acumen and the extent and spread of his influence in the East Indies. So he had married his first daughter, Teck Neo, to him. Teck Neo spoke Teochew, for Wei's first wife had been brought from China and Cheng had renewed his ties with the family tongue. When Wei's son had died of fever, Cheng had become the principal male in the family after Wei himself. Thus were fortunes made over time through judicious marriages and kinship ties.

Cheng's first wife, his two sons, with their wives and children would continue to live in Riau and attend to his business interests there. With Teck Neo he had had five daughters, all married judiciously throughout the Indies to the most influential Baba families. Teck Neo had died a year ago in an epidemic of smallpox along with his beautiful Javanese concubine, a court dancer, whom he had loved most dearly. Now he was here in Singapore with the daughter she had given him, his favourite child, the child of his love, Jia Wen.

He walked to her room. She was seated at the mirror. She rose and bowed to her father as he entered. He looked at her a moment. She was dressed in the clothes of a Javanese court princess, a gold and brown sarong and a tight black-and-gold tunic. Her ears had rings of gold and her head carried a golden diadem. Her black hair was gathered at her neck with diamond pins. Her eyes were her great beauty, large and lustrous, curved at the edge, dark with kohl. She looked like her mother and Cheng's heart felt sorrow for this lost love.

'Daughter, when I send for you, you must make a good impression. He may bring great good fortune to our house.'

'Father, I will obey you.'

Jia Wen bowed her head to him. They spoke in Chinese, which she had learned from her father and from the tutors he had brought in to teach her. He had wanted her to learn to read it too, so as to read to him from Chinese books which he could not understand. She and her Javanese mother had lived separately from his wives in a peaceful kampong amongst the Malays and it was his pleasure to visit them and watch whilst the old scholar made her write out the characters. In consequence of her quick intelligence and many years of such tutoring she had become proficient and she read to him from *The Dream of Red Mansions* and *The Romance of the Three Kingdoms*. He had given her the Chinese name of Jia Wen, though he rarely used it, and he liked her to dress as her mother had.

She had grown up in this unusual way, surrounded by Malays and their religion amongst a group of Javanese women who taught her beauty secrets and graceful dance and obedience, especially to her father.

She felt a small quiver of excitement. Her father had talked only briefly to her of this man. She knew her father loved her and trusted him absolutely. If this man was to be chosen for her, she very much wanted to see him. Cheng kissed his daughter's cheek.

Zhen looked about him. The house was richly decorated with an eclectic mix of Chinese and English elements. Two large Venetian mirrors adorned the walls of the reception room above a Chinese table, which held an ornate French clock.

Cheng entered and Zhen bowed low to him as befitted a young man to an elder. Here they were not in the kongsi.

'Thank you for honouring me.'

A servant brought tea and the two men discussed trivial things for a while.

'Hong has been to visit me, to pay his respects.'

Cheng pursed his lips and waited.

'He would not reveal what he intends to bid but I got the impression he wants to win. What you have said strikes me as correct. I believe he is involved in smuggling chandu into Riau, perhaps into Singapore. I have heard he has a headquarters on one of the islands in the Lingga Archipelago and runs chandu from there throughout the region.'

'How does he obtain the raw opium?'

Zhen shrugged. 'Doubtless piracy. Junks from China deliver their cargoes of coolies and leave here empty and scour the region. The British cannot stop them. The law does not permit it. As an important coolie broker, the captains of these ships need him. He finances them, they waylay the opium ships from India as they leave the Straits of Malacca and rob them. The chandu is easy to make on any of a thousand islands and everyone gets rich. Who can prove he is behind it?'

Cheng shook his head. 'The man is a thief and a pirate.'

Zhen glanced at Cheng. We are all thieves, he thought. We take the goods of the native populations for as low as we can, abuse their labour, make addicts of them and go about our business. Only a fine line separated himself, Cheng and Hong. But Hong was a pedlar of human flesh, flesh like his own and others he cared for, and Zhen disliked him.

'If you could prove it, the British would prosecute him for piracy and interfering in the legitimate activities of the revenue farmers.'

'Prove it? How?'

'That is not my problem. But I imagine it worries him somewhat so that is why he wishes to be the legitimate farmer. Otherwise he would just carry on as usual.'

'It worries him. Yes. So he is vulnerable in some way.'

'Seems like it. There are junk captains involved, and then there are the Penghulu, the island headmen, who all have to get a share. The Malays and Chinese rarely get on for long. Perhaps there's been a problem. Only takes one disgruntled or jealous Penghulu to take to piracy himself. Murder the crew of the junk in some isolated river mouth, sink it, decide to keep all the opium to his own account and what can Hong do? He can't police the islands which the Penghulu controls. He needs the cooperation of a lot of uncontrollable people over a wide area. You see?'

'Yes, yes. You're right.'

'I imagine he also wants the face. The recognition as the syndicate head. He has asked me to back him with the government.'

'Will you?'

'No. I will back no-one. This is about money. The government might listen to me because they don't want anyone to default on payment and might believe I can guarantee that. But I won't do it. I was backed into this role by you for the only reason that I am impartial. So that is what I will be. If you want the farm, you will have to outbid Hong.'

'Even though if Hong takes the farm it will cause trouble with Tay?'

Zhen shrugged. 'I can order the brotherhood to ignore certain things perhaps, rally behind others, but, at the end of the day, their employers are their leaders. If they are told to smuggle they will, especially if there is a financial incentive. It is not my role to interfere in such matters. Actually it is very unusual for the leader of the kongsi not to be the opium farmer or at least the major plantation holder. You, Hong or Tay are the natural leaders.'

Cheng looked sharply at Zhen. 'Yes, true. You know the reason you were asked ...'

'Yes. And I will do it. But my interests don't lie in the farming business, not opium, not gambier, not pepper, not spirits. When the excise leases are sold, I will resign. This role has already led to some regrettable problems in my private life.'

Cheng nodded. 'I am sorry. I am grateful; we are grateful for your compliance. Come. Let us enjoy some dinner and rice wine. I also have brandy.'

Zhen relaxed. He had said what he wanted to. Cheng was the best man to take the Singapore opium farm. He was of Teochew origin, like Tay, so there would be less resentment between them and he was the son-in-law of Wei, the friend of Tay. But it was up to him now, as to whether he could raise the funds. Zhen was convinced the governor would not take less than sixteen thousand a month for the Singapore farm. For Hong, Zhen knew it was a matter of pride, of face. Hong might bid for Johor but Zhen had no doubt that the Temenggong would not accept even if it was high. Abu Bakar had grown up in Singapore and seen what havoc the riots of 1854 had wreaked. He would want a man he trusted to keep the peace as well as pay him the tax. So with Tay most certain to win Johor, the bad blood between the men would mean Hong had to win on this side of the straits.

He meant to ask Cheng to include Qian, with his backing, into the syndicate. Advancing him credit which he had to pay back might curb a little of the lifestyle he had chosen to adopt. It was the last thing he would do for Qian and he did it only to try to better the life of Ah Soon and, by extension, that of Lian.

He had thought long about her and was, indeed, worried that Ah Soon would not be able to father a child or conduct himself as a husband ought. He had seen, at first hand, what a barren and miserable marriage had done to Lilin. At this moment, this was the only way he could think of to find a solution to the problem.

Dinner was copious. Cheng had brought his cooks and they knew their business. Cheng was a pleasant companion and the two men talked of their childhoods, so very different. Cheng, ostensibly Chinese, yet ignorant of his roots and an Indies native, asked many questions about his great grandfather's homeland. Zhen found himself enjoying the evening speaking of things long forgotten, and his own recollections of China. They talked of the mad Christian convert, Hong Xuiquan, who claimed to be the younger brother of Jesus Christ. He and his followers had cut their queues and had risen up against the Qing government. They caused havoc in the countryside, crops failed, villages were burned. The rebels held Hangzhou and Suzhou but had failed to take Shanghai so far. Men poured out of China and into Singapore in their tens of thousands.

Cheng found Zhen knowledgeable on the subject for the English papers reported on it in detail. This knowledge of English, Cheng saw clearly, was an immense advantage in the colonial cities of the British empire. Perhaps his grandsons should be tutored in it, alongside Dutch, rather than, like himself, turning to Chinese in an attempt to somehow dig into his distant roots.

As the servants laid the final dishes, several others came running holding a long Chinese zither which they placed on two low stands.

'I hope you do not mind. My daughter will play for us. She lives here with me.'

Zhen was taken aback. To see an unmarried daughter of such a man was unexpected to say the least. But he did not fully understand the habits of the Baba of Riau.

'It is a great honour.'

'Her music is pleasing. It is not the custom to praise a daughter, I know, but I cannot help myself. She has a gift.'

Jia Wen entered and bowed to her father and his guest. She kept her eyes down, never once glancing up. She sat on her knees before the zither.

Zhen was surprised to see, not a young nonya in her baju and sarong but a Javanese woman, fully eighteen or nineteen, with a curvaceous figure and the large limpid eyes of the Javanese beauty. It was unexpected and Cheng let out a small laugh at his expression.

Then he received an even greater surprise. She took up a paper and read in fluent Chinese a poem he knew, *The Painted Zither*, by his favourite poet, the enigmatic, complex, passionate, mystical and ever entrancing poet of love, Li Shangyin.

Why does the painted zither have fifty strings?
Each string, each bridge, recalls a year of youth
Vast sea, bright moon, pearls with tears
Indigo mountain, the warm sun, jade forms smoke
This feeling; does it have to wait to be a memory
This moment, as it comes, already lost in a trance

This was so charmingly read and with such grace that Zhen smiled and Cheng clapped his hands lightly.

She began to play. The zither music is like water, now soft and bubbling like a stream running over stones, now strong like wind in trees. Zhen watched this woman at the zither, her fingers plucking the instrument. Her touch was as light as gossamer yet the music was strong and melodic.

She played a Chinese melody on a Chinese instrument yet she

had all the freshness and warmth of the southern climes. Her skin was a smooth pale brown, like honey.

Cheng clearly loved this daughter and had chosen not to marry her away at a very young age. Zhen saw the bloom on her cheek, the glossy blackness of her hair, her full red lips. Her gold diadem flashed in the low candlelight. For the first time in many years he found himself not entirely immune to the charms of youth and beauty.

She played so well that Zhen saw many of the servants had gathered in the corridors to listen as if she were a siren on the shores of some mystical island. The last notes were plucked. She lifted her head and looked at him with the deep darkness of her eyes. It was a glance, an instant only, before she lowered her gaze. Cheng beckoned to her and she rose in one fluid movement and came forward.

She sank to her knees in front of Zhen and bowed deeply, her hands on the floor, her head just above them. It was an attitude of absolute respect and abandonment to him and Zhen felt it like a lightning strike. She was pure Yin, dark, yielding and liquid.

Cheng smiled slightly.

'My worthless daughter, Jia Wen.'

13

'Wake, Miss Lian, wake up.'

Lian felt her shoulders being shaken and opened her eyes to see her old maid trembling by the side of the bed.

'Ah Fu, what …'

'The mistress. Come quickly.'

Lian yawned. What on earth? What time was it?

Ah Fu's voice was filled with fear and the hand which she extended trembled. Lian and Ah Fu were as close as mother and child, for without her Lian knew her life in this house would have been infinitely worse. She had been raised by Ah Fu, an old woman now, but a girl once who had been brought from China as a bondmaiden and raised in a Hokkien merchant's home. She, not being pretty, was perhaps saved from the brothel and passed from place to place, sold on each time until finally she had come to rest in the house of Baba Tan and given into the service of Noan, the eldest daughter. When Noan had died, she was given Lian to care for, moved into the household of Lilin, and poured her love onto the little girl.

Lilin paid no attention to Lian unless she wanted something. Approval, perhaps, as she paraded the streets with her little girl and received the smiling murmurs of the other women. Love, or at least its false outward expression. Respectability, for married women without children were pitied and secretly despised and since she had driven away her husband, a fact which everyone knew, Lian had been the bedrock of this respectable life. But neglect was her usual attitude and Ah Fu had taken her and kept her sane.

Lian rose and followed Ah Fu's candle. Two other maids emerged from the darkness and joined them. Together they went towards the light which glowed in the bedroom of Mother Lilin.

She turned into the room and put her hand to her mouth. Lilin floated on a pool of red-stained silk bed clothes. Ah Ma was by one side of Lilin, wrapping a bandage around her left wrist. Lian rushed forward.

'Is she dead?' she cried, and the housekeeper shook her head. 'Alive.'

She looked at one of the maids who was hanging back, her mouth opened, half terrified. 'Water,' she said. 'Lots of it. Hurry up, silly girl.'

'A doctor ...' Lian began but the housekeeper looked up sharply.

'She will live. No doctor. No scandal. Your grandmother will have my head.'

Lian knew Ah Ma was the spy her grandmother kept in the house. She had not kept this fact a secret. The woman was sensible, sanity in an insane house and was kind to her.

Ah Ma finished the bandage, which was itself now stained with blood.

'Xiao Lin heard her screams,' the housekeeper said. Xiao Lin was Lilin's maid and slept in the room next to her, always on the alert for some change of mood in her volatile mistress.

'She had the guts only to slash one wrist and then set up a hue and cry. Perhaps it would have been better if …'

The housekeeper did not finish the sentence and exchanged a glance with Lian.

Ah Fu came up to Lian and put an arm on her shoulder. Lian took her hand and together, all the women looked down at the white drained face of this crazed woman. In this house of women, all sympathised with Lian and none wished to lose their place. Here, within reason, they did as they pleased for no man lived in the house to order them about. Their job, they knew very well, was to keep Lilin quiet and stifle any scandal.

'If my grandmother knows,' Lian said, staring at Ah Ma, 'she will tell my father and then he will be forced to do something.'

Ah Ma rose from the bed as the maid brought water. Ah Ma and Lian raised Lilin, forcing water down her throat. She spluttered but drank.

'Go back to bed,' Ah Ma whispered. 'I will take care of this.'

The next morning when Lian woke, she went instantly to Lilin's room. She was half-conscious only and Lian knew Ah Ma had given her opium pills. Xiao Lin was applying a paste of tamarind and honey to the wound. Lian went forward. The slash which had bled so copiously seemed like nothing, but that thin line was like a mark in the sand in Lian's life.

How long before it became known that Lilin was suicidal? Ah Ma, Ah Fu and the upstairs maids would not tell, she was sure, but the cook and his young boy, the scullery maid and the syce, all the others would wag their tongues. Such delicious news would go from the house through the hawkers and tradesmen who called and within a day or two to the ears of her grandmother.

The news about her father had come to her in just this way. The servants told the cooks who told the seller of noodles who told their supplier of wood who liked one of the housemaids.

Like a long siren's song it reached the ears, of course, of Ah Fu, a woman so enamoured of gossip her very life seemed to depend on it.

Her father had visited the house of the old man Wei Sun Wei, where there was a young girl, the pretty daughter of the son-in-law Cheng, who spoke Chinese though she was from Java, or looked like it, and she had played music for him and kowtowed before him and there was talk all over the house that she would be his bride, for otherwise why had the father shown her to him, which was really a scandal anyway. Lian recalled her father's words at the graveside of her grandfather.

Am I not free to take another wife if I choose?

'Ah Fu,' she said as they walked towards the Institution. 'After school I will go to visit with Miss Xia Lou.'

Ah Fu smiled. Her teeth were like a picket fence with one or two railings missing. Ah Fu loved to visit this English house. She had a friend in one of the cooks and she would eat sugary English cakes and drink tea and find even more wonderful gossip about the European town.

Accordingly, that afternoon, Lian and the old woman turned their steps to North Bridge Road and Lian rang the bell. The Indian majordomo despatched Ah Fu to the kitchen, showed Lian to a chair in the hall and went in search of his mistress.

Lian could barely contain herself. She felt this might be her last hope and her hand shook with anxiety.

Within a few minutes he returned and she followed him into the garden, her legs wobbling with nerves.

'Lian.' Charlotte rose. She could see the girl was distressed. Her body was shaking and her face was covered in sweat.

'My dear, are you ill?'

She took Lian's hands and helped her to a chair. Lian took

deep breath and threw a beseeching look at Charlotte.

'I cannot marry him. He is addicted to opium, he consorts with women in the town, he is a degenerate.'

'You talk of Ah Soon. I know this. It's a terrible thing.'

'I beg of you. You must speak to my father again. Please.'

Charlotte shook her head and Lian's heart fell.

'Lian, my dear, it will serve no purpose. It is all I can do to convince him how to act with Lily and ...' Charlotte held her tongue. She had almost spoken of Alex.

Tears welled in Lian's eyes and she put her hands to her face in utter despair.

'Oh, my dear, I'm sorry. At the moment my relations with your father are ... well ... perhaps not ... There are some things.'

'So it's true?' Lian asked, staring at Charlotte and wringing her hands.

Charlotte frowned. 'True? What's true?'

'That he will marry that girl, the Javanese daughter of the merchant Cheng. She is to be the new bride he spoke to me about.'

'Your father spoke of taking a wife?'

'Yes, yes.' Lian's agitation increased and she made as if to rise then sank back to the chair. 'I am doomed. He will think nothing of marrying me off as quickly as possible so he may get on with his new family.'

Lian burst into tears, her entire being concerned so entirely with herself, she thought of nothing else.

Charlotte was so shocked she could neither move nor think. She stared at Lian and time seemed to slow.

'If you do not help me, I will kill myself.'

Something in the hushed tone dragged Charlotte's attention back to the young girl. She put her hand to Lian's.

'No,' she said, 'don't say such things.'

Suddenly Lian rose. She turned and ran into the house. Charlotte watched her go, feeling like a ship that had come loose from its moorings and set adrift, ragged and aimless, far out to sea.

For days Charlotte tried to make sense of what Lian had said. She had no reason on earth to suspect Zhen. In all the time they had been together he had never lied to her. But she could not speak to him and dared not go to his house. And he had not replied to her letter. There had been no communication between them for almost ten days and she felt the strain of it and a deep, dull resentment.

Her heart grew heavy and she more distracted until one morning, as massed clouds gathered in the south, her eyes fell on an article by the editor fulminating about the state of Chinatown and the evils of human trafficking, especially the degrading spectacle, in one of her Majesty's colonies, of young women forced into prostitution. She remembered that Zhen had told her Qian had moved to Hong Kong Street, where he ran some of these brothels.

Prostitution was so commonplace on the other side of the river that hardly anyone gave it a thought. Miss Cooke took in prostitutes who, through their diseases, had been abandoned to their fate. Some ran away, from time to time, but Charlotte knew it was a dangerous thing to do. Many were murdered by the thugs.

She wanted to get to the bottom of this gossip about Zhen's marriage and at the same time she wanted to speak seriously to Qian about Lian and Ah Soon. These were the reasons which impelled her to rise and take up her hat. But she was curious too and longing, hoping, to see Zhen.

She left the syce at the corner of South Bridge Road. He made a small objection but quickly relented. He did not want to go into the town where the cholera killed you in three days. She walked slowly down Hong Kong Street which was lined with low taverns cheek-by-jowl with opium dens and brothels. Two beggars approached and tugged her gown and, alarmed, she moved away. A gaggle of little children with filthy faces and clothes wiped their noses, pointed and ran away. Two men lay, cadaverous, down a filthy alley. The smell of effluent was strong and rubbish lay strewn the length of the street and in the drains. She had not been in this street in her life, rarely now ever came to Chinatown. It was degraded and foul and she regretted her unconsidered decision.

Min fanned herself and watched Charlotte from the verandah of the Heaven's Gate brothel. She knew exactly who this woman was. Min had been crazy for Zhen when he first came to her brothel and he had saved her life after she had been half beaten to death by an English sailor. He had secured her release from the *kwai po* through a combination of bullying, influence and money, and she had gone to Malacca as a *tap tang*, a free agent. She had served Qian in the brothels there and made a great deal of money. Enough to give up the life but when Qian had fallen on hard times, Zhen had sent for her and she had remembered her obligations to him and returned to take charge of Qian's four ah ku houses.

Her obligation to him and Qian was therefore deep and not just because she had burned the yellow paper and sworn an oath to the kongsi. They had saved her from the ultimate degradations of such a life.

As a dirt-poor girl of fifteen, she had been sold by her parents to the dealer and shipped to Canton along with thousands of others. This sale condemned her to a life of sexual slavery from which there was little chance of escaping, except by death. It was in Canton that she, along with hundreds of other virginal young girls had been turned over to the highest bidder and been deflowered not too gently by a fat old Mandarin. She had been terrified and cowed, as they all were, surrounded by heavy-set thugs.

Having made the first part of his money from her, the virgin price, the pimp then sold her on for shipment to Singapore where she had been forced to have an abortion, a job so botched, there had been no more pregnancies. A small mercy she supposed, growing hard in this relentless life. For two years she had served in a *loh kui chai*, a high-class brothel in Smith Street reserved for the well-off Chinese tradesmen and merchants who could pass the night with their favourite. Then she had been moved to the brothel for the foreigners, ones with money, the government officials and officers of the regiment for she was still pretty and only seventeen. These establishment were, at least clean, but she had got the pox, of course, all the women had it and she had successfully concealed it. The pox could mean you were sold on down instantly into the lowest class brothels, or even simply murdered or abandoned.

After a time she had been put down to the second-class brothel. Here she had met Zhen and ultimately been saved from what followed. Usually, after six years, women like her were moved along, to the very low-class coolie brothels, the *pau chai*, firecracker brothels, so named for the swiftness with which the prostitute dealt with her clientele of drunkards, poor coolies, sailors and soldiers. Within a couple of years they were sold out of Singapore and moved to Malaya or Borneo, or the Indies and as they aged, to lower and lower places, the huts on the plantations of gambier and pepper and the tin mines until they were worn out. The women were never free, always indebted to their owners, until they died of disease or despair.

There was always a steady stream of new young women arriving to replenish those moved on. As a *kwai po* with a decent heart, Min tried to mitigate to a certain extent the misery of the girls in her charge, but there was only so much she could do. She trained them in the life and if they didn't work, they were moved on or beaten. They were like dust, carried on the wind and their graves could be anywhere.

Min could see the Mah Nuk woman was distressed. Doubtless her blue eyes never saw such sights in the quiet spaces of the European town. What she was doing here was a mystery, but she was Zhen's woman so Min rose and went down the stairs. She whispered to one of the samseng slouching in the verandah and he raced away.

'Can I help you?' she said in Malay and Charlotte turned.

The woman she saw was Chinese, slight and dressed in a colourful baju and sarong. Her face had been hurt at some stage and the scars were obvious.

'I seek Sang Qian. I was told he lives here.'

'There,' said Min and pointed to the small house squeezed between two of the brothels opposite Heaven's Gate. Charlotte stared in dismay at this poor-looking establishment. She knew Qian had fall on hard times and taken Ah Soon out of school, but she had not seen him for at least two years.

'Thank you,' Charlotte said to Min and turned towards the house.

'He's not at home,' Min said and Charlotte paused. 'At this hour he is upstairs with the accounts.' She pointed to the Heaven's Gate brothel.

Charlotte stared and tried to think what to do. She felt afraid. Then she saw one of Robert's peons talking to some men on the corner and this sight, irrationally, reassured her.

'Can you ask him to come out?' she said.

'You're his woman,' Min said. 'Master Zhen's. They call you the English Concubine.'

Charlotte felt the blood of her face rush to her cheeks. My god! She was known to even the lowliest whore. Mortified, she turned away, ready to fly back to the carriage. The two women had now become the centre of attention. Several of the prostitutes hung over the verandah and men emerged from the small shops and taverns.

Min knew Zhen wouldn't like this. She took Charlotte's arm and ushered her into the hall of the brothel.

'Wait here, I'll get him.'

Charlotte now knew not whether to stay or to flee, but at least no eyes were peering at her. She calmed herself and had only an instant to wait as Qian came down the stairs.

'Miss Xia Lou, what?'

'Qian, oh, I am so happy to see you.'

Charlotte looked around her. Faces had appeared at the doorway. Min came down the stairs and opened the door to a room, ushering them inside. Qian moved slowly and she saw that he was drugged. She stared at him and at the red cotton cover on the mean little bed and swallowed.

'I have to speak to you about Zhen.' She took her fan and moved it briskly. The room was insufferably hot.

'Yes,' Qian said warily.

Suddenly Charlotte knew she could not ask this man about his friend. Zhen would never forgive her and he might well lie. And his mind was flying somewhere else. But she persevered for Lian's sake.

'Actually about Lian, his daughter.'

Qian nodded, waiting, blinking slowly.

'She has spoken to me about the marriage you are planning with Ah Soon. She begs not to be married to him because he is … he is …' Charlotte found her courage. 'He's an opium addict.'

No sooner had the words fallen from her lips than she realised the stupidity of talking about an opium addict to an opium addict. She was floundering in a world of vice and filth and attitudes she could not begin to fathom.

'What you say?' He lost control of his English and began to rant at her in Hokkien.

Charlotte backed away from. She had made the most dreadful mistake. What had she been thinking? This Qian was not the man she had known. These men did not care about some young girl and her wishes. The evidence lay all around her. They were surrounded in these whorehouses by thousands of them whom they prostituted for money.

She turned to go when suddenly the door flew open and Zhen walked into the room.

'Go,' he said and Qian scurried away. Zhen shut the door and turned to Charlotte.

'What are you doing here?'

'How ... ?'

'I know everything in Chinatown.'

Her eyes opened with surprise. Did he? Was he so powerful? She felt a tremor of fear. Over here she understood nothing.

'What are you thinking being here, wandering around brothels and dens? Everyone knows who you are.'

'So you have spies everywhere, is that it?'

'Kongsi eyes are everywhere if that's what you mean. The whole town will know I have come here to meet you when I gave an oath not to do so.'

'I see. So I have embarrassed you in ways I can hardly begin to understand. You and your oaths which are so hurtful.'

He was heartily sorry he had ever agreed to this arrangement but on top of her other transgressions, she had made him look utterly ridiculous, wandering around like this. To be the pawn of a woman was to be the laughing stock and was the end of authority. But how could he express this to her? Why had she come here?

He ran his hand over his face in utter frustration.

'I came to speak about Lian, but I realise now that my words will carry no weight, with you or Qian. I find you both disgusting. You might as well put her here in this whorehouse as marry her to Ah Soon.'

He stood impassively. Charlotte found his face impenetrable. He kept his emotions under tight rein and sometimes she took it for stubbornness or indifference, even though he had told her that in China, for a man to show his feelings was weak, impolite and impolitic.

'How you insult me. I am disgusting. I see. And what of you and your inexcusable behaviour with another man in front of the entire Chinese community?'

Charlotte felt her temper flare.

'My behaviour was not inexcusable. The man was an old acquaintance. I am not Chinese. I am not to be bound by foot and by mouth. I will speak to whomsoever I wish.' It came out in a rush, hard and angry.

Zhen felt his own temper and made an effort to suppress it.

'You made me look like a fool. The fool they all think I am because of you. And you shame me more by visiting his ship.'

Charlotte's hand flew to her mouth and she was momentarily lost for words. Then the full import of this statement came upon her.

'My God!'

'You spent hours on the ship of another man, alone, when all the world knows you are my woman. If I lose the respect of my fellows, my power is nothing. Now you come here asking about my daughter, interfering and speaking about things which are not your concern. Again you shame me. I warn you.'

Charlotte looked him in the face and a feeling of deep resentment crept over her.

'Warn me? Warn me? Of what? That you will have another bride, is that it? You have already selected a suitably grovelling and obedient mare to give you more sons.'

She spat the words at him. He was utterly amazed. What had she heard?

'I have made no such selection. Who has been talking to you?'

'Never mind. Is it true? Have you been presented with such a girl?'

Zhen felt nonplussed. He hesitated.

Charlotte saw it and walked up to him and with the swiftness of all her anger, slapped him across the face, her nails raking his skin.

'So it is true. You liar.'

She lifted her hand again. She wanted to strike and strike him until her anger and despair drained out of her. But he took her wrists in his hands and in one movement pinned her to the wall, her arms above her head. He stood over her, his eyes angry, blood pouring from the wounds on his cheek. At that moment she felt they were like two rivers which had poured into each other, filled with both fury and lust. Her breathing became short and shallow. She saw that he knew, that he could read it in her. He put his mouth to hers and kissed her hard, crushing his lips to hers. She tasted his blood on her lips and felt a rage of passion. He took her waist in his arm and pulled her tight against him and grabbed her hair, holding her face to his and kissing her until she could hardly breathe. She abandoned herself, her mind black, her blood on fire.

He pulled his lips from hers, threw his head back and roared, a great shout of anger and frustration, filled with the fever in his blood. Charlotte, afraid, tried to pull way from him, but he held her fast.

'Zhen, stop.'

He looked at her with a gaze so black she could not be sure he even saw her. He pulled back his hand and threw his fist at the wall by her face. The wall crumpled under the blow sending splinters of wood spinning away. She screamed, a piercing scream of terror and he released her. She scrambled away from him.

He smeared the blood on his face with the back of his hand. She heaved air into her lungs.

He sent a stream of Hokkien over her until he felt a calm return.

'You cannot humiliate me,' he said. 'Do you hear me, woman?'

'I …' she began, the blood in her veins still on fire, a sudden fear of his anger filling her and her breath not yet fully returned to calm.

'You are not my wife and even if you were, I would not have to answer to you. I am a Chinese man, and we do not kowtow to our women. If I choose to take another wife, and another, and another, I will.'

Charlotte gazed at him, fear left her, and the trickle of doubts which had been seeping into her over the last month, rushed into a flood.

'And so, without telling me, you are choosing to do just that. If I know it, the town knows it.'

Anger was not Zhen's natural state and the blood fever went off him as quickly as it had come. He realised what he had said.

'But I do not choose,' he said. 'We … '

'There is no "we",' she interrupted. 'There is no "us". We are a figment of our imaginations, a dream. We have no reality. I am Scottish and you are Chinese, we are impossible.'

Zhen was thunderstruck.

'I make one last appeal to your decency, if you have any left. I am warning you that this situation with Lian is very serious. I no longer care about your rules and strictures about your Chinese family. That is nothing to me now. I talk as a human person. You cannot marry Lian to Ah Soon. You will kill her.'

Charlotte walked to the door.

'Be warned. Deal properly with this situation whilst you have time.'

As swift as a panther he cut her off. He took her by the shoulders, his hands gripping her hard.

'No, you may not speak like this. There is no bride. Listen to me.'

'You met no man with a daughter who played music and simpered about you?' Charlotte's felt her breath short in her throat again and fought it away.

'I met a man who has a daughter. It is common practice. Xia Lou, you know it.'

'Can you honestly say you have not considered this one?'

They stood, eyes locked.

'She has not been offered to me in marriage. You mistake.'

'You told Lian that you would take another wife.'

His eyes narrowed. 'Lian has no business doing such things. You have no business listening. Why am I plagued by disobedient women on every side?'

He dropped his hands from her. 'Will the gods not send me one woman who will do as I wish.'

Charlotte dropped her eyes. 'Perhaps you have found her.'

'Stop this. I don't mean that. You, Lian, Lilin, you are driving me mad. I know this separation is hard but why, Xia Lou, why are you saying these things? Why are you meeting men on ships, which makes a fool of me. Why are you coming here where you know nothing, to speak of things that are not your concern?'

Charlotte tightened her lips. It hardly mattered what he thought, or whether there was a bride in prospect or not. One day there would be. It was only a matter of time, as she aged, that he would stray. Not immediately, no, but a year from now, perhaps his gaze would fall on a girl, or their own lives together would be just too complicated. Gradually he would come to her less, and then one day he would not come at all and he would have slipped away from her like a wave. A death of a thousand cuts. And all in the gaze and on the lips of the gossiping tongues of Singapore.

She looked directly into his eyes.

'I don't trust you anymore,' she said.

She knew she had shocked him. He stared at her as if she was an old, old friend he'd come across suddenly in an out of the way place who had been transformed in ways he couldn't fathom. She felt herself begin to shake with emotion and longed to leave the room but he blocked the door. She did not trust her voice to say another word to him.

Then, in an instant, he turned, flung open the door and disappeared. Charlotte felt the liquid in her body rise like a tide and the urgent need to vomit.

14

The storm that lashed the island had gone on for three days. The streets were awash and river sloshed over the quayside. Houses collapsed in Kampong Glam and a great chunk of Bukit Larangan came crashing down onto Hill Street.

Charlotte stood at the window and watched the water flooding down, so strong she could see nothing outside. The day was like night.

It hurt like a knife hurts, slicing into the skin, severing the nerves, sending searing pain throughout her body. She had left on her terms. But she loved him still. She felt emptied of blood, as if the knife cut had drained her dry.

She took up the letter from Batavia. It was from Matthew, Tigran's son from his first wife. Nicolaus, Matthew's brother, who had run the affairs of Manouk & Son for the last ten years had died of malarial fever. Matthew, with the help of the office manager Pieter de Vos and two Eurasian clerks, was handling affairs for the moment. But things were bad. The company had suffered in recent times and the sugar lands of Semarang were under threat from debtors. In addition, the tea plantation at Buitenzorg had been affected by the liberalisation of the new ports of the China trade. The list of problems went on and Charlotte realised that the company might very well be in serious trouble.

She called for her carriage though the rain was still cascading against the windows. She needed to get out of the house. She had found a terrible resolution and knew if she could lose Zhen then to find an iron resolve with Alexander was almost nothing.

At Robert's house, the housekeeper opened the door and Amber, who had seen her aunt's carriage draw up, rushed to kiss her.

'Send for Robert, Shilah,' she said, as Shilah, heavily pregnant, came to greet her. 'We have to speak of important things.'

'Is it the divorce?' Shilah said, a light glinting in her eye.

Charlotte sighed. 'No, of course not. Shilah, Robert cannot divorce Teresa. You might as well get used to it.'

Shilah's face fell and Charlotte regretted her tone. Amber went to her mother's side.

'My dear, I am sorry. But it is the truth. Robert can love you and live with you and your children but, under the laws of England, he cannot marry you.'

Shilah said she felt unwell and took to her room. A servant was sent for Robert, who arrived in a state of undue excitement which turned to annoyance when he found out his child was not in the process of being born and he had had to struggle through the rain. When he came from Shilah's side he looked pointedly at his sister.

'Well, well, Kitt. What is all this? You send for me when I am busy and in such a storm. I have a town full of addicts and criminals and more each day pouring in. I have no money for …'

'Robbie, be quiet. I have come to make a proposition and it concerns Amber.'

Robert listened, walked a little around his living room, and listened some more.

'I am not against this plan, Kitt. After all, they are not even cousins so it is even more appropriate.'

Charlotte threw a glance of warning at her brother.

'All right, of course, they will never know. And it does serve, it does serve. Amber is sixteen and must marry in any case. But will Alexander have her? There's the rub.'

'I have no more patience,' she snapped. 'He will accept it or he will not. If he does not he may find he has no finances. I will settle his debts in Scotland for Aunt Jeanne is worried sick, but beyond that he may have to find work as a clerk in Bousteads or Jardines. Serve him right.'

'This is a change of mind, sister. You have always spoilt him.'

'Agreed. And now I have come to realise it. I have financial troubles in Java. Such things have a way of settling the mind. If nothing is done, no-one shall have a fortune.'

'A whisky, sister?'

'A wee tot, perhaps.'

Brother and sister shared a smile. She felt the emptiness at the heart of her but she had made up her mind. She would cover it all up and go away on *The Queen of the South* and settle her business like a clever Scottish woman. It was almost a relief. Love was such a slavery.

'If he agrees, they shall be married,' Charlotte went on, 'at Brieswijk, under Dutch law. Alexander will be given responsibility for the estate and share in its profits. If he agrees and proves himself, it will all pass to him, Amber and his heirs when I die.'

Robert handed the glass of whisky to his sister.

'This is a new resolute you,' he said and raised his glass.

'Robbie. I have had a terrible fright. Three years of complacency and now, sudden upheaval. First the Caldwell business. I lost a lot of money.'

Robert turned down his mouth. They had still not located Caldwell, the Court Registrar who acted as agent for land purchases and had run off with a hundred thousand dollars.

'We continue to search. We will find him, but of the money …'

Charlotte raised her hand. 'Never mind. I have accepted that. But I have neglected everything in Batavia and I must straighten it out. Nicolaus, Tigran's eldest son, has died, God bless him. He was a good man and it seems that he has not been forthcoming about some of the decisions of the company. I need to understand. If it is too bad, I may have to sell off some parts of the business for I cannot run such an enterprise myself.'

She turned the whisky in the glass.

'I have broken with Zhen.'

Robert was so startled he put his glass down with a thud.

She put up her hand. 'I can't speak of it.' Tears sprang to her eyes and she brushed them away quickly.

'Sister, why?'

'No, not now,' she said. 'Please, Robert.'

Robert nodded his head and stayed silent.

'But there is Lily. I have to tell Alex immediately. He will not be in Singapore five minutes and he will find out.'

Robert nodded. 'Yes. For heaven's sake just tell him. What will he do? Sulk? Run away? Cry?'

Charlotte smiled ruefully. 'Frankly, at this moment, I don't give a damn.'

Robbie settled in a chair. A silence fell between them.

'Since you are in such a frame of mind, perhaps you can speak to Teresa?'

Charlotte glanced at her brother who smiled.

* * *

The rain had done nothing to dampen the trade at the Heaven's Gate brothel. Men were lined the length of the corridor and out under the five-foot way, huddled against the rain, but, Min thought, it had not been a good day. Another girl had eaten opium, ending her life in drugged oblivion. This one had been so very fast. She had been only three weeks in the brothel. Sixteen and dead. In one month seven girls had taken their lives, two had died of beatings by a client and one had stabbed her attacker to death and been taken away.

Min looked over at Zhen, passed out on her bed.

He had been half drunk when he'd arrived and had drunk even more, pouring the arrack down his throat. When he needed to do this, to find some sort of oblivion, he came here, to her. He had not been in almost three years and she knew it was about the fight he had had with the Mah Nuk woman.

She fingered the paper that informed all members of the Grand Triad that Zhen was the new leader.

Ironfist Wang stood downstairs, guarding his Lord. The whole town knew he had broken with the English concubine but it was not enough. She had humiliated and hurt the Shan Chu. He lay upstairs in a drunken stupor because of her. She was dangerous and Wang's job was to eliminate those he considered dangerous to the kongsi leader.

15

In the pale dark before dawn, Alexander Manouk stood on the deck as the ship ploughed white-lipped furrows on the dark waters of the Straits of Malacca.

Three years of icy Scottish winds had dulled his memory of the soft warmth of the breezes. The rhythmic splash of the paddle wheel casts its hypnotic spell and he lost himself in this moment of pure, cool happiness. He knew it would not last long. The sun would burn it up.

His home, Singapore, was ahead. He had cast off the shackles of childhood and the irksome constrictions of Scotland's tiresome morality.

He saw Miss McNair approaching. She was joining her brother, the private secretary to the new Governor, and they had sailed from Calcutta together. He had flirted with her briefly but he had curbed the natural instincts and impulses of his nature. He had not tried to seduce her. She was pretty enough but he was in such trouble he had no wish to add to the store.

Nevertheless he ran his lips over her hand and smiled his handsome smile and knew that, at virginal sixteen, she would be so easy to seduce. A kiss perhaps, no harm in that, he thought, as she gazed into his eyes.

But he was saved, as was she, from the dangers of such thoughts with the arrival of her nanny, a woman of ample figure and voice.

'My dear,' she said and Miss McNair, with a brief look of disappointment, turned away. Alexander forgot her instantly. He turned his face eastwards and his thoughts to what awaited him in Singapore.

An angry mother, no doubt, but at least no overbearing father to set him straight or force him into the navy or some such. Uncle Robert might have a word with him, but on the whole Alexander thought he might be quite lucky. His mother, at the first sight of him, would forget all about his past sins in the pleasure of having him home. Then he would, as quickly as was seemly, renew his acquaintance with Min, the brothel keeper in Chinatown to whom his honorary Uncle Zhen had introduced him when he turned thirteen.

Alexander knew well that it was this early introduction to the fleshpots of Chinatown which had made him itchy. That's what it was. His schoolfriends, of whom he had many, all said so. He was an itchy boy. Women were the balm.

Alex smiled. The sun came up, bursting onto the sea, scything its long golden rays into the vast green jungle. A jabbering of monkeys echoed down the hillside. The ship's men called in Hindustani and the Javanese crew began a song.

He felt intensely happy, the call of the East bringing him home.

* * *

Charlotte stood at the end of Dalhousie Ghaut upon which the passengers would disembark. It stood almost exactly where she had lived with Robert when she first came to Singapore. The police offices had stood on this very spot and she looked over at the fort and down towards Tanjong Rhu, remembering her first nights in this beautiful place.

Her gaze went out over the harbour. HMS Valiant was still there. She had thought of writing to Edmund but had rejected it. What was the point and it was unworthy to think of him simply because her relations with Zhen had gone so terribly wrong.

Her mind slipped to him and she closed her eyes, willing tears away. She heard nothing of him or from him. The river was like a wall of silence between two towns, two cultures, and she had never felt it more intensely than now. From here she was glad that she could not see his godown, way beyond the bend in the river. She waved the fan before her face and settled her emotions.

Robert and Amber came to her side.

Amber was smoothing the flounces of the blue organza over the hooped petticoat. The top hugged her figure emphasising the slenderness of her waist. Her hands moved in constant, convulsive motions. Her face was flushed and she never took her gaze for a moment off the water.

The sampans and lighters were jostling for place in the river mouth. The tremendous rains had washed away the filth in the gutters and the canals. The tide was high and the air smelt crisp and clean.

'There, there,' Amber squealed and hopped up and down with excitement.

All eyes turned and Charlotte saw him, standing, holding the mast of the sampan. Instinctively she raised her hand and Alex saw his mother and waved wildly.

As the sampan knocked against the steps of the Ghaut he leapt out and ran quickly up to his mother, picking her up in his arms.

Charlotte's anger at him fled. She was so happy to see him. He appeared like a breath of air, filled with vigour, tall and handsome. She could see Zhen's features in him. It seemed so obvious, but perhaps only to her eyes.

'Welcome home, my love,' Charlotte said, her voice thick with emotion.

'Welcome home, Alex,' Robert said and Alex grinned.

'Thank you, Uncle. I'm prodigiously glad to be here.'

Alex's eyes strayed to the young girl standing at his mother's side.

'Amber?' he asked hesitantly. He slowly looked her up and down.

Amber was delighted at this response and curtsied elegantly to him. He had grown more handsome than a god and she was somewhat breathless, but she pulled herself under control.

'Why Alexander Manouk, did you not recognise me?' She cocked her head on one side and smiled widely.

He went up to her and took her hand, putting it to his lips. She smelled of roses and he took her in from beneath his lashes, the slenderness of her waist, the swell of her bosom, the fine skin of her cheek, the deep brown of her eyes.

Robert coughed. 'Alex, you shall dine with us tonight.' He turned to his daughter. 'Come with me, Amber. Leave the boy and his mother.'

Amber began to protest but she saw her father's face and curtsied obediently and left with small glances backwards.

When the carriage arrived at Charlotte's town house, the servants gathered round. Many had known him as a boy and Alex greeted them enthusiastically.

When these duties were done, he threw himself into an armchair in the drawing room.

'By heavens, Mother, Amber has certainly grown up.' His accent, Charlotte noticed, had taken a decided Scottish turn.

'Why yes, my boy, that's what girls do, they grow into women. You have grown too, you look well.'

And he did. His shoulders were wider, stronger, his waist was narrow and he looked well in the tight-fitting jacket and breeches which were the fashion. His black hair had changed. He no longer wore it long. It was shorter but she was glad he had not taken to the beard. He was fine featured, the dark eyes and the strong jaw those of his father. But he seemed utterly unaware of the storm he had unleashed on Jeanne and on her and his insouciance was irksome.

'I am well, very well and very happy to be home.'

Charlotte took a deep breath. Alex waited. He knew she must have her say.

'I am sorry you have returned under such a cloud.'

'Mother, you will forgive me. I have been somewhat liberal and headstrong I admit, but oats must be sown, Mama.'

'You have caused Jeanne great anxiety. You have behaved badly and become indebted. It won't do, really. So I hope you have sown all the oats you intend.' She turned away and rang for tea.

Alex gazed at his mother. She looked prodigiously well.

'Well, Mama, I am still very young so it is hard to say.' He laughed and Charlotte's face became serious.

'It is no laughing matter. You have consorted with a married woman, been ejected disgracefully from your school and Jeanne is hounded by your creditors.'

'Straight to it, then, Mother. Well for the first, the married woman was quite consenting, even demanding. For the second, the college was increasingly pointless; and for the third, I had not thought money to be such a concern.'

Charlotte gazed at her son. 'The morality of your actions with the Dean's wife, I shall not dwell upon. You know very well. Your lack of concern for your Aunt Jeanne seems to point to a certain heartlessness. As for money, well it is never a concern for those who do not earn it.'

'I am not heartless. I am sorry if Aunt Jeanne has been worried, naturally.'

'Not enough to curb your behaviour apparently. Really, Alexander.'

'I had not realised that the money was so important. I had presumed you would pay it. So what are you saying? That those who do not earn money do not understand its value. So am I to earn it then?'

'Yes. If you want it from me, then yes.'

Alex's eyes opened wide. He had expected to be met with a small wall of annoyance but his mother seemed determined to make a mountain out of a molehill.

'Mother, I am hardly arrived.'

'No time like the present.'

The tea tray arrived and for the space of several minutes neither mother nor son spoke.

Alex rose and went to gaze down on the street. A series of Chinese coolies passed in the distance carrying goods on their long poles. He smiled. He had missed Singapore and the Chinese girls especially. He was sobered by the extraordinary sight of a line of black-hooded monks parading along the street. Monks? He shook his head.

'I should be most obliged if you would settle down and marry Amber.'

He turned. 'Amber?'

'Alexander, you must marry. It will settle you from all this ... this womanising you seem to have adopted as a profession.'

'I see.'

'I want you to agree to this marriage which Amber most decidedly wishes. I think the girl is madly in love with you.'

'Is she?'

Alexander smiled. He had always known Amber was in love with him. It allowed him to disdain and ignore her as it suited him. There was that in him, the disregard for women who chose to adore him.

'If you agree, then you will take her to Brieswijk. You will assume control of the estate. Things are not as they should be in the company. We must see to it.'

'Well, Mother. My head is reeling. May I have a moment to consider.' Alexander sat and took up his tea cup.

Charlotte gazed at her son. She realised she had absolutely no idea what, if anything, was going on inside his head.

'In a fortnight the *Queen* will be here and I shall set sail for Batavia, with, I hope, you affianced to Amber. The wedding will take place in Brieswijk and you shall learn how to take care of a great estate.'

'Well, I see you have thought this through. I am somewhat stunned.'

'No you're not. You have known half your life that Brieswijk is your destiny. And yes I have had ample time to think this through. In return for all this I will settle all your debts and you shall prove you can be a master.'

Alex smiled wryly. 'And if I do not?'

'Then I suggest you find work with Bousteads as a clerk and look for lodgings in the town.'

Alexander laughed. Charlotte had expected a variety of

reactions but amusement was not amongst them.

'Well that is a horrid alternative. May I take a day or so to think about it. Unless Mr. Boustead is in urgent need of a useless clerk.'

'You may take a day or two, of course. But no more. I need your answer.'

The mother that confronted Alex was not the one he had left. They had not met for more than three years and he had left as a young boy. Perhaps she had always been more resolute than he remembered her. It was something of a shock and he realised that she was serious.

'You understand that I am not in love with Amber.'

This caused Charlotte to pause. Alexander saw it. 'Do you wish me to marry a woman I do not love?'

Charlotte frowned. 'We marry for many reasons, Alexander. I did not love Tigran when first I married him, but I grew to do so. Marriage and children will settle you, give you something to strive for.'

Alex gazed steadily at his mother. 'Why *did* you marry him, Mother?'

Charlotte shot a look at her son. 'That is not the question at hand and don't change the subject.'

Charlotte turned away.

'There is something else,' she said and went to the window.

She watched the Malay gardeners moving slowly across the grass clearing the great quantity of branches and leaves which lay, tossed and broken from the storm.

'I have a child, a daughter.'

Alexander stared at his mother's back. It was tense. She drew her shoulders together and turned her neck, almost imperceptibly, to one side as if her head was heavy.

'What on earth do you mean?'

'I mean I have a daughter.'

'You mean you have remarried? To whom?'

She whipped round, her dress sweeping her ankles. 'I am not married and I have a child. The father is Zhen.'

Alexander burst out laughing. What on earth was she saying?

Charlotte had had enough. It had to come out and she had to do it all, headlong, like water rushing and tumbling over rocks.

'I hardly think to shock you, with the tales I have heard of your doings in Scotland. I have for some years had a relationship with Zhen. It is …' She hesitated, the words sticking in her throat and swallowed hard, turning her face to the window.

'It is over now, but we have a daughter.'

Alex stopped laughing.

She waited until she felt her emotions under control, then turned to face him. 'You would have found out within the hour. I'm very notorious.'

She went forward quickly and stood in front of him.

'This does not mean your behaviour can be excused. You are a boy and I am a full-grown woman. I make my own life. I have said all I wish to say to you on this matter.'

Alex rose. She raised her chin defiantly.

'Doubtless you are tired. This is a lot to take in. I will see you at dinner. We dine with Robert. And Amber.' She gathered her skirts and swept from the room.

16

Alex bathed and rested half an hour in his old bedroom. Everything his mother had told him settled in his brain. What hypocrites they were. He had never thought to think this of his mother, but what other conclusion could he draw.

All this posturing about his wild ways, all these demands to marry and lead a righteous life. All this was complete hypocrisy. His mother was, or had been, the lover of a Chinese man, lived with him out of wedlock and kept it all a secret from her children, her aunt and all her acquaintance in Scotland. What did the town think of her? What did his uncle Robert think of her?

He wanted to empty his head of these thoughts and left the house. He turned his steps to the house of his old friend, Ah Soon, on High Street but to his astonishment, the huge old Chinese compound which occupied the entire corner from High Street to the river, was no longer his home.

He crossed the river into Chinatown. Nothing very much had changed here. It was bigger of course, but still filled with the endless busy world of hawkers and hustlers and shopkeepers, tradesmen of every hue, the bullocks plopping hot steaming turds on the street. He addressed a few shopkeepers in Hokkien and their mouths dropped open with astonishment. He had hardly forgotten it at all, the sounds popping in his mouth. He loved to speak Chinese. No-one knew of the old Chinese compound, almost everyone he spoke to had arrived in the last three years. Finally he found an old man, an apothecary, who knew of the old Sang property and the owner Qian. The son was always in the den, he said, every afternoon after four o'clock. Alex frowned. The den? The opium den. The man told him the address.

Alex consulted his pocket watch. It was only three and he wandered slowly, savouring all the noise and bustle around him, occasionally alarmed at the rubbish and filth in the streets and the sight of an emaciated coolie propped up in a ditch. Things had gotten worse over here since he'd left. More men, the crowding and poverty appalling. A procession with noisy drums and a lion dance was progressing round the streets. He knew they were chasing away evil of some sort. He turned his feet to Hong Kong Street and the ah ku houses of his uncle Qian. He stood outside number 23, Heaven's Gate, the house of Min, the brothel keeper and friend of his uncle Zhen.

Uncle Zhen, he thought and grimaced. Turned out Uncle Zhen had been the lover of his mother. He had had no time to take this in but now he found it annoyed him. When had this happened? How had it happened? What could have drawn a European woman to a Chinese man? Of course they knew each other, the way he knew Ah Soon and his father. And Zhen was a close friend of them all and spoke good English.

He put it away. Alex was not one to dwell for long on the mysteries of others. He looked at the upper windows and the faces of the girls who stared down at him. He grinned and they waved. He felt the itch. He'd not had a Chinese woman in three years.

He went inside. It was hot and sticky, airless.

'Min,' he asked, 'the kwai po, is she here?'

She ignored him though he spoke in Hokkien. 'You want girl?' she said in Cantonese.

He didn't understand a word.

The toothless crone rose and bowed. She ushered him into the next room. Here sat five or six young females, none older than fifteen.

They were all dressed in a shift of cotton and looked at him silently, their eyes blank, their lips red, their skin white with powder. He felt repulsed, not attracted. This was not how he remembered the brothel. He had been brought here by uncle Zhen, and taken in hand by a girl, older than him, sweet and tender, and taught the ways by Min, her hand guiding him, her words in his ear as she told him what women liked.

The old crone stared at him, sucking her teeth. 'You want girl?' she said in Hokkien.

He left the building and walked with more purpose and found himself, at last, at the door of the opium den. A man staggered past him. He stood and gazed at the entrance and felt a sudden thrill. The girls in the brothel, the vice and the dirt and the heat were overwhelming. The feelings of shock which had assailed him at the brothel evaporated. This was the East.

The awful cold morality of the Scottish kirk, the dull order of each passing day, had no play here. The east was vivid, the people a cacophonous mix of every race, the vibrations of the day filled with a riot of sin and violence and colour. He sniffed the air and the sweet odour of opium assailed him. It drew men in, into the dark, hot rooms and the oblivion and dreams which lay inside.

He had taken opium once, when he and a friend had spent the term interval in London, whoring drunkenly from morning to night until their money ran out and they were forced to return to Aberdeen. It had made him sleep and he had forgotten all about it.

A girl appeared at the door, her face deformed and carbuncular, the nose half eaten away. Alex stepped back. He recognised the face of the poxed child as they were known, those born with the French disease. Alex had contracted the pox but ointments and a series of doses of calomel had been effective in ridding him of the chancre and he no longer gave it a thought, except when he saw these faces. The child was no older than fifteen he guessed. She beckoned him in and lifted the curtain.

'I seek a man, a friend,' he said in Hokkien. She looked alarmed and dropped the curtain. A few moments later an older man appeared. He was thin, the ribs lying like shadows on his sallow skin.

'Sir,' he said deferentially.

'I seek Ah Soon, of the old Sang House, the son of Qian.'

The old man's face showed no expression. Perhaps he wanted money, thought Alexander, but currently he did not possess Straits dollars. He hardened his tone. A touch of colonial arrogance might induce the fellow to speak.

'Speak up, man. Ah Soon, is he here?'

'Who seeks me?'

Alex turned and looked into the eyes of his old friend. He was shocked. At seventeen, Ah Soon looked like an old man. His eyes were bloodshot and his skin was grey.

'Ah Soon, it's me, Alex.'

Ah Soon stared at the man in front of him. Alex went forward and clasped his arm.

'Ah Rex?' Ah Soon said. 'You're here? My God.'

Alex clasped Ah Soon in his arms and felt his bones, as fragile as a bird. When they released each other Ah Soon took Alex's hand.

'Come, we shall have a pipe or two and you will tell me about your life.'

Alex glanced at the doorway of the den. He realised that Ah Soon would not be deflected. This was his habit, his need, his desire. It had taken over his life.

'We shall talk. You will smoke, but I will not. It does not agree with me.'

Ah Soon smiled. His teeth were yellow and his breath exhaled a fetid odour. 'Come then, old friend. We have much to discuss.'

Ah Soon put his arm through his friend's, the old man drew the curtain aside and the darkness of the den swallowed them.

* * *

The house in North Bridge Road rested somnolent in the silence of the hot afternoon when nothing stirred, when animals and humans alike rested from the oppressive humidity of the day. The only sound was the shrill trill trill of the cicadas in the shrubberies.

Charlotte sat in the chair under the trees. Lily was in her hammock, the little Chinese maid seated by her side, pushing it, her fan moving to and fro over the child. She reread the letter on her lap. It was from Edmund, arrived on the steamer from Hong Kong this morning. She was in his thoughts, he said, and when this war was done he longed to see her again. More, he had written, he loved her, had always loved her and wished to marry her. She had not absolutely told him she was not free when he had left Singapore. And so he permitted himself to hope. When she felt able to do so he begged her to write to him. She touched her neck where a small rill of sweat ran into her collar. The sudden memory of Zhen, of that last afternoon they had spent here flooded her and she dropped her head into her hands.

She felt drained of energy. She slept badly, dreams into nightmares, and now the heat sucked the life out of her. She needed sleep. She rose and pointed to the house.

'Amah, I go.'

The young Chinese maid had been engaged from Miss Cooke's school. She had been a prostitute of fourteen who had got sick and been abandoned and found her way to the comfort and protection of the girl's school. After a year she had recovered and now had been engaged by Charlotte for she spoke Hokkien and Charlotte knew Zhen wanted his daughter to speak his language. They had both agreed on her hire.

The maid continued to rock Lily as Charlotte walked away. When she was alone with the child, she rose and took the basket, which had been placed by the fence. She came back and dropped the contents into the hammock with Lily.

* * *

Alex wiped his brow. The heat was intense; it boiled your blood. He went to the bathroom and eased his burning skin with water then to his room where the curtains were drawn against the assault of the sun.

His head was filled with the fumes of the opium pipes and pounded incessantly. He lay down in the dark.

Ah Soon, his childhood friend, had smoked. The first pipe had revealed Ah Soon's loneliness after Alex had left. Their friendship had been severed and he had wished, also, to go abroad, to go to Scotland or England to school but his father would have none of it. Alex felt a great sorrow for his friend. He had departed, his eyes fixed on adventure, and never given Ah Soon a thought.

Ah Soon's relations with his father had become terribly

strained. Qian had taken a young man and Ah Soon had discovered the truth of his father's homosexuality. It had been a shock to discover the strange facts about the household. His mother had a lover, the carpenter who lived within the compound. He found out that his two younger sisters were by this man, a servant. Ah Soon could not even be sure of his own paternity or of his younger brother who had died of whooping cough at four.

And Qian had become distant, indulging the young man, neglecting his family. And then his mother had died and he had mourned her beyond anything for she had been an extraordinary woman who held the entire family together. She had loved him, been so proud of this son who spoke English and was a scholar. Then everything had erupted like a volcano. Within six months, the business had failed, the compound sold; he'd been summarily removed from the Institution, his education curtailed, and thrown into the brothels like some filthy pimp.

By the second pipe, Ah Soon wept on Alex's shoulder and Alex held him and read between the mumbling lines. He had taken to opium, perhaps to forget all this, perhaps to spite his father and now the drug owned him body and soul.

By the third pipe, Alex's head was reeling and Ah Soon had sunk into the torpor of his dreams.

Alex longed to help Ah Soon but he had no idea how to do it. He dozed and the vivid dreams of the opium fumes filled his head, the brothel and the girls' faces, drawing him in. He was wrenched from slumber by a hue and cry from below. He rose, his hand to his temple.

He opened the door and went onto the landing. A group of servants was talking loudly in the middle of the hall, the women wailing. Alex was about to open his mouth and tell them all to shut up when his mother came out to the landing.

'What is this noise?' she cried as Dr. Little came rushing through the door.

Malik ran into the hall, a child in his arms, and Charlotte let out a scream. Alex watched as his mother raced down the stairs.

Dr. Little spoke quickly to Charlotte, and Malik carried the child into the living room.

'What is it?' Alex cried and Charlotte looked up at him, her face so distraught and distorted, that he gasped with alarm.

'Mother,' he shouted and raced down the stairs.

She collapsed against him and he held her tightly and led her to a chair.

'What is it, Mother, for heaven's sake?'

'Lily,' she said. 'She's been bitten by a snake.'

She began to sob, her chest heaving.

Alexander had no idea what on earth was going on. He rose and went to the door. Dr. Little was leaning over the child examining her.

'What is it? Who is this child?'

The younger servants were screaming, the Chinese nursemaid tearing at her hair, the Malay maids beating their cheeks.

'Be quiet,' Alex yelled and a shocked silence momentarily fell. 'What is going on? Who is this girl?'

His mother rushed into the room and with a face as pale as a ghost and stood, waiting. Dr. Little rose and shook his head. Charlotte screamed and screamed.

Alex was utterly rooted to the spot.

'Lily,' Charlotte wailed.

Alex suddenly remembered. The daughter, the child his mother had with Zhen, was lying dead. He went to his mother and took her in his arms.

17

'Were you alone with the child?'

The Chinese maid looked at the big Englishman and listened to the interpreter. She nodded.

'Did you see the snake?'

The maid shook her head. 'Only when it bit the child,' she said.

The coroner returned a verdict of accidental death. Lily had been asleep in the heat of the afternoon on the low hammock outside under the trees where it was cooler. The mistress had gone into the house. The Chinese maid had just stopped rocking her and fallen into a slumber for the day was so hot and airless.

She was awakened by the child's cries and found a viper slithering away, its long tail disappearing into the bushes. The snake had slithered over Lily and, it was presumed, she had moved under it and, surprised, it had bitten her on the face, delivering a fatal dose of venom. From the maid's description, the snake was identified as a Malayan pit viper, an ill-tempered, poisonous serpent known for the sudden rapidity of its strike.

Evangeline took Charlotte's arm and led her away from the gravesite. For three days they had come. The flowers for Lily were curled and rotted and Evangeline took them away. The tombstone had been put up and Charlotte stared down at the grave of her and Zhen's child. It was a tombstone not only on Lily, sweet little Lily, but on them. She realised that Robert, who had ordered the stone, had named her Lily Manouk, though on her birth certificate Zhen was marked as the father. They were not married and so Lily was not considered a Tan, the name he had adopted when he married his first wife. She felt it terribly. Why had they not given this child his name? Lily was no more a Manouk than Alex, but two of his children carried another man's name. She felt the terrible injustice of it and a sudden deep understanding of his feelings.

He had not come, not to the funeral, not to see her, not to grieve with her, not now, even when their daughter lay dead in the ground. She had received no letter from him. It felt as if he had simply cut away all that part of his life.

She turned and went to George Coleman's grave and touched it. Evangeline waited then wandered away to the grave of a friend. A figure approached and Charlotte looked over, hoping it was Zhen, but she recognised the slight and lonely figure not of him, but his daughter, Lian. Her maid waited by the entrance to the cemetery, fearful of entering this ang moh spirit ground.

Lian knelt at the little grave and placed a lotus bud against the stone. Charlotte watched from a distance then walked slowly over to the girl.

'Thank you,' she said, and Lian turned. She put out her arms and Lian fell into them.

'I loved her too,' Lian said. 'I wanted someone from her other family to be here.'

Lian wiped the tears from her cheeks and Charlotte put her arm around the girl's waist.

'Why, why does he not come?' she said and Lian felt so sorry for this woman who had tried to do something incredible for her.

She had heard from Ah Fu about the visit to Hong Kong Street. It was the talk of all the Chinese town. Zhen, the new leader of the kongsi, had broken with the English concubine in a great fight at the brothel. She had interfered and shamed him and, white woman or not, she had been summarily dismissed. His prestige had soared.

'Miss Charlotte, come.' Lian led Charlotte to the stone bench under the banyan tree.

'I have to explain some difficult things to you and some of this is secret. You must not speak of it to your brother or anyone for if you do they will know it and they will know it is me and that is dangerous. You understand.'

Charlotte nodded.

'My father has become what they call the lord of the kongsi. You understand. It's like a sort of prince. Prince of the Chinese. Does that make sense? Thousands of men swear an oath of loyalty to him.'

'Lord? This is what he had to do? This is why he couldn't be with me? Because I'm not Chinese. And because of this he cannot mourn his daughter?'

Lian shook her head. 'A man like that, who becomes such a prince, he cannot have women he does not control, who defy him publicly. It's impossible. You see. Ah Fu says that in China you would have been killed.'

Charlotte's eyes opened wide with shock.

'There is that part, and then it is forbidden, in Chinese tradition, to openly mourn a child who dies young. You see, if a child dies young it is considered bad luck on the family and the child must be put away and not mourned or talked about as if it had never lived. '

Charlotte stared at Lian. What tradition did not mourn a

beloved child?

'As the mere daughter of a concubine, in a Chinese family she is considered worthless. Forgive me, Miss Charlotte, I'm trying to explain. Perhaps he doesn't feel that in his heart but for all those reasons he cannot show any public grief for her.'

She could hardly believe what she was hearing. She shut her heart from him.

'Mother.'

Charlotte turned to see Alexander approaching. She rose and so too did Lian.

'Alex, oh my boy.'

Alex put his arm around his mother's shoulders and kissed her. He walked to Lily's grave and placed the orchids he had gathered next to the lotus bud. Lian and Charlotte followed. He rose and looked at Lian, suddenly remembering her.

'Lian?' he asked, putting his head to one side.

'Hello, Alex,' she said. 'I heard you were back.'

He smiled. He'd forgotten how beautiful she was. He felt pierced by her slender grace, her quiet assurance. Lian ignored him and turned away, back to the grave.

'I don't care about what I said to you. That is my father's affair. I'll come here and be her Che Che, her big sister, and light joss for her.'

Charlotte took Lian's hand. This thought was a great comfort. Lily would not be alone.

'Thank you. Lily thanks her big sister.'

'Thank you, Miss Charlotte, for what you tried to do for me. I will never forget it.'

Alex opened his mouth to speak but Lian turned and walked rapidly down the hill.

18

'Things are so terrible in Aunty Kitt's house.'

Amber put her handkerchief to her eyes. Sarah and Lian sat on either side of her. The three girls were seated under the branches of the great banyan tree which spread over the edge of the stream. On the ground, behind the tree, lay their three maids. Ah Fu's snores punctuated their conversation.

The tide was out and they all gazed out over the vast mud flats and the small army of pickers, all concentrated, heads down, gathering the creatures that appeared at every low tide, clams, crabs, sea snails and whelks. A squawking flock of gulls wheeled above the flats, one occasionally diving down and snatching up its prey. Lian recalled doing this picking with Ah Fu when she was a child.

'No-one talks of my marriage to Alex.' She began to wail, a high keening with occasional great sobs.

Sarah stared at her friend in astonishment.

'You are to marry Alex, your cousin? Why, he has just arrived. When did this happen?'

Amber ceased her wailing and shot a look of annoyance at Sarah.

'Well, Aunty and Father spoke of it. It is Aunt's wish.'

'Oh, gosh, really,' said Sarah. 'Did they? But now it's off?'

Amber quietly sobbed anew. 'I hope not. I love him.'

'I knew it,' crowed Sarah. 'You have been such a liar.'

'Does Alexander want to marry you?' Lian said.

Amber stopped sobbing and shot a sharp look at Lian. Then she lifted her handkerchief to her eyes.

'I ... I ... I don't know. It doesn't matter.' She looked up suddenly, defiantly. 'If Aunt Charlotte says he must marry me then he must.'

Lian watched the pickers amid the constant screeching of the wheeling birds. Since the sea wall had been built, children rarely came to play on the beach anymore. The Malay Orang Laut, the sea people, with their blithe spirits and happy dispositions, whom she remembered from her childhood, had disappeared from the town. It was sad. The town here, on the European side, had lost any liveliness it might have possessed and, in its empty, quiet vastness, felt half-dead.

'Goodness, Amber. If he doesn't love you, it would be jolly horrid,' Sarah said, her eyes flashing with pleasure. 'You always said we should marry for love, didn't you? Doesn't that mean Alex too?'

Amber stood up, angry.

'You're the one always prattling on about marrying for love. Well I am. I love him so it's all right. Anyway people marry who do not love each other. Look at Lian. She must marry Ah Soon, whom she despises.'

Lian looked at her friend. She raised an eyebrow.

'And if it came to pass I would hate him. Do you want Alex to hate you?'

It was as if Lian had stuck a dagger in her friend's heart.

Amber staggered backwards, her eyes blazing, then turned

and walked quickly away.

Sarah shot a glance of triumph after Amber but Lian regretted her words.

Sarah and Lian parted, the mood of their easy friendship soured, and Lian made her way along the edge of the sea, Ah Fu trailing her and yawning noisily. The air was cool and clouds obscured the sun throwing a greyness on the scene, bleaching colour from the day.

She had hurt Amber. Had she meant to? And why? What did she care if Amber married Alexander? She had barely said two words to him at the cemetery, but that did not mean she had not taken him in. He was not bluff and red and pompous but tall, broad-shouldered and handsome. He was, perhaps, a little arrogant, but also had an easy charm and she recognised in him the boy she had known and liked so much. She knew instinctively that Amber, so rigid and worried, was not right for him.

She felt sorry and gave a deep sigh. Too much was happening. Lian had been brought up in such chaos, in the uncertainty of strange and unpredictable behaviour, that she craved peace and quiet. Mother Lilin sometimes forgot she was around, especially in the morning when she was busy with her Chap Ji Kee betting slips or with the shamans who visited her daily, two nonyas and one Malay, leeching money out of her, or with the jewellery hawker who always came by to listen to her incessant chatter knowing he would end up the richer. These were the happy hours. At noon the mee hawker and the Tamil fried cake seller and the dumpling man would call and she would eat everything she could lay her hands on. Then she spent hours in front of her mirror, combing her thinning hair incessantly, the comb filled with strands, then blood as furrows of scarlet formed on her scalp.

Lian knew her aunt would sleep at three o'clock and tried to stay away until then. It gave her an hour of calm before Mother Lilin needed her to prepare the sireh and make Lian sit with her whilst she raved, or play cards with her which always ended up in anger, or play the piano which she had bought, or bring her sweets and crystal ginger and read in English which Lilin could barely understand. Then there would be the half an hour when Lilin was virtually inconsolable, howling, and could only be calmed with the opium pills in wine. She was ill, Lian knew it, and it had got so much worse recently. She needed to speak to her father of it but with the tension which lay between them and the loss of his child, no matter what outward manifestation he made, she dared not.

A feeling of desolation crept over her and she walked over the footbridge at the river's mouth to get lost in the noise and bustle of Chinatown. Ah Fu trailed along, chatting to acquaintances. One such stopped her and Ah Fu, lost in her chatter, ignored her charge. It happened so often that Lian no longer gave it a thought. She wandered amongst the shops and the food stalls, the hawkers calling their wares, the shoemakers banging, the clacking sound of wooden clogs a constant refrain. A pack of mongrels began fighting over a scrap and she went into the Thien Hock Keng temple to escape and sit with the Buddha, who asked nothing from her except serenity, resting in the peace of his smile, listening to the women chant, until three o'clock, when she turned for home.

On the corner of Philip Street a voice addressed her.

'Hello, Lian,' said Alex.

She was utterly beautiful, a slender and graceful goddess, with her perfect skin and straight black hair falling down her back. He had left her at twelve and now she was almost sixteen. Since he had laid eyes on her at the cemetery he had not ceased to think of her.

'Alex,' she said and looked around. 'You should not be here.'

'I should,' he said and she felt an unaccustomed thrill. He had said something totally unexpected and it had the ring of truth to it.

The silence lengthened between them. The town went about its business around them but two eyes gazed on them. Lilin, at the window, watched the young man standing with Lian. She knew who this was. This was Zhen's son and he was back in Singapore. She smiled.

Lian shook her head. 'If my father knows I am with a man, especially without my maid, he will never let me out again. You don't know who he is.'

'He was the lover of my mother.'

Lian shrugged and moved away from him.

'He's more than that. Don't come again.'

She walked quickly to her house and went inside. Alex followed her with his eyes then turned and lost himself in Chinatown.

19

Zhen, eyes closed, sat cross-legged in quietness. He had come to Circular Road, to his old house, which was a place which held memories of peace and tranquillity. His thoughts were of this lost child, the daughter he and Xia Lou had formed out of such oblivious passion. He wanted to speak to her, to hold her, but could not. That comfort, that love, was lost to him by this position which had been thrust upon him.

In a few weeks the auction for the opium farm would take place and this would be over, but what comfort was that? She was gone from him and so, for eternity, was Lily. For what? Nothing as he could see. As a Taoist he had not sought this role. He had not wished to stand out but it had been thrust on him and in Taoism that too was his lot in life. It had come to him unbidden and he had to pick it up.

Alexander had arrived, he had seen him embrace his mother on the quayside. He felt a terrible emotion swell inside him and sought to empty his mind.

Two children lost to him. And Xia Lou's words had stung. Was he to condemn Lian to a kind of whoredom with Ah Soon? This too was not the way of the Taoist sage who should be charitable and seek happiness in the natural flow of life. This marriage was a

Confucian concept that he had fallen into. He felt his whole body out of alignment, a constant battle between his Taoist beliefs and the needs of commerce, of family and now the kongsi.

He closed his eyes and tried to concentrate on the light of the candle wavering in his mind but he felt as if he was crumbling to dust and the pieces of him were blowing away. He fell to the floor as the strain of iron control burst and all these feelings poured out of him. He sobbed, his chest straining for control but it was as if a river had opened up inside him and tears coursed.

He knew Lian had gone to her half-sister's gravesite and he was glad. But he knew, too, that she had been greeted by Alexander. Eyes were everywhere. He did not even have to order it. It was done as a matter of course. Wang had taken it upon himself to be the guardian of his life. A life he did not want.

He cried until no more tears could come, allowing himself to fall into the stream of grief. Exhausted, he rose and washed away his sweat and tears. He touched the marks on his cheek where her nails had cut into him. He was glad she had made these marks, he wanted her mark on him. He wanted her back but it all seemed so impossible.

He dressed in the white clothes he had brought, pure white, to make the offerings for Lily's soul and her release into the void.

On the altar table stood a lamp for the light of wisdom, on either side two candles for the light of the sun and the moon; their light would burn unceasingly for the next ten days. Before them stood cups of tea, water and rice, to represent Ying and Yang and their endless union. He had made a circle of five fruits, green papaya, red banana, yellow mango, white lychee and black dates, which symbolised the five elements of wood, fire, earth, metal and water. Inside the circle, he placed the incense burner. He lit the incense and brushed the smoke over his head and face and visualised Lily's face. Then he began the prayer.

* * *

Charlotte pointed to the dressing table.

'There, a picture of her. We had it painted for her third birthday.'

Alex rose and took up the picture. He brought it back to the bed.

Charlotte stroked the face and Alex gazed at his little half-sister. She was pretty, a pretty little girl with her dark eyes. She looked a little … what was it? He could not put his finger on it. She did not resemble Lian, whose features were wholly Chinese.

'The Taoists believe she has not died, you know, merely passed to another existence, one we cannot see. Her body is not here but her spirit has joined the river of life beyond this veil of tears. They have no concept of God, or heaven and hell. It is comforting.'

Charlotte turned the picture down on the bed and let her hand rest on it.

'Mother, please. Let the maid bring some food.'

'No, not now.'

She put her hand to his cheek.

'Let me grieve how I must. I will be all right. Aunt Jeanne told me how to do it once, long ago. But how I should dearly like to see Zhen.' She closed her eyes.

Alex went downstairs where Robert and Amber were waiting in the living room.

'My boy,' said Robert.

'She is better. A sleep will improve her.'

'Yes, yes, good, good. Well, we shall be off.'

'I shall stay, Father. May I, and see Aunt Charlotte later?

Perhaps Alex will keep me company?'

Before Robert could respond, Alex turned to Amber and took her hand, bowing.

'Forgive me. I must go out.' He bowed to Robert and left. Amber stared at his back, a look of misery on her face.

'Come, child. Well, well,' Robert said. 'I shall take you home. I have things to do.'

'Father, what of the marriage? You said …'

'Yes, yes, well. We shall see. After all, now is not the time. Your sister or brother is about to be born. You must attend to your mother.'

With a pout of annoyance Amber took up her hat and followed her father.

Alex made his way to Chinatown, crossing the river at Thomson Bridge and turned on to Boat Quay.

Before the Tan godown he stopped, watchful. The coolies were unloading bales of Indian cotton and great quantities of pepper. He went up to the gang leader.

'Master Zhen. Is he here?'

The man drew back in astonishment at the Chinese words issuing from the white man's mouth. A samseng loitering at the corner of the godown looked up. The coolie leader glanced at the samseng. The man took off. From the quay to Market Street where the Shan Chu lived and worked was a matter of minutes. He spoke to Ironfist Wang.

Alex could not understand the man's silence. He repeated his question then, as the man shrugged, he turned his footsteps towards the interior of the godown. A man appeared out of nowhere and barred his way.

'Get out of my way,' Alex snarled, adding a string of the filthiest Hokkien insults he could muster. Work on the quay came to a halt at the happy prospect of a fistfight.

'Ah Rex,' Zhen said and Alex turned as the man he had sought strode towards him. 'Your Chinese is still versatile, I see.'

Zhen waved a hand and instantly the coolies returned to their tasks. Wang took up a stance on the edge of the quay.

'Come inside,' Zhen said.

The interior of the godown was cool and vast. Alex looked around. He had spent hours here, whiling away time with Ah Soon and his Uncle Zhen. Zhen gazed at his son. He was fine looking, tall and strong and handsome.

'I heard you had returned. I am very happy to see you.'

Alexander faced Zhen. They were almost the same height and Zhen knew that in a few years, Alex would be as strong and muscled as him. Kai would never look like this. He was not tall and he tended to Noan's plumpness, not helped by the fact that his grandmother fed him anything he liked.

'Uncle, my mother wishes to see you.'

Zhen turned away from the boy.

'Sit,' he said in English. He had no wish for this conversation to reach the ears of all the coolies.

'I do not wish to sit. I have come only to tell you that your absence hurts mother. She mourns for your daughter.'

'Ah Rex, at the moment I cannot come to see Xia Lou. It is not possible.'

'Uncle Zhen, I don't understand. You and my mother, what has happened, all of that, it is not my business. But that you do not comfort her in this time, it is heartless, sir.'

'So it must seem. But I am not heartless. You must trust me on this.'

Zhen could see curious eyes staring at them as the coolies unloaded their goods in a steady stream. All this would be around the town in an hour. Alex opened his mouth to speak.

'No,' Zhen said, his tone harder. 'You do not understand my position and you must leave now.'

He turned on his heel. Alexander followed him, unable to believe the man so cruel but Wang stepped in front of him and the look he gave him made Alex stop abruptly. Zhen disappeared and within a moment so did Wang. The quay returned to its bustle as if nothing had happened.

He wandered away, bewildered. What was going on here? He did not notice the man following him at a discreet distance.

It was nearing three o'clock. He knew Lian came home at that hour. He felt the most intense need to see her. And to speak to her, for she must surely know more of what was going on between Zhen and his mother.

He waited and felt the eyes of the shopkeepers turned to him. He moved away, fingering some cloth goods and keeping an eye out for her. He saw her maid first, the old Ah Fu. Then she appeared and he smiled.

At that instant a hand shot out, grabbed his arm and pulled him swiftly sideways so hard he stumbled.

'You can't do this,' Ah Soon hissed to him. 'Come on.'

Alex was so astonished he allowed himself to be led.

'We need to go over to the European side. Too many eyes and ears here.'

For a man in Ah Soon's cadaverous condition, he walked fast and within fifteen minutes they found themselves over the wooden footbridge by the fort and quickly onto the beachside of the padang. Ah Soon slowed, sweat pouring off him. He mopped his face and Alex fell into rhythm beside him.

'The Institution. We can talk there. The old fives court.'

The fives court had been turned into a storeroom of sorts

with a rough roof over it. The two men sat.

'My God, Ah Soon, I thought you were half dead with all that damn opium. You're fitter than I am.'

Ah Soon grinned. 'I've had a pipe. One invigorates you. You should try it.'

'No thanks. I have other addictions.'

'Yes, and Lian cannot be one of them. Everyone knows you talked to her. Zhen has sent me to speak with you.'

'Has he? That was fast. Why doesn't he just talk to me himself?'

'There are reasons I cannot tell you but it is all to do with Chinese stuff. You understand?'

Alex did understand. Chinese stuff was the triads, the secret societies. Slowly Ah Soon began to explain to Alex the events during the years of his absence in Scotland.

'Your mother went away to Batavia just after you left. When she returned it was with the baby. My father told me it was Uncle Zhen's, and that he and your mother were henceforth to live like husband and wife but not together. They lived separate lives socially but everyone knew what was going on. They were talked about all the time. I suppose it has taken its toll.'

'You never thought to write and tell me all this?'

Ah Soon threw a glance at Alex. 'Write to you? You went and it was like you had forgotten about me. When did you send one letter to me?'

Alex looked down. 'I'm sorry. The voyage to Scotland, the newness of it all. And then I was so free. Sorry.'

'Free to do whatever you liked. But that isn't possible here. You can't see Lian again.'

Alex rose and began to pace.

'Do you love her?'

Ah Soon burst into laughter. 'Of course I don't love her. And she thinks I'm a dope fiend.'

'So why ...'

'Wake up. She's Chinese and she's his daughter and what he wants she must do. That's the way it is and always shall be. Here endeth the lesson.'

Alex threw a look of resentment at Ah Soon.

'Don't sulk. What did you think? You would marry her? How would that ever happen? Don't be stupid and don't try to see her again. You will ruin her and they will punish her. My father will not let this go away. He needs to be related to wealthy, successful Zhen so he can get hold of money. The man is a fool and I despise him.'

'You don't have to marry her. You could refuse.'

Ah Soon rose and pointed to Alex's head. 'What you got in there? No-one can refuse anything. How would I live, eh? What do I know how to do? And I don't care who I marry. What's the difference?'

Alex stared at Ah Soon. What was the difference between them? He must also bend the knee, marry a woman he cared nothing for so as to keep his wealth and status. The only difference was that Alex felt that he was falling in love with Lian, and Ah Soon was in love with opium and whatever it took to get it he would do.

'The difference is, I love her.'

Ah Soon laughed again. 'How? You met her a couple of days ago.'

'I met her years ago. I think I might have been in love with her for years.'

Ah Soon shook his head. 'Then it's a tragedy,' he said. 'Like Romeo and Juliet. Remember. Mr. Holstead made you play

Romeo and you did the first act in Hokkien just to annoy him. Impressed the hell out of the Chinese merchants and the governor though.'

Alex smiled then shrugged and made his way out of the shed and began to walk through the gardens to North Bridge Road. Ah Soon rose too and stared at his friend's back.

'There's a tiffin room in Bonham Street. Meet me there next Friday?'

Alex raised a hand in acknowledgement but continued walking, his head bowed, staring at his boots.

20

The house was silent. He had taken dinner alone. His mother was still in her room. He had grown up in this house with his brother Adam who now, unaccountably, wanted to be a priest. What had happened to the simian Rajah Brooke that his mother had brought back as a baby monkey from Sarawak? And what had happened to Tarun, his guardian, who had taught him Malay and with whom he had had so many adventures? He had not given them a moment's thought. No more than Ah Soon. He felt sorry for that.

He went to the living room and poured a brandy. Malik advanced with a tray.

'A letter, sir,' he said and departed silently. The letter was addressed in English in spidery handwriting to A. Manouk.

Alexander threw himself into a chair and opened the letter. It was written in Malay and though he had not spoken it or read it for three years, it was still a familiar language to him.

Come now. Lian waits. Back door. Be invisible.

There was no signature.

He felt the thrill of adventure. He threw a cloak about his

shoulders and disguised his hair under a cloth hat.

He walked through the cool evening from the dark, silent streets of the European town, past the Europa Hotel, which glowed inside its grounds on the corner of High Street, music faintly emanating from its halls. He hugged the shrubbery which formed its fence and across Thomson Bridge to the streets of Chinatown.

The dim coconut oil lamps threw barely a glow but he was glad of the obscurity. On Boat Quay a Chinese opera was taking place, the firebrands throwing a brightness on the river and the assembled crowd. The high-pitched wails fell on his ears and faded as he moved towards Lian's house.

Once there he went down the pitch-black lane behind the house. The only light came from a bright moon and from some small lamps and the fires of cooks making fried goods for sale in the morning. A line of coolies gathering the night soil passed by with their fragrant cargo.

He knocked quietly at the door and it swung open. The small Malay boy ushered him inside the darkened hall. There was a light somewhere but the house was silent. The boy melted into the darkness, then a candle glowed and he recognised the hunched form of Lian's maid, Ah Fu.

She beckoned him and he followed her light. She opened a door and there, in the main room of the house, stood Lian. The paraffin lamps glowed brightly and the room was a pool of light after the darkness of the rest of the house.

'Mother Lilin sent for you. Ah Fu told me. It is incredibly dangerous for you to be here. For you, and especially for me. The Malay boy brought the letter to you and he is young and not interested in things he doesn't understand. Ah Fu won't tell. She's a gossip but she won't tell this. She knows what will happen. You know that my aunt is mad.'

'I don't know she is mad. I know that I have been warned not to come near you. But here I am.'

Lian could not prevent a smile. He was so cocksure, so arrogant. It was appallingly attractive.

'Listen, Alex. I am guessing Mother Lilin saw you the other day. She wants to meet you, apparently and has sent out this message. But you must understand, she is not well. I would rather not do this but if she is refused anything she becomes distracted.'

'I see. You are beautiful.'

He spoke the truth. In this half-light, she was all beauty, her hair shining, her skin like silk. Her face fell into an attitude of absolute seriousness and she hardened her voice.

'Stop it. This woman is visited by demons, you have to understand. If I had known about this I would never have allowed it. Now you must meet her or she will be mad all night. But be careful.'

Lian spoke with such hushed gravity that Alex frowned, suddenly realising that this evening was taking an utterly unexpected turn.

Lian led the way into the sitting room. Lilin rose as Alex entered. He had expected to see a raving lunatic but she was dressed neatly in the fashion of the Straits Chinese in a flowery baju and sarong, her hair tightly pulled back and several diamond pins in her bun. She was quite calm. Her hair, Alex saw, was thinning and the scalp covered in raised scars. He had remembered her as beautiful but the creature before him was like a hideous witch.

Lian sat nervously on the edge of a seat. Alex bowed to Lilin who stared at him, then suddenly smiled. Her teeth were red and decaying.

He addressed her in Hokkien then remembered she spoke

Baba Malay. He looked at Lian.

'Mother Lilin speaks English.'

'How do you do?' he said.

'Sit,' she said imperiously, pointing to the seat next to Lian with her long painted fingernail.

'You came back,' she said staring at him intently.

'Yes.' A silence fell. Alex wasn't sure what to do.

'You shake hands with Lian.'

This was unexpected. Lian looked at Alex and frowned. He put out his hand to Lian's and she took it.

Lilin began to laugh. 'Why you not kiss her? She your …' Lilin stopped abruptly and put her finger to her lips slyly. 'Ha, ha.'

Lian dropped Alex's hand.

Lilin looked at them intently, peering, and a sudden movement of confusion contorted her face. 'Zhen,' she said.

Lian made a warning sign to Alex.

'Ah Rex must leave now, Mother Lilin,' she said in Baba Malay. Lian indicated to Alex to stand. He rose but before he could make another move, Lilin flew forward. She put her arm round Alex's neck and pushed her lips against his. Her other hand took him between the legs, rubbing.

'Ah,' she said as Alex tried to pull away.

Lian was frozen in horror. Alex's eyes flew to hers.

Lilin pulled at his clothes, ripping his shirt, then sank down in front of him and put her face to his groin.

Alex leapt back as if burned and Lian let out a scream. Lilin was like a tigress. In one swift movement she tore at her clothing, revealing her breasts. The pins in her hair flew out and she flung herself on Alex, holding him, ripping her nails down his chest. With a supreme effort Alex flung her off. She landed in a heap on the floor, but in a moment was up again. Lian's hands were in front of her face in shock.

The door flew open and Ah Ma came in and grabbed Lilin's shoulders. Lent abnormal strength by her dementia, Lilin spat and bit and scratched. Lian screamed and Alex took her hand and dragged her from the room.

'Get the doctor,' he said to a half-dressed servant who had appeared in the hall and stared at Alex.

'The apothecary,' Lian said, her voice shaking. 'Quickly.'

The man bolted. From inside the room, the sound of struggle continued. The syce arrived, a big Indian man. Lian nodded at him and he went inside. Gradually the sounds subsided as the apothecary rushed into the house. Lian felt every nerve in her body quivering. Alex was covered in blood, seeping from the scratches to his chest.

'Come,' she said and led him to the bathroom. She took a cloth but her hands were shaking so much she could not control them.

Alex put his arms around her. 'Calm down. There. It's all right.'

Lian lay against his bloody chest, felt his heart beating as hard as hers. 'I don't know why. What …'

'Just wait. We'll talk about it in a minute.'

She lay in his arms until she felt some control returning, then made to pull away but he did not release her.

'It's all right. I'm all right,' she said and looked up into his eyes.

He dropped his head to hers and kissed her gently on the lips.

Lian could not help herself. She returned his kiss. Alex pressed more urgently, pulled her more closely into him and she ran her hands around his waist, deepening the kiss.

There was a knock at the door and Alex released her.

'The apothecary, miss,' the maid said through the door.

'I'm coming,' she said. She looked at Alex then down at herself. 'What a sight we are. You're covered in blood.'

'I'll clean myself up.'

Lian nodded and left the room.

She put on a long tunic to cover the blood and went to speak to the apothecary. This man was quite used to her aunt's bouts of insanity.

When he left, she went to her room and cleaned up and changed her clothes. Mother Lilin was sleeping. She took a paste which was good for wounds and went in search of Alex. He was in the sitting room. He had arranged his clothes as best he could.

She sank to her knees and took a little of the paste on her finger. He watched her touching his skin, wincing as she moved over the scratches, but feeling, more intensely, his arousal.

'This will heal them. You should not have kissed me.'

He took her wrist in his hand, putting her palm on his chest. She did not resist. The darkness of passion filled his brain, but scything through it came concern for her. She was in trouble.

'I should kiss you a hundred times a day. Until you can hardly breathe.'

Lian flushed and felt her face grow hot.

'I would marry you. I want you,' he said.

She pulled her hand from his and moved away from him.

'I love you, Lian. I won't lie, I've said it before to lots of women.'

She threw him a dark glance.

'But I've never meant it. Don't you feel it too? We belong together.'

'Stop saying these things. In the morning my grandmother will know of your visit and what has happened here. She and my father will punish me somehow.'

He took a step forward and pulled her into his arms and put his lips to hers. She sighed and ran her arms around his neck. He picked her up. She was as light as air yet as substantial as the weight of this feeling for her that had suddenly come upon him.

He ran kisses along her neck and she dropped her head back and savoured them, the small trails of heat of his lips on her skin. She felt blood pound in her temples, swept into longing for him.

'You love me too,' he said. He put her feet back to the floor. 'Lian?'

'How can I love you? What is it, the kind of love that can come so quickly. We met only a few days ago.'

'We met years ago. I think I've loved you for years.'

He gazed into her eyes, staring into them and she could not move, almost mesmerised by his intensity and his will.

'Yes,' she said quietly. 'Incredible as it seems, I love you.'

He smiled and put her hands to his lips. 'Then I shall make a plan. I am good at plans. Whatever happens tomorrow, trust me. Somehow we will be together.'

She shook her head. This was mad. She heard the sounds of the servants coming. 'You have to go.' She pushed Alex towards the back door.

'Trust me,' he said and disappeared into the darkness.

21

The two men sat facing the Resident Councillor. Blackwood, behind his desk, fingered the envelopes in front of him. He had hoped for more syndicates to come forward. The government had advertised all over the town but no more offers had been forthcoming. Of course he could not know who was in the syndicate. Could be half the merchants in the town for all he knew. The leaders and public faces of the syndicates were before him and he avoided any expression.

Hong sat, oozing off the chair, uncomfortable, and glared at Cheng who looked straight ahead. Blackwood looked at them both. Really, it was distasteful this business of dealing with the Chinese on such matters but what other choice was there.

'Thank you,' he said. 'Mr. McNair, would you be witness to the validity of the sealed bids.'

McNair came forward and stood by Blackwood as he opened the first envelope and read the figure there. Neither man reacted but McNair saw Blackwood's fingers grip the paper a little more intently. And not surprisingly.

The second envelope was opened. McNair nodded to Blackwood and went back to his chair.

Blackwood laid the two sheets of paper on the table and

looked up at the two men.

* * *

Zhen watched Cheng pacing, fuming and agitated. 'How can he make a profit at such a bid. It's impossible,' Cheng snarled.

Cheng's shoes squeaked on the floorboards, the coat of his gown flapping wildly.

'Twenty-four thousand dollars a month. It's not possible.'

Zhen shook his head. He too could not work out the sums Hong was assuming.

'What did you bid?' he asked an increasingly agitated Cheng. 'Sit down. You'll have a heart attack.'

Cheng looked at Zhen beseechingly, as if Zhen could somehow explain the logic of Hong's actions. 'Sixteen thousand. That's generous with the price of raw opium as it stands.'

'Perhaps Hong has some other means of obtaining raw opium than through the legal channels. If the price of the opium is nothing but the cost of a few pirates, then the profits will be enormous. We assume he is capable of it.'

'Yes,' shouted Cheng. 'Yes, that's it. The man is so devious and foul that he is capable of anything. We must report him to the governor.'

Zhen stood up and went to Cheng. 'Sit down, Lao Cheng, and calm down. He hasn't done anything yet.'

Cheng sat. As his heart began to find a decent rhythm he noted the 'Lao' that Zhen had added to his name. It was the mark of friendship and respect.

'No, no. You're right.'

Zhen called for tea. Cheng took a cup and felt better.

'Johor has gone for $2700 a month, did you see? To the Tay

syndicate. It was reported in the Straits Times. Hong did not even bid so the Temenggong had no choice and is not well pleased.'

'No. It's Hong's game to smuggle opium to kill Tay's farm. That's why he didn't bother to bid. It is a certainty.'

'You would do well to contact Tay,' Zhen said. 'Offer any help. Warn him of Hong and perhaps supply chintengs for his police force.'

'Yes, I will do that. It will mend fences with the Temenggong, perhaps.' Cheng smiled ruefully at Zhen. Silence fell as the two men sipped their tea.

'What does this mean for me? I have no desire to continue in this post.'

'I am sorry. This was entirely unexpected. I am sure the Deputy, the others would want you to continue until things straighten out. Until the spirit farm comes up. I have decided to bid on that. Another two months.'

Cheng waited, hoping.

'I apologise for my tone on the previous occasion. I don't like to make threats, but I did not know you then. I cannot oblige you but if you step aside Hong has all the power now. He will certainly take over. Do you think?' Cheng glanced at Zhen.

What fine sons he and Jia Wen would make. The man was magnificent. The body and the heart of a lion. He had five granddaughters in Riau but not yet a grandson. Cheng had no wish to take another wife. A concubine perhaps, for companionship, when he was settled here in Singapore, but no more wives, and the thought of such a family with this man as his son-in-law, gladdened his heart. He had given Tan a magnificent funeral. The whole town still spoke of it. He would honour him in life and in death. He gazed at Zhen with something like adoration.

'The spirit farm too has been divided,' Zhen said. 'Tay will certainly take Johor. If you bid on the Singapore spirit farm, bid high. Once you have that you are in a better position to take over the kongsi as Tay will probably agree to keep out Hong.'

'Yes, yes. Don't worry. There is plenty of money in liquor, I can go high. Make Hong's head spin.'

These old men and their rivalries. It was precisely this sort of thing that made him steer well clear of these syndicates. But it jogged his memory.

'If I do this, I need a favour.'

'I'm listening.'

'I have a friend. He has fallen on hard times but I want you to stake him into the spirit syndicate. It would mean you advancing him credit which you could recoup against his share of liquor profits, but it would also mean he would be seen to be a trusted individual who has found favour with you. You are not his friend, it would carry more weight.'

'Naturally. Your friend is mine.'

Cheng nodded to Zhen and made for the door. Then, as if a thought had just occurred to him, he turned back.

'My daughter is eighteen. A woman, not a girl. She must have a man of course, before much longer. She has the passionate nature of the Javanese. She is the daughter of my Javanese concubine. Now that I am establishing myself in Singapore I would like her to have a husband.'

'Yes,' Zhen said. 'I see. You taught her Chinese ways. It is a wonder. If you permit me to say so, she plays well, wonderfully well.'

'Thank you. I am so new here, I don't know the right people. Is there a matchmaker whom I should speak to?'

'There is. Lao Liu is the most respected. I will ask him to contact you.'

'Thank you, Master Zhen.'

Cheng bowed and departed.

Zhen went slowly back to his seat and put his head in his hands. The floating sounds of the zither came to him and he looked up.

22

The plan grew almost fully formed inside Alex's head as he stood next to his uncle Robert at the font of St. Andrew's Cathedral. He had not slept for two days and nights, his thoughts in a constant ferment. And then it came to him.

'You are a diabolical and clever bastard, Alexander Manouk,' he said to himself.

The baby, a four-day-old boy, was baptised, the mark of the cross made on his forehead and he was given the name Robert. His uncle's nyai was not present. Naturally, as an unmarried woman, she was not in the church. Furthermore, Alex had been told, Shilah had suffered a great deal giving birth and was in bed with a fever, attended by Dr Little.

The ceremony and the Sunday service ended in the sparsely populated church. Charlotte held the baby in her arms and all she could think about was Lily and had to force herself to stop the tears she felt about to overwhelm her. Still no word from Zhen and with each day her heart grew colder and colder to him.

Now she wanted to leave, for what was there to stay for. The *Queen* would, by her reckoning, be here in two days. The time to take on new crew, load the holds, would be two or three more days. Within a week she would be on board and leave this misery behind her.

They walked back to Robert's home on Queen Street, the baby now in the arms of his Malay ayah. Charlotte linked arms with Robert.

'Shilah is unwell. Did you not do as I asked? I gave you the frankincense oils and the paste from the Malay bomoh.'

'Dr. Little, well, he said, all that was stuff and nonsense and had a frightful row with Dr. Cowper who says the native medicines are efficacious.'

'Did he? It is what all the women do here. Shilah would know that. Why did not a midwife come? Or why not use Dr. Cowper. He is a good man. He gives medicines to the poor and the missionary families for free.'

'Dr. Little would not have a native midwife. Said the birthing women were no more than sorts of witchdoctors. And after the row with Cowper, he refused to talk to him.'

Charlotte shook her head.

'They do nothing but fight and argue. In the meantime lives are lost.'

'Surely Dr. Little knows what he's doing,' Robert said, looking aggrieved and distressed.

'I had all my children in the Indies and the midwife always made me use smoke or oil. They birth in water too, which is quite different to here.'

'Charlotte, for heaven's sake, that's enough. I can't talk about such things. I can't tell Little his job. Surely Shilah will be well.'

Charlotte frowned. She could not pursue this with Robert, for whom the subject was clearly embarrassing and distressing. She had no proof that the Malay and *Indische* midwives knew better than British doctors. But she suspected it. She regretted not attending on Shilah before now, but the birth had begun so suddenly in the middle of the night and by the morning she was delivered. Robert said it was all very fast and she was resting peacefully. So indeed she was when Charlotte had gone to the house the following evening.

Robert moved ahead and joined Arthur Graves, his new inspector from Penang. A small baptismal celebration had been prepared in his garden, to which many of Robert's policemen had been invited.

Alexander joined his mother. 'Mother, how are you?'

She put her arm through her son's. 'Grief is slow to part, son.' She smiled at him. 'But you have been wonderful. Thank you.'

'Are we friends again?' he said. He had not told her he had been to see Zhen. It was cruel to relate the man's cold-heartedness.

'Yes.'

'Good, then I shall please you more. I have decided to bow to your wishes. I shall marry Amber and go with you to Batavia.'

Charlotte examined her son. He seemed genuine.

'Well. Good.' She hugged his arm and he smiled.

The plan, he thought, had begun. He intended to marry Amber as his mother wished. Amber was so besotted with him that he could do anything with her. Once she was pregnant, he would while away his time with the local women. Such dalliances were quite acceptable in the Indies where wealthy men had as many nyais as they could afford.

Then, when Lian was married to Ah Soon, he would make the offer to bring his friend to his estate where he would work with him at something Alex hadn't thought about yet. She would come and then he would have her. Why would Ah Soon not agree? He would escape his father, have a life of luxury and opium, have women, as many as he wanted. And in return he, Alex, would have Lian, virginal Lian, for he did not intend Ah Soon to sleep with her. He would write to him this very afternoon.

'There is a condition, however.'

She looked at him, wary.

'On the day I am married to Amber, Brieswijk, all of it, will come to me.'

Charlotte gave a laugh of astonishment. 'What a request. What do you know of running such an estate?'

'I shall learn much faster if it is mine.'

Charlotte hardly knew what to answer. 'But you need time, a year or two, to learn ...'

'Mother, I will be the master or I will not go. A man needs respect.'

She saw he was adamant and heard it in his voice. He waited whilst she reflected. He was almost certain she would give in. Adam was never going to inherit, and who else was there?

'I shall draw a percentage of the profit whilst I live,' she said.

He smiled. 'Yes, of course, that is not an issue. But all the control, all the decisions will be mine and mine alone. I will not consult you unless I need your advice.'

'And the company. It is still mine, you know. Nicolaus had charge of it, but it is mine.'

'The company, Buitenzorg, the fleet, these you must decide about when you are there. What is profitable keep, what is failing sell. It is all too big anyway.'

She was slightly impressed with this attitude of authority. And he was right. The trading company of Manouk & Son, which was Tigran's heritage, had been wealthy and well run when he had taken it over. He had added to it and by the time she had married him it was a vast enterprise with interests through the East Indies. Without him, it lacked the hard and steady hand it needed and had become too vast to be controlled by his sons, the best of whom had now died.

'Well, well. I suppose this is a good thing. You are being sensible.'

'Very. And you shall have grandchildren. As many as Amber can bear.'

Something in his tone sounded strange and she glanced at him. But she sensed a resolution, even a maturity in him that had not been there a few days ago. And he would relieve her and an aging Takouhi of the responsibility. To go to Brieswijk, to see Takouhi, see her son married, these were truly joys. Suddenly a life without this Zhen, so cold and untrustworthy, seemed perfectly possible.

'We shall go to the lawyer and draw up the papers tomorrow,' he said.

At the house, as the guests gathered in the garden, Charlotte went up the stairs to Shilah's room. It was darkened and she pulled the curtain a little. She signalled the maid to leave and went to Shilah, taking up the water and the cloth and bathing her forehead. She was hot, feverish, shaking. Charlotte locked the door and went back to the bed. She pulled back the sheet and raised Shilah's nightgown and pulled away the wadding holding the blood. It was smelly and she knew instantly.

She called for Amber, who came promptly. 'Listen. She is very sick. Dr. Little is like all the men. He won't listen. This is women's work. You must go to my house and ask the maid for my small red leather case. Hurry.'

Amber was annoyed to be asked this. She wanted to be with Alexander but she obeyed and left the house.

Charlotte took away the bloody cloths and called the maid back. Together they washed her. Charlotte added the tea tree oil to the water. This was a Malay remedy she had learned for cleansing. The Javanese used turmeric and honey too but she did not have these at hand.

By the time Amber returned, she and the maid had cleaned away the foul-smelling blood and Charlotte took the frankincense oil and applied it all around the vaginal area and as far as she dared inside. Shilah had split and the wound was horrible to see, swollen and purple. The labour had been fast but, she could see, it had also been brutal. The maid put back clean cloths and they pulled the sheet over her.

'Keep bathing her,' she told the maid. 'I will come back this evening.'

She leant over Shilah who had opened her eyes. She had been prescribed tincture of opium. The bottle stood on the bedside table. 'Take heart. I'm here.'

Shilah closed her eyes.

She washed her hands and went downstairs. She sent a note to Dr. Cowper, for Dr. Little was so arrogant and greedy that she did not trust him.

Amber was next to Alexander, hanging on his every word. Alex ignored her and Charlotte frowned. Was this the right thing to do? He clearly did not love her.

But she joined them and for several hours the house was filled with the pleasures of the baby. Charlotte looked up at the window where Shilah lay. She had come to her four days after the birth. Was it in time?

Dr. Cowper arrived and went upstairs. When all the guests had departed and Robert had gone to see Shilah, she called Amber to her.

'My dear, Alexander has asked for your hand in marriage.'

Amber's face was so filled with light and joy that Charlotte's heart went out to her niece.

'Oh Aunt Charlotte. I am so happy.' She rushed into

Charlotte's arms.

'You must make your goodbyes. We shall all depart when the *Queen* is ready. Perhaps six or seven days from now. You will be married in Brieswijk. All your trousseau will be prepared over there as mine was.'

Amber left Charlotte and danced around the room. 'Married at your estate. I have heard it is marvellous. Is it, Aunt?'

'Most beautiful, and Alexander will take charge of it and you shall be its mistress as I was.'

Amber, suddenly serious, threw herself at Charlotte's feet.

'I have wanted Alex all my life. I will make him the best, most devoted wife. Thank you.'

She took Charlotte's hands and kissed them. Charlotte was moved but a sudden shadow crossed her mind. Amber loved Alex but Alex did not love her.. She dismissed this thought. Love could blossom anywhere. And Brieswijk had made her love Tigran. Hand in hand the two women went to Shilah's room.

23

'The servants have told me of … ' She waved her hand. 'Episodes.'

Zhen sat silently as his mother-in-law spoke.

'The child can no longer stay there. A report has come of scandalous things.'

The old woman chewed her betel and let slip a long stream of spit into the pot. Zhen found this habit unpleasant. Noan had chewed sireh and it gave her breath an odour that he found repugnant. But it was a ritual with the nonya and they carried their splendid sireh sets of silver and tortoiseshell and gold when they visited their friends. Like his hair, Zhen took prodigiously good care of his teeth with herbal rinses and pastes made from his own compounds.

'What things?'

'A boy, the English boy, came to the house. It is the greatest scandal. From what I have heard, Lilin asked him to come and then she attacked him. It is too much. The whole family's reputation will be ruined.'

Zhen showed nothing of the shock he felt. The English boy must be Ah Rex.

'This is punishment. This child dying. A child of an abominable relationship.'

Zhen rose and the old woman looked away. He was the head of the household, but she had to have her say. The child with the English concubine, well, of course she had died. A child like that, made from this white woman. She remembered her own child. Noan, the sweetest, most obedient child any woman could have. She had died giving birth to his son. It had killed her husband and she, herself, had taken a long time to recover. But he had never married again. Never honoured the family with more grandsons.

Now her second daughter, Lilin, was insane and she wanted her here with her. Lian she wanted gone, married away as quickly as possible. The girl was hideous, disobedient, and a freak with her English education.

She waited but Zhen said nothing, staring out of the window.

He ignored her views on Lily. She was a beloved child and this superstitious and ignorant old woman's ideas meant nothing to him. The news of Alex and Lian was shocking but not in the way his mother-in-law imagined. He knew now that Alex wanted Lian. In his youth he had intimated it and now he was seen hanging around her as if the years between had not happened. He knew everything about obsessive love. He had felt it for Xia Lou for twenty years. And it had not gone away, not for him. He knew there was bad feeling between them, but surely, when this obligation of his was over, surely they would find a way back to each other.

The widow Tan waited as the silence lengthened, chewing. A gob of red spittle landed with a plop in the porcelain spittoon.

He turned towards her. 'Lilin will come here. She is beyond our reach and you must take care of her.'

She nodded, glad he had finally spoken.

'Lian will come here also. Arrange the Cheo Thau ceremony.

Lian and Ah Soon shall be wed as soon as possible.'

The widow Tan bowed to her son-in-law. He had made the correct decision. As he left the room she rose and called the second concubine. When her husband had died, this girl had been twenty and obligated to a life of servitude to her, the principal wife. She had done her best to make this girl's life misery and she did not intend to stop now.

Zhen knew he had to speak to Xia Lou before something terrible happened. In the carriage ride back to town he thought hard and long how he could meet her. Now he knew he had to, he wanted to with all his heart. He had left her in anger and anguish and they had lost their child.

But he had never been more supervised. Wang had his men everywhere and since the public break with Xia Lou he did not want more interest in his private life. He called at Hong Kong Street and greeted Min. She smiled, happy to see him.

'You feeling better?' she said.

No-one was more familiar to him than Min. They were friends. He shared more with her than anyone, not Qian, not even Xia Lou. He and she had come together as lowly creatures in a hard world and had helped each other along the way. He went into her room and lay down on her bed.

'Eyes everywhere. I'm not enjoying my job,' he said and she grinned.

'Hard to be adored,' she said. 'Ironfist Wang thinks the sun shines out of your arse.'

He laughed. 'I need to meet her. Privately. How?'

Min nodded. She knew who he meant. 'After that fight, won't be easy. Not here. Over there somewhere. Kampong Glam?'

'Plenty of Chinese living there.'

He remembered the house in Katong. Her brother's cottage

by the beach. The whole of the area had been opened up since they had been there last. It was no longer necessary to sail there. A road led to Katong. He would write and request a meeting there. He rose and kissed Min on her forehead.

He walked from Hong Kong Street down towards the harbour. He needed a clear head, and looking at his ships always reassured and buoyed him. He made his way to Johnstone's Pier and gazed out.

There were his ships, two sail, two steam. Three bound for China, one for Semarang. Then he saw it. The black ship with white sails, the white flag with a black panther. It was the most distinctive ship he had ever seen. It was her ship, *The Queen of the South*. This ship rarely called at Singapore for it plied the local Indies trade. It came here only when its mistress called.

He went quickly back to Market Street and called Wang to him. 'Her ship is the black brig. *Queen of the South*. Find out what is happening with it.'

Wang disguised his annoyance. Still the master thought of this woman. The stupid maid was supposed to release the snakes, both of them, near her. Instead she'd got scared and dumped the damn things on the child. Since that death, he'd had her sorely beaten and now she was back in the brothel. Served her right. Within an hour he returned.

'It loads a cargo of iron goods, English cloth, guns, gunpowder and opium and sails for Batavia in three days. I cannot be sure but the gossip is that she will be on board with her son and her niece.'

Wang was disconcerted by this news. On the one hand she would disappear, on the other, she had not received the justice he believed she deserved.

Zhen thought furiously. In a few days she was leaving, sailing away with Alex. What was happening?

* * *

The tiffin rooms were new. A trader named Ellington had given up his business and started these rooms where one could eat Indian food, drink India pale ale or porter and read the newspaper. They were already crowded at eleven o'clock with the English, Armenian, Chinese and Eurasian merchants from the quay, the streets and the Square or Raffles Place as it was now known.

He ordered rice and curry and looked around. The noise was tremendous. He greeted several of the merchants who recognised him, and waved as he saw Ah Soon.

'We are being watched,' Ah Soon said as he took a chair. 'Beer,' he said to the boy who came up. 'I got your letter.'

Alexander waited. Ah Soon was ditheringly slow. He waited until the food and beers had arrived. Then he took two pill boxes from his pocket and took two pills from each which he drank down.

'What's that?'

'This one is Du Fu Ling. Zhen makes me take them. He says they prevent the pox and help with the sores and sweats I get. The other I forget, herbs all mixed up which he says will stop me craving the opium and improve my qi.'

'Have you had it, the pox?'

'Course, everyone's had the pox.'

'Me too, got it in a whorehouse in London.'

Ah Soon nodded. 'Nasty, isn't it. I'm not bothered about sex, not really. Got rid of all that in my father's whorehouses when I was sixteen and then found a new love.'

Alex raised his eyebrows. 'I love sex. Randy as a goat all the time. Hand over the pox pills. You can get some more.'

Ah Soon laughed and handed the pill box to him. Alex

swallowed two pills and set about his beer. 'Randy, but no whoring for me. I don't want to get it again and give it to Lian. I need to be clean for her.'

The two men sat and watched the crowd for a while.

'So, what do you think of my plan?'

Ah Soon grinned. 'I think it is a diabolical and brilliant plan.'

Alex laughed, a great guffaw of pleasure that made eyes turn onto him.

'But Lian must know too. She must agree,' Ah Soon whispered, his head close to Alex's.

'I will tell her. She has been moved out to the old grandma's estate at River Valley Road. I will go there and tell her. I know she wants to be with me.'

Ah Soon looked surprised. 'How do you know?'

'Never mind.'

Ah Soon looked doubtful, his lower lip falling between his yellow teeth. Alex grimaced.

'You can't touch her. You marry her and pretend like the marriage has been consummated. Take some blood into the bedroom somehow. I know what these old bibiks look out for. As soon as you are wed, you will show your father the letter I will send offering you a position at Brieswijk as a manager. I will pay the passage for you both.'

Ah Soon nodded. The plan seemed foolproof. 'What shall I do at Brieswijk?'

'Whatever you want. Grow rice, live in a kampong. Smoke opium all day if you wish. Have young maidens hanging all over you. Make lots of brown babies, or Chinese babies. I will endow them all with money galore and your children and mine will grow up together as we did.'

Both men grinned but a sudden doubt wormed into Ah Soon's

brain. 'But you will be married to Amber. What will she say?'

Alex waved a hand in disdainful dismissal. 'She will do has her husband tells her.'

'But Lian is her school friend. I don't know.'

Alex attacked his curry and rice, his face set hard. 'Shut up. I want Lian. That's all. You agree or not. If you don't, I'll come and get her anyway and if you've slept with her, I'll kill you.'

Alex shot Ah Soon a look of pure venom. Ah Soon drank the rest of his beer. He knew Alexander meant every word.

24

The house at River Valley Road was one he remembered well. He had come here with Ah Soon, Qian and other children to play, for his Uncle Zhen always invited him and taught him Chinese expressions and how to do tai chi.

He left his horse tethered beyond the lake. When darkness fell he made his way to the house and watched as the evening meal preparations took place. Lian was in the kitchen with her grandmother. Lian never said a word as the old woman's mouth moved constantly and she raised her finger time and again. Lian kept her head bowed and cut vegetables. The food was made and the odours of it wafted to him. Of the mad aunt he saw nothing.

He trailed Lian and finally saw where she slept. It was a small bedroom off the verandah. These houses were all built the same way. The shutters were locked with a small lever and, if it wasn't more closely bolted inside, it was a matter of slipping a knife through and flicking it up.

The old woman seemed insomniac and he watched as she chewed her sireh and played cards with another old woman. A pretty young nonya seemed to be at their beck and call, preparing sireh, bringing drinks and snacks, hanging there, obediently waiting at the old woman's elbow for the next order.

'God,' he thought, 'will they never be done.'

It was two hours more before the lights were extinguished and the house settled down for the night. He took a close look at her room. On the verandah, directly under her window was an Indian guard on his cot. These guards were everywhere in the houses in the country for everyone feared Chinese burglars. But as a Chinese family, and the family of someone like Zhen, this house would never be attacked. English houses, Indian houses, Malay houses, those were the targets of the Chinese gangs.

Which meant the ancient Indian guard was the most relaxed man in the world and lay snoring, sleeping the sleep of the dead, on his cot on the edge of the verandah.

Alex stepped over the man and within a second he had opened the shutter and slipped into the room.

'Lian,' he whispered. 'It's me, Alex.'

The darkness was so total that he only heard her feet patter lightly on the floorboards and then she was in his arms, the soft material of her nightgown, her body against him.

'Alex, my goodness. I've been so frightened,' she whispered and he held her tight. 'They will hold the vowing ceremony in three days. I shall be married.'

She began to cry quietly and he held her more tightly. His body craved her but his mind gave it pause. He wanted their first time to be wonderful, not fast, here in the dark like furtive creatures.

'Come on. We need to talk.' He climbed outside and lifted her into his arms, over the guard and onto the grass. 'Go, quickly, to the pavilion.'

He closed the shutters and raced after her. They ran and ran, down to the Chinese pavilion by the lake, where the half moon lay resting in the water. Panting, they stood next to each other, her hand in his, looking at the beauty of the scene.

'Listen to me. We have no time.' Quickly he told her the plan. When he finished, she turned her gaze on him, pulling her hand from his.

'Are you mad? I shall be your whore. That is your plan? Amber, my friend, will be your wife, and I will be your whore.'

'No, you will be my wife in all but name, honoured and loved.' Alex began to pace. 'Lian, don't think this way. What else can I do? Do you want to have Ah Soon's brats, live a life of misery with him, under the constant eye of your grandmother or your aunts. Don't you want to be with me?'

An owl hooted loudly and the wind rose and sighed in the trees. It made them jump but somehow the tension drained away.

'How can we know the future? You must come and get away from here. We can decide when you are there.'

'I can't think. Oh God. Everything is going so fast. I don't know what to do.'

'I do. You will marry Ah Soon like a good obedient girl. You will not consummate the marriage. You will come to Batavia and we shall begin our life together, far from here, far from parents and grandmothers on my estate, where I will be the king. You understand.'

She said nothing and he felt all her fears and doubts.

'My father …'

'He has no power once you are married to Ah Soon. As his wife you must follow where he goes.'

'But Amber …'

'Don't think about Amber. You go twenty steps ahead. I can divorce Amber. Right now I have to get you away from Singapore somehow.' He took her hand, willing her to stay these objections. 'I love you. Do you love me? That's all that matters right now.

Not a week from now. Right now. Don't you see?'

She suddenly felt the iron enter her soul. She had endured chaos and misery living with her aunt. She did not even know her sisters or her brother. She had been given a certain kind of life, and now it was to be snatched away. The voice of her grandmother rang in her head. Other than the day all her wedding clothes had been chosen, when the old *sangkek um* was present in the house, she had not ceased to berate and bully her. Everything had been organised so fast she hardly had time to breathe, like some kind of military operation.

She and her aunt had been taken from their home and installed in River Valley Road. The date for the marriage ceremonies had been chosen. It was all done with unseemly haste. Within a fortnight she would be married.

This is what it would be like. Ah Soon was too weak to stand up to anyone. He would probably be dead of his addiction in a few years. And she would be here, with children, under the eye of her grandmother or aunts. Never free again. Alex was strong and resolute. He knew what he wanted and nothing would stand in his way.

'Yes.' She came into his arms and he breathed a sigh of relief.

'I will write to you. The letters will be at the Post Office and Ah Soon will collect them.'

He took her hand and led her back to the house, walking silently, the feeling of absolute union fizzing through their hands. They loved each other and they were in this together. It was thrilling and wonderful. In the shadows he put her palm to his lips, then released her. She climbed into the window and pulled the shutters closed. He smiled, a feeling of triumph rilling through his blood.

25

Charlotte found her brother's house in disarray. Robert was distressed and incoherent. Amber had sent for her and she had come as quickly as possible. Amber rushed out to greet her, trembling with agitation.

'She is deathly sick, Aunt,' she said hysterically and burst into tears.

Her distress for her sick mother was real but it was mingled with the disappointment at Alex's proposal to her. He had not gone down on a knee, nor even declared his love for her. She knew he didn't love her yet, but she had hoped that he might at least show some affection. But nothing like that. The ring had been on the table, when she had entered the living room. He had taken it and put on her finger, just like that.

'There,' he had said with not even a smile, 'we are engaged.'

She had looked at the ring and up at him, smiling and he had looked so coldly down at her, then, as if he had recalled something, he put her hand to his lips and kissed it. She had come close, turned up her mouth to his, wanting his kiss. He had dropped her hand and turned, and, without a word had left. She had stood in the middle of the room, bewildered and withered.

Charlotte ran up the stairs. Shilah lay in the semidarkness.

The room was oppressively hot and the fan the maid was moving across the bed did nothing to cool the air.

Dr. Cowper was in attendance. He shook his head as she entered. They had all got to Shilah too late.

Shilah was burning hot, the sweat pouring from her. Her face was waxen and Charlotte knew that she was on the verge of death. She had seen this before. The fever burned you up from the inside and left nothing. She hardly moved, the rise and fall of her breath barely visible.

Amber came and put her head on her mother's thin, hot hand. Charlotte took the cloth and bathed her forehead and face. Shilah opened her eyes. Amber sprang forward and put her lips to her mother's cheek.

'Mother, don't die. Oh please. Look, I am engaged to Alexander. We shall be married. You mustn't die.' Amber put the ring in front of her mother's eyes and began to sob. Charlotte put an arm around her shoulder.

'Amber, kiss your mother. There is no time.'

'Mama,' Amber sobbed and put her lips against her mother's skin, her tears splashing down over her lips onto the dying woman's cheeks.

Shilah closed her eyes and took her last breath, a small rattle in her throat. Amber fell away from the bed onto the floor and pulled at her hair and screamed and screamed.

The screams resonated throughout the house and Robert fell to his knees and put his hands together and prayed for her soul, tears pouring over his cheeks. He was to blame. Charlotte had been right. Why hadn't he listened?

Charlotte took Amber from the room and ordered the maid to stay with her.

She came to her brother and took him into her arms. 'Stop

praying, Rob, for heaven's sake. This is not God's but the British medical establishment's doing.'

He put his head on her shoulder and held her. 'Don't go Kitt, please. Stay.'

'I will not leave until you feel ready,' she said and he nodded.

Alexander arrived and rushed to his uncle's side. 'Uncle Rob, I am so sorry.'

Robert rose. 'I want to go to her.' He staggered from the room. Alex made to follow him.

'Leave him,' Charlotte said. 'He will grieve how he must. You had better comfort Amber. She will need you.'

Alex threw himself into a chair. 'Yes, of course. Let her have a good cry first.'

Charlotte raised an eyebrow.

'You too, eh? A grieving woman does not earn your sympathy. You are more like your …' She stopped abruptly and turned away. 'I will go to her.'

Alex rose, shamed by her words. 'No, sorry. I'll go.'

'Yes,' she said. 'She is to be your wife, don't forget; she is due, at least, if not your passion, then your compassion.'

He threw a dark look at her and left the room. Charlotte sat heavily. She felt as if a shadow lay over the house and she herself was mere air within it. She took the letter from her purse. He asked her to meet him at the cottage in Katong this evening. She read it again and again, his handwriting conjuring him in her mind. She crumpled the letter and called Raja, Robert's Tamil majordomo.

'The mistress has died. Have the salon prepared for the lying in and send for the Reverend. And have the maids bring water to wash the body and get the muslin winding cloth. There is a quantity in the store.'

He bowed solemnly. These Indian majordomos were all so similar. Stoic, quiet, unfathomable and endlessly efficient. Houses without them simply did not run.

She rose with a sigh. There was no time to wait. In the tropics a body would rapidly decay. She had to pull Robert away from Shilah and get on with the business of her funeral. Mr. Tivendale, the shipwright, also made coffins, and she sent a boy to fetch him.

As she went to the hall, the door opened and Dr. Little appeared.

'Ah, Doctor,' she said. 'You have done your worst. Just in time to sign the death certificate.'

He threw her a look of bewilderment.

'Well,' she said. 'What's one more dead mother more or less.'

He spluttered slightly but she ignored him. She looked up and out of the window at the head of the stairs. The sky was as blue as the shallow island seas.

'Merely a passage, isn't it, anyway?'

* * *

'A most propitious choice,' the old *sangkek um* said.

Widow Tan looked over the costumes she had chosen. Rose and white for the lunch for the female guests. The most spectacular for the wedding day – red silk embroidered with gold thread, resplendent in peonies and butterflies. Purple for the third day ceremony. The jewellery of the Tan family lay spread out, gold and diamond necklaces and earrings, a spectacular array of diamond pins which would form the bride's headdress. The child had no idea how to embroider so an array of slippers had been arranged from a family who specialised in such high quality items.

Though she cared nothing for this girl, she cared for her own pride and reputation. Nothing but the finest would be allowed. It was a credit to her abilities that such a lengthy and monumental event as a Baba wedding could be organised so well and on such short notice. Of course, money helped.

The exchange of gifts had taken place and the announcement had been sent out by Wak Chik and her helpers to be taken to every Baba house in the town. The wedding would take place inside the house on China Street that Zhen had leased for Lian and Ah Soon. Here they would be wed and live. Qian, when he found out how quickly this was happening, had been surprised but pleased. Also Zhen had told him about the liquor syndicate. Things were looking up. Now if only Ah Soon could stop smoking long enough to do his duty as a husband.

Widow Tan looked nervously at the clock. The tailor had yet to come for the cutting of the cloth for the vowing ceremony. The importance of this hour was such that even a few seconds either side meant bad luck.

She rose and looked outside to the verandah and breathed a sigh of relief to see her carriage carrying the tailor. He entered, sweating copiously and wiping his face, and laid the white cloth and large scissors out on the table. At the exact time chosen for maximum good luck, this cloth would be symbolically cut and from it the tailor would make the identical simple pyjamas for the vowing ceremony. The house waited silently, all eyes on the clock. As the clock struck eleven, the tailor rose and snipped the cloth. Widow Tan felt a small tear come to her eye. She recalled the costumes made from this cloth for her vowing ceremony. She had buried her husband in one pair and she would be buried in the other and in death the cloth and they would come together again. It was the most moving ritual.

The tailor rose, mopped his sweating brow, bundled up the

cloth and got back into the carriage. The actual sewing would be done at his shop. The second concubine was set the task of beading and embroidering the triangular handkerchief which Lian would wear attached to a gold ring on her hand. It was what all the guests would look at and had to be prepared in the house. It carried enormous prestige. The widow estimated that the second concubine would need to forego a great deal of sleep to finish it on time.

'Now,' said the widow. 'The food for the Guests' Day. It is in five days' time. It will be held here as will the vowing ceremony. We shall set up the Sam Kai altar in the ancestral room. But you,' she said indicating the *sangkek um,* 'you shall take charge of the bridal chamber in China Street for the final ceremonies will be there. Make sure everything is done properly.'

The old *sangkek um* had never in her life had such a rushed wedding and she felt quite light-headed. She was glad to depart a house so suddenly filled with noise and bustle. Usually she took charge but the widow was having none of it on this occasion.

In particular, the wraith-like figure of the lunatic daughter threw her head into a spin and she jumped whenever this woman walked along the verandah.

Lian watched from the garden as utterly detached from all this as the sparrow in the bush. She was glad to be out of the house, to be permitted to be out of the house whilst all these women rushed here and there. Her aunt was kept constantly in a state of drugged calm. This was her grandmother's answer to this particular problem and she recognised her own selfish relief that she no longer had to deal with it.

She knew all this was going on with Ah Soon, too; the costumes, the noise. On the wedding day he would walk in procession from his home to their new house, dressed in his red jacket with gold dragons, his skull cap with diamonds, mincing along as he was told by his *pak chindek*, waving his huge fan. He would look ludicrous. She had seen plenty of these processions, with lanterns and a noisy band wailing. She almost smiled, then didn't.

A vast array of tradesmen had turned up, to sew, stitch, cut, hammer and decorate and when she saw the hawkers arriving with the trays of food, she left and walked down to the peace of the lake, taking with her the only book she had had in her possession when she and Mother Lilin had been bundled away from town. She had taken it from the lending library of the reading rooms run by the American trader, Wolf, whom everyone said had been a pirate. This library had all sorts of unsuitable American books unvetted by more puritanical eyes and Lian had chosen *The Scarlet Letter*, the story of Hester who, punished for adultery and pregnancy out of wedlock, must struggle to create a new life of repentance and dignity. She found it entirely fitting and thanked all the gods that no-one here could read a word of anything, least of all English.

She was so effectively cut off from everything out here she had no idea of what was going on in town and there was no way to find out. Ah Fu had been left at the house in town, judged a malefic and ignorant ally in Lian's misbehaviour.

She settled into the pavilion and drew her legs under her chin and opened the book to the fifth chapter.

Hester Prynne's term of confinement was now at an end. Her prison-door was thrown open, and she came forth into the sunshine, which, falling on all alike, seemed, to her sick and morbid heart, as if meant for no other purpose than to reveal the scarlet letter on her breast.

26

'Mrs. Manouk, each day we delay costs you money.' Captain Elliot opened his hands.

Charlotte knew it. Each day the *Queen* stood loaded in the harbour, fully crewed and idle, did cost money. But there was nothing to be done.

'James, there is nothing I can do. Robert has gone to pieces and Amber cannot be consoled.'

James Elliott nodded. He had grown old before the mast, Charlotte thought, much of it in Tigran's service. He was perhaps sixty-five years old. He deserved a rest. She had offered to buy him a small house in Batavia but he had refused. He wished to return to Somerset, to his village where he still had brothers and cousins. He would not be sailing again on this ship for the P&O would be carrying him home in ten days. So she had rewarded him handsomely with a generous pension for the rest of his days.

'If I may make a suggestion, ma'am.'

She turned her gaze onto the man James had recommended and who was the new captain of her ship. He was John Hall, an American from New York. She had been surprised and distrustful. She had known another captain from America and he had tried to kill her. But James said he was a good man, so she believed him.

'Yes, Captain. Any suggestion is welcome.'

'The ship is loaded with guns and powder, opium, iron goods and cloth, commodities I can trade anywhere. If you permit I will go to Pontianak, Benjamarsin and into the Moluccas. I can trade on your account, then come back here in six weeks.'

James nodded. 'Good. John knows his business. He can get pepper, gold and diamonds in Banjarmasin, rattans, pearls and bado oil in Makassar. Pontianak has gold too.'

He can steal my ship, Charlotte thought. But what other choice was there but to trust this man? What choice but to trust any captain who set off onto the vast oceans loaded with goods. She thought for a moment.

'John, if you trade on my account, and show a good profit you shall have a percentage and the crew a bonus.'

'Yes, ma'am,' he said and smiled. He knew what she was thinking. 'You can depend on me, Mrs. Manouk.'

'You are a young man, Captain Hall. Try not to go adventuring.'

He touched his cap. 'No, ma'am.'

Despite herself she smiled. He had a lazy charm and good looks. He was no older than thirty, she guessed, only eight years younger than herself.

'Well, well, we shall settle it then. You will sail as soon as you have the ship's orders ready and inform the Master Attendant. I will expect you back in six weeks' time.'

John touched his cap again and departed.

'Can I trust him, James?'

'Aye, Mrs. Manouk. He seems loose and easy but he has sailed these last three voyages with me and knows the sea and the stars. And he is good with the men and, for an American, speaks Malay well.'

'Very well, then. Will you stay with me these next days?'

'That's kind of you, but you have trouble in the family. And an old salt like me needs the company of sailoring men. I shall stay at the Sailors' Home.'

She watched him depart with his dog, Tasty, at his heels. Old companions.

* * *

Amber, head low, walked along the street.

'My dear,' Charlotte said. 'Come in.'

Shilah had been laid to rest yesterday and Charlotte had invited Amber to stay with her, away from the noise of the baby and the dark mood of her father.

'Is Alex here?'

'No, he is in town.'

Amber went to the living room and threw herself on the sofa and promptly burst into tears. 'I am so unhappy,' she wailed.

'I know, of course. Your poor mother...'

'Yes, Mother. Of course. But Alex ... he's so distant.'

Charlotte raised an eyebrow. The mother so quickly set aside for the young man she desired. Until they learned a little more of life, children were the most ungrateful creatures.

'You are distressed. It is not a good start for either of you. And give him some time also. You need to get to know each other in a quite different way.'

'But how can we? He is never around, never. I have been engaged five days and have barely seen him upwards of an hour or two.'

'I am sorry, Amber. I will speak to him. Do you still wish this marriage?'

'Yes, oh yes, Aunt.' Amber's eyes had filled with tears.

'Tonight we shall all dine together. I will order it and tell cook to make the beef Alex likes so much.'

'But when do we depart, Aunt, for Batavia? I so long to be married to Alex.'

'Yes, but we are delayed here six weeks, Amber. I must stay for Robert and have sent the ship away. When it returns we will depart.'

Amber shot a look of such horror and disappointment, Charlotte thought she might rise and strike her. 'No, no. It's too long. He must marry me here.'

Charlotte rose. 'My dear, you are grieving. You need time to recover. And I will not have you married under English law when you plan to live under Dutch.'

Amber burst into tears again and ran from the room.

Charlotte went to her room and gazed into the mirror. She touched her belly. Zhen's child, another, lay within her.

When Alex returned Charlotte called him to her.

'You must pay attention to Amber,' she said. 'She is distressed and misses you.'

'Oh Mother, really. We shall be married soon enough.'

'Alex, don't be naïve. A young girl likes to be wooed. And we are here for the next six weeks. Pay her a little court.'

'Six weeks?'

'Yes, the *Queen* has gone to trade. I can't leave Robert and the baby. I need to talk to Teresa. Robert needs her now. At least I think he does. Anyway …'

Charlotte looked severely at her son and lifted the paper on the desk. 'This is the marriage agreement. I have not yet signed it. Woo her.'

Alex smiled at his mother. 'You are right, of course.'

Alex went to his room and bathed. He had spent the morning with Ah Soon whose marriage was to take place the next day. This delay was actually more than he had hoped for. Once they were married, Ah Soon was expected to only stay the night. Such was the peculiarity of the Baba wedding rites. The groom must arrive under cover of darkness, his face covered and leave well before dawn. Alex had no idea why this should be, but he meant, as much as he was able, to profit from it. He wanted to be with Lian. There would be no need for false blood. He felt his excitement at this prospect and rose, agitated. He knocked at Amber's door. 'Come out. We shall walk before dinner.'

Amber flung the door open and rushed into his arms. 'Oh Alex, I love you so much.' She pulled him into her room and closed the door.

'Amber, you minx. Don't you think we should wait?'

'No.' She pulled his head to hers and rubbed her lips on his, her desperate ardour a sad testimony to her adoration of him.

He allowed himself to be kissed in this childish way for a moment, then his thoughts flew to the nights he would spend with Lian. He took Amber in his arms and showed her what a kiss really was, making her half swoon. She clung to him, pressing her body against his. It was quite pleasant and he could play this game for a while if it kept his mother off his back.

27

From the upstairs window Zhen watched the procession arrive before the main doorway of the house in China Street. He had leased this house for his daughter and her husband because he could not bear the thought of Lian locked up with the Widow Tan and Mad Lilin out in the country. Here she would at least be mistress of her own home in the centre of the town and could entertain her school friends, keep up her English and have a semblance of the life she had been wrenched from.

Ah Soon was dressed as he himself had been twenty years ago, but the man was so skinny and sallow, he could not help but feel sorry for Lian. He knew she would never love this man, so he wanted to do as much for her as possible. Give her riches and certain freedoms.

As Ah Soon stepped over the basket in the doorway, the firecrackers started to pop and sent a volley of deafening noise up and down the street. A crowd had gathered to watch.

Zhen went to the hall of the first floor and looked down. Various dances and rituals took place, then the matchmaker stepped inside the hall and called *sangkek um, si kau lai chim pang*. The appointed time had come for the bride and groom to meet.

Lian was led from a side room into the hall, bound in her wedding clothes with a black veil over her face. As Ah Soon lifted the veil most of the assembled party averted their gaze. Zhen did not. She was beautiful.

The new bride was traditionally supposed to keep her eyes down and not gaze on her new husband but Lian kept her look steady, unsmiling. The couple, flanked by the *sangkek um* and the *pak chindek*, walked slowly upstairs to their bedroom. Lian looked neither right nor left and certainly not at him.

The next part of the ceremony, Zhen knew, involved the candles that must not go out but which had been blown out on his own wedding day by Noan's sleeve which signified that she would die first. And she had. He did not join the press of guests around the couple.

Qian had not joined them either and came to his friend. 'It is a good day.'

Zhen said nothing.

'Cheng has offered me a part in the syndicate. He will advance me credit and I will pay back from the profits. It is a good start."

'Yes, make the most of it.'

'I know you are behind this. Thank you. As part of your family I can get credit from the English bankers and start to rebuild the business.'

Zhen looked at Qian a moment. 'Don't think of it. Stick to what you know. The ah ku houses and this syndicate for which you have to do nothing but collect.'

Qian pulled a face. The ah ku houses held no prestige. To be part of the syndicate, to deal with the Europeans carried all the cachet. And his catamite – he deserved more, more jewels, more clothes, for Qian had never loved a young boy so much as he did this one.

The guests buzzed noisily out of the room. It was time for the groom to leave and for the bride to rest. All the guest went downstairs, chattering, to admire all the gifts and *ang pow* displayed on the hall tables. Zhen had presented a tray of jewellery for Lian.

Qian left, for the next part of the ritual involved Lian and Ah Soon paying their respects to him at his house. Qian offered the wedding dinner too, although Zhen had paid for it all. The men would all get very drunk and tease the bride and the young maidens. Zhen had no intention of attending. Following the dinner, the bride went home and the groom would depart only to return under cover of darkness to find himself finally alone with the bride.

Zhen turned his feet to Boat Quay and gazed over the river. She had not replied. He had had a moment of anxiety when her ship had departed but soon learned she was still in Singapore. Robert's nyai had died in childbirth, and she had stayed to console him.

The Baba wedding went on for twelve days, and, on the fifth, it was customary to present the bride and groom to the greater community, the merchants of all races and all of the Europeans so that they could pay their respects and leave *ang pow*. Invitations had been sent but whether she would come or not was uncertain, especially with a death in the house.

He walked back to Market Street. The signs of trouble had already begun. A gang fight had broken out two nights in a row and Zhen knew it was Tay and Hong's men. The police soon broke it up but it would get worse. Wang had reported smuggling activities on the Straits. Both men were already trying to import cheap chandu to undermine the other's monopolies.

'Keep an eye on it,' he'd told Wang. 'Find out who's doing the smuggling, set spies to find informers here and in Johor. But do nothing else. Gather information and report back to me.'

The *chintengs*, the revenue police of both Tay and Hong, were numerous. Their job was to keep an eye out, report illegal storing and smuggling of chandu and exact their vengeance. The *chintengs* could raid houses and often did. It led to a lot of bad blood and this blood spilled out onto the streets of Chinatown and in the plantations of Johor. The fact that Tay was Teochew and Hong Hokkien made it worse. The clans fought each other for greed, vengeance and pride, the men fought because they were violent and bored or for money.

Cheng had given generously to the married couple. He had invited Zhen to dine at his home and Zhen knew very well what was in the air. He intended his daughter for him. Zhen didn't know what he thought about this. Xia Lou was angry and distant and she intended to depart although he did not know if she meant to return soon. He needed to know that.

In two months the liquor farm bids would come up and his obligations would be coming to an end. Whilst her ship was not in port he knew she would not go. He hoped she would come to the open presentation of the couple. If she did not then he intended to go over the river secretly and speak with her.

* * *

Alex felt light-headed. Amber had hung on him from morning to night and finally, after dinner, he had simply left. To play billiards, he said, at the Hotel London and perhaps drink in the town with the men. And there he had headed for an hour or two and, as night set in, he made his way slowly to Chinatown.

The house in China Street was an elegant house, built as many of them were on three floors. The front had a deep verandah and was decorated with dragons and fish made of turquoise and rose tiles. The back gave on to an alley where the night soil collectors came in the early morning. The back alley always had a door to the small courtyard where the traders and hawkers came.

Into this back door Ah Soon would be smuggled, his head covered, accompanied by the master of ceremonies. This much he knew. Once the master of ceremonies had left, the house would be silent as the bride and groom were given the utmost privacy. This man would come back just before dawn to collect Ah Soon.

He watched as Ah Soon arrived at around nine o'clock. Eyes would be everywhere at that time, Ah Soon had told him, for what was supposed to be secret was known to everyone. But once he had entered they would go to bed until he was obliged to creep out in the morning.

Alex waited. A light moved behind the shutters here and there. Servants he guessed. He watched as Ah Soon went through this ritual, rushed through the alley to the back door, head covered. The door closed, the lights one by one were extinguished. At eleven o'clock the back door opened and he slipped inside.

'Does she know?'

'No. You said don't tell her and I haven't.'

'Where will you be?'

'There is a small closet attached to the bedroom. I'll have a pipe and sleep there. When it's time come and get me.'

Two young maids were snoring lightly in the kitchen. Ah Soon took him to the closet and opened the door to the bedroom. Alex closed the closet door. The bedroom was lit with a low lamp. The bed was Chinese, a square of elaborately carved wood from which silver decorations and heavy embroideries hung. The shutter to the street stood ajar allowing a small breeze to enter.

He went forward and saw her. She was sleeping in white pyjamas, her black hair spread about the embroidered pillow.

This was her wedding night and he intended it to be the most wonderful night of her life. He undressed and lay next to her. She must have sensed movement for she turned suddenly and slapped out. 'Ah Soon, no.'

Alex took her in his arms, still fighting and then she realised. He kissed her lips and ran his hands through her hair. She looked around, dazed.

'Where is Ah Soon?'

'In the closet. So be quiet.'

She laughed lightly. It was funny to think of Ah Soon spending his wedding night in the closet but then she grew alarmed. 'You should not be here. Are you insane? We agreed.'

'I don't care what we agreed. I can't wait. We are here for six weeks more and I can't wait.'

She thrilled to this recklessness. He had waited and waited, risked discovery and all for her. She heard the urgency in his voice and felt him grow hard against her leg and looked down. She had seen the dirty pictures, but what could prepare you for this? She gazed at him and put her hand to him.

'Ah,' he sighed.

'You feel wonderful,' she whispered.

He smiled and kissed her lips lightly.

He took off her pyjama top and put his lips to hers in a deep kiss, pulling her breasts against his chest. She returned the kiss, feeling the excitement growing inside her so strong she shivered.

He felt it and held her tight, putting his lips to her ear. She felt like silk and the increasing passion he felt was as natural as breathing.

She held him tight, loving the feel of his skin on hers then lifted her face and put her mouth to his.

He ran his hand under the pyjamas, between her legs and she looked down, feeling the trembling of her body and the violence of her emotion as his fingers touched her.

'Don't be frightened. I won't hurt you. You will love this.' He put his mouth to her breast. She let out a low moan and ran her hands over his back, gripping him tight. She had no fear and abandoned herself utterly to this sensation.

28

'Wake up, sleepy-head.'

Alex turned over and tried to ignore the voice. He was dreaming of Lian. They had made love all night. He couldn't get enough of her. She had bled a little the first time and she made sure it was on the pyjamas. She was not shy and silly but bold and lusty, wanting him as he wanted her. In every thought they were complicit, as if they were one. It made him light-headed and insane for her.

'They take it away,' she said, her lips to his neck, her body tight against his, as she recovered her wits from the intensity of this incredible experience. 'And test it with lime. They say that lime will wash away all blood but a virgin's blood.'

He kissed her and turned on his back, carrying her with him, her hair cascading around his face. 'Sounds like nonsense to me. But no matter. It's virgin's blood all right. Shall we do it again?'

'Alex, wake up.'

He groaned and turned over. It was Amber. He couldn't believe it. He was stark naked and the day wasn't yet up. He must have been asleep only two hours. He grabbed a sheet and covered himself. How long had she been standing there?

'What are you doing?'

'Can I come in to bed with you?'

Alex sat up, pulling the sheet about his body, like a scandalised virgin. 'No, are you mad? Get out.'

For answer Amber dropped her nightgown to the floor, exposing her naked body, climbed onto the bed and threw herself against him, raining kisses on his neck, gripping him as if her life depended on it.

'Alex, please. Please. Why wait? You did it with those other women.'

Alex pushed her away and rose, the sheet about his lower limbs. 'Get dressed. Stop acting like a complete whore. I'm tired.'

Amber looked at him in shock, burst into tears, then grabbed her nightgown and flew out of the room. He locked the door and went back to bed.

* * *

He woke at mid-day, bathed and went downstairs. He took up the red invitation to the reception for Lian and Ah Soon and strolled into the dining room.

'Well, here you are,' Charlotte said, examining her son. He had returned home very late but she did not scold him. In towns like these young men just did these things but she was concerned nevertheless.

'Keep yourself clean,' she said, and gave him a piercing gaze.

'Mother,' he said, actually shocked. 'I was playing billiards and drinking a little too much.'

She gazed at him a moment longer then went back to her lunch.

The servant brought curry and rice, a roast chicken and vegetables and a large plate of fruit. He began forking food onto his plate. 'God, I'm starving,' he said.

Charlotte contemplated him.

'Have you seen Amber this morning?' he said between mouthfuls.

'Yes, she went back to Robert's. She said she'd rather be there at the moment.'

Alex nodded, relieved. He tapped the invitation on the table. He wanted to go to this. He wanted to look at her knowing she was his, that the wedding night had been his, to have that secret between them in the face of all her family.

'This reception, I should like to go. Congratulate Ah Soon you know. Will you come?'

'No,' Charlotte said and placed her knife and fork in the plate.

'Mother, because of Zhen?'

'I can't understand even receiving this. He knows how I feel about Lian marrying Ah Soon.'

'You don't approve.'

'No, I do not. The girl came here scared witless but he is immune to my appeals. He has become as cold-hearted as a lizard.'

'Do you dislike him, Mama?'

Charlotte shook her head and drank the glass of water at her side. His child was here in her belly and she had no answer to that. Alex saw her distress.

'Sorry, Mama. May I go? I am Ah Soon's oldest friend.'

'Yes, go,' she said and rose.

He picked up the paper, finished his lunch and decided he needed to sort Amber out once and for all.

He walked to her house. Raja let him in and he went into the day room. His uncle was out, returned to the police station. Several gang fights had broken out in the town, so he had read, and a spate of burglaries in Chinese houses. The baby was crying somewhere in the house.

Amber came into the room, her face shut down, resentful. He went to the door, locked it and came back to her swiftly. He put his two hands to her bodice and ripped it, the tearing sound shooting like gunshot through the room. Amber gasped. Alex dropped his mouth to her exposed bosom, biting and gripping her roughly, twisting her nipples. She cried out, desperately trying to pull his hands away.

He pulled her hands behind her back, holding her tight and hard, then with the other pulled up her dress and ran his hand between her legs, through the pantelletes and into her so hard she let out a cry of anguish. He dropped his hand and pushed her away. She was in disarray, half naked and trembling.

'Like this? Is this what you want? To be treated like a whore?'

She whimpered and pulled the tatters of her bodice over herself.

He pulled her towards the sofa and took her on his lap. 'Or this?'

He released her hand from the bodice and gently touched her, moving his tongue around her breasts, sucking lightly on the nipple, kissing her neck. Her head fell back. He stopped.

'Which one, Amber?'

'Oh Alex, I'm sorry.'

He remained hard-eyed. 'Which one?'

'This, this.'

She put her arms around his neck and dropped her head against his shoulder. He allowed this for a minute, stroking her hair. Then he put her off his lap and stood. 'Then you will not act like a whore, do you understand?'

She dropped her eyes.

'You will behave like a lady. And when I choose, *after* we are married, when I choose, then I will come to you. As little or as often as I like. No man wants a whore for a wife.'

She looked at him with eyes of total adoration.

'Do you understand, Amber? Or do you want to break our engagement? Now is the time.'

She came to him and fell at his feet. She took his hand and pressed it to her lips. 'No, no. I want to marry you. I'm sorry. I'm sorry.'

He walked to the door, unlocked it and left the room.

29

She did not come to the reception and Zhen waited until all the foreigners had left. Alex had come and presented his congratulations in the manner required. Zhen could see clearly what perhaps no-one else could. His daughter never once looked up, as ritual decreed. Her eyes stayed resolutely on the floor as the guests passed by murmuring congratulations. But Alex's eyes ate her up. He couldn't help himself.

The next morning Zhen spoke to Wang. He nodded and departed. Ten minutes later Zhen walked across the footbridge unrecognisable as the wealthy towkay. He was dressed in coolie trousers and an open jacket, with a straw sunhat on his head and sandals on his feet. He walked quickly along the padang to the great banyan tree by the creek. There Wang was waiting with the driver of his covered gharry and Zhen slipped inside.

Zhen knew Wang well enough now to know he would do anything for him. Wang was a romantic. He believed the myths of the Triads with their warrior ethics of strength and undying loyalty. To him, Zhen was Lui Bei and he, Wang, was Zhang Fei, undying companions of Guan Di, a sworn brotherhood sprung complete from the pages of the *Romance of the Three Kingdoms*.

The gharry pulled up under the porte-cochère. Zhen leapt

down and rang the bell. Malik opened the door. He gave a look of horror at the sight on the doorstep.

'Back entrance,' he said and made to shut the door. The coolie put his foot against it and gave it a shove.

'Where is your mistress?'

Malik was about to shout when he recognised the voice and his mouth dropped open in surprise. Zhen took off his hat and Malik, intimidated by his tone and shocked at his dress, pointed upstairs. Zhen took the stairs two at a time and opened her bedroom door.

She was lying on the bed in semi-obscurity. He went to the shutters and opened them.

'I need to talk to you.'

She sat up, pulling her robe around her. She stared at him, looking him up and down. He was dressed the way she had met him for the first time in her life. His jacket swung open over his chest, the hard muscles, the tan skin, the tattoo of Guan Di. Ordinarily she might have been thrilled to see him like this but today she felt too sick to even care and filled with anger at him.

'I haven't seen you for months. Why are you dressed like this?'

'Never mind.'

She felt nauseous. The morning sickness was strong and she still concealed it from everyone. 'Go away.'

He ignored her. 'Get dressed. You're going for a ride. Alone. To Katong. I will meet you at the cottage in one hour.'

'Get out. ' She lay back on the bed in an attempt to stop the nausea. He frowned. She was pale and wan.

'Are you sick?' he said, suddenly worried.

'What do you care?'

He came towards her and she sat up and put her feet to the floor.

'Shut up,' she said, 'and get out.' Her anger was real and deep. 'Get out. I had no right to shame you in Chinatown and you have no right any more to be here.'

He regretted his sudden incursion and his absence from her. He regretted everything. 'I'm sorry, Xia Lou.'

'Go away,' she said and walked to the closet.

He wanted to go to her but something in her attitude gave him pause. And he dared not stay longer. 'Something is going on between Lian and Alex. Please come.' He left the room and raced down the stairs.

Charlotte stared after him. What could he mean? She went into the closet and threw up. The new maid she had engaged was Malay. She never wanted a Chinese servant in this house ever again. Thank goodness, the Malay maid knew nothing of her and disposed of everything without a thought. She lay back down on the bed and waited. The nausea would pass. She drank some tea and felt better. The nausea was worse in the morning and gradually faded in the day, coming back with a vengeance in the evening. It had never been like this. She had never felt so ill and she thought it was, perhaps, about her age.

Finally it passed. She dressed and arranged a hat to protect her from the sun. She had to go and not only to find out why he had come to her in such an extraordinary manner. She wanted to have it out with him. All this. All the pain about Lily.

She called for her carriage and took off quietly along North Bridge Road. She crossed the Rochor and then the Kallang on the new iron bridge, passing the gangs of Indian prisoners digging ditches and repairing the roads. She turned down the road which had been made for the fort Collyer had mapped out at Tanjong Rhu but which had been abandoned, as all his constructions had suddenly met with resistance even in India, where they were judged too extravagant and unnecessary. This road led to the dirt track which led to the cottage by the beach Robert had constructed years ago. He had built two more further along the coast but this had been the first.

She hadn't been here in years and neither, by the look of it, had anyone else. The wooden verandah was eaten away by white ants and sagged into the sand. The roof had fallen in. She pulled the horse to a halt and tied it where it could eat the grass.

He appeared out of nowhere.

'It's falling apart,' he said.

She turned to look at him. 'A metaphor for our lives.'

He frowned, not understanding her English. The paleness of her skin had gone. She looked flushed from the ride, her cheeks pink. Her hair was in vague disarray, just as he loved her, all mussed up from him. He had difficulty not putting his hands on her.

'What do you want?' she said, her voice hard and cold.

He turned and looked out, through the leaning coconut palms, out to the glints of the sea. At this hour it had no colour, only brilliance.

'Something is going on between Lian and Alex,' he said.

She ignored him, the urgency of what she wanted to say overwhelmed her. 'You do not say sorry?'

He turned around.

'For Lily? For not coming to me?'

'I mourned Lily. I mourned her and prayed for her. I could not come to you.'

'We lost our child and you could not come to me. What kind of thing are you?' She raised her hand. She had begun to feel sick again and wanted to stop it. 'Never mind. What is it you want to say about Alex?'

He gazed at her. It was taking strength for her to be here. He saw it and felt terribly sorry. He could not explain about Lily and he did not wish to upset her further.

'He is in love with Lian. I know it. I recognise it.'

Charlotte shook her head. He had made no reaction to her condemnation of him. That he no longer cared was blatantly obvious. She collected herself and a note of steel entered her tone. The nausea abated.

'I don't understand. Lian is married, is she not? As you decreed in your vast wisdom. Condemned to a life of misery with Ah Soon.'

'It does not change the fact that Alex is in love with her. And they are sister and brother.'

'Alex will be married to Amber in Batavia. My ship will return in five weeks and we shall all depart. Then whoever loves whomsoever will not matter one whit for we shall all never see each other again.'

Zhen's English was good but this speech defeated him. So he ignored it.

'You must tell him.'

Charlotte turned, sick of it all, and walked back to her carriage.

He took her arm and turned her towards him. She looked at his hand on her arm as if he was a cockroach whose filthy passage had been left on her dress. He dropped his hand. He had not expected her to genuinely hate him and he felt it in his gut, and a wave of panic overtook him which he had difficulty controlling. Only the knowledge of Wang in the trees stopped him from beseeching her.

'So much has happened,' he said softly. 'But it will soon end. My obligations will soon end. I'll be free again. Will you come back, Xia Lou? I should like …'

She turned. 'I don't care,' she said and got into the carriage. 'I will not tell Alex anything. We will depart and he will never see Lian again.' She picked up the reins. 'And I will never see you.'

She clicked the horse into movement. Wang emerged from the trees ready for some idiotic act of heroic loyalty to his lord. Zhen signalled to him to leave her.

She drove the horse forward, fast, and a great ball of dust spat from her wheels.

30

The Malay police peon turned as he heard the blood-curdling cry suddenly cut short. He raced down South Bridge Road and turned into Cross Street. He saw the man lying in a pool of blood. Several shopkeepers had attacked the two thugs brandishing knives, slashing and running as they went.

He stopped in his tracks. At least ten men, armed with clubs and staves, were setting about each other. They didn't pay him enough. He blew his whistle which might bring another peon but had no effect on the gang fight taking place in the middle of the street. A great crowd had gathered and all commerce ceased. An Indian driver pulled his bullocks to a halt, slipped a quid of sireh in his mouth and sat, waiting and chewing, spewing blood red spittle onto the dusty ground from time to time.

Alex, on the corner of China Street, peered along the street at the fight but quickly walked away. He did not want to be seen in this street by any of the policeman or any other eyes that might be watching.

When the Indian jemader from Telok Ayer station arrived with two more peons, the men, buoyed by numbers, ran towards the thugs. In an instant the attackers melted away down the back lanes of Chinatown and the police were left with wounded shopkeepers, a dead man and little else.

The jemader looked at his men. No-one would be caught for this. It was Chinese gang violence between the two dialect groups.

'The Teochew man, sir,' the jemader said to the new European officer, Inspector Graves, 'was murdered by two Hokkien thugs. That's what the shopkeepers say.'

Graves listened. The Tamil was translated into Malay for the Malay scribe to write down the jemader's report. The Malay scribe translated as he went along so that by the time the story came to Grave's ears in English it had, like fine oil but without its benefits, passed through several strainings. He had been in this job for four months and disliked it intensely. Robert Macleod was a good man doubtless, but the job had no real pay and the town was a constant soup of incomprehensible violence.

'The day after tomorrow, I am guessing, a Hokkien man will be murdered by a couple of Teochew.'

This went back up the line and the jemader smiled slowly. The white officer was new but he was quick.

Graves dismissed the jemader with his thanks. He would make a report but there was nothing to be done. If these Chinese insisted on murdering each other willy-nilly, there was nothing he could do.

He turned his attention to the more important matter of the burglary at the town house of Hong Boon Teck, the opium farmer. This man had claimed the burglars were Teochew gangs working for Tay, the opium farmer in Johor, but no proof was forthcoming. Graves sighed.

* * *

Lian wound her way slowly up the wooded slopes of Mount

Erskine. Alex had just left her. She felt a warmth invigorate her limbs and the wetness of him between her thighs. He was exciting, sex was exciting. In all the misery of her life, she had never felt so alive and he was the cause. Her want of him was constant.

But that was impossible. Her grandmother had examined the bloody white cloth and the very stained bedclothes, raised an eyebrow, but had pronounced herself satisfied as to the consummation and then it had been a slow wind down to the twelfth day and the end to the wedding period.

The most difficult day was the open reception for all the town. She had seen Alex watching her out of the corner of her eye and grown truly scared. He was too reckless. But he had not come again. Ah Soon said it was too dangerous and that since the reception, the house had been watched.

So today they had met, not in China Street, but in an old storehouse attached to the back of a shut-up sago shop at the end of Amoy Street. It was half broken down and unused and it could be approached from the heavy woods of the hill behind. They had crept into the shop and fashioned a bed out of sacking and to the muted thump of the rice pounder in the shop next door and the clank of the tinsmith opposite, surrounded by the hawking, calling, spitting populace outside, the sun had slanted in through the broken roof onto them and they had wound themselves around each other, their hearts pounding and their bodies slick with sweat until they were exhausted.

As she rose to the top of the hill, the wind caught her hair and cooled the heat of her body. She put down the basket of beading and embroidery she had bought and gazed down at the town and out to the sea. She would go there, she thought, out on the ocean, on a ship, which was new and exciting to her, and begin a new life in this strange place, this Dutch place she knew only from the maps in the school.

'Lian.'

She jumped back and stumbled towards the edge. The fall was straight here, where the trees had been removed to construct the new harbour, straight down onto the heavy boulders below. The edge crumbled away and she lost her footing and screamed. An arm caught her, strong, and pulled her to safety.

'Father,' she said with a look of immense surprise.

Zhen looked steadily at his daughter. She was flushed with surprise and fright from the near fall, he supposed. The samseng had reported that the boy Alex had been seen in Chinatown, in China Street, but had returned to the European town. His daughter was not in the house. She had gone out at least two hours before. He had not followed her. He had not been ordered to. Zhen had sent the cowering samseng away with orders to scour the town and finally, the man, exhausted and grateful, had found someone who had told him she was on the hill.

Zhen looked out, like her, across the sea to the smudgy islands lying on the horizon. He recalled coming here after Xia Lou had left him. He knew about youth and passion and love and sex and the heady obsessions they filled you with. And Alex was his son, every inch of him.

'Where have you been?'

'Here,' she said.

'For two hours?'

Lian followed his gaze.

'I walk on the hill, then I practice the beading and embroidery which my grandmother insists I must learn, up here where things feel fresh and clean.'

She picked up the basket and showed him its contents. She had taken the precaution of pricking her fingers several times and putting the blood on the cloth. She was glad she had. She knew he had eyes everywhere. They could never come back here again. Each time would be more dangerous, each time it had to be somewhere new.

'I'm not very good.'

Zhen was unsure what to think.

'It won't surprise you to learn that I dislike being married and being in that house.'

He closed his eyes. Xia Lou's words resounded in his head.

'Would you deny me every pleasure, Father? Even this?'

The marriage had been consummated. The old woman had told him only that. The husband had done his duty. Zhen did not dare contemplate what that had been like for her. It was not seemly to consider such things about a daughter. He was rather astounded Ah Soon had managed it.

He took her basket. 'Come, I will walk with you. Shall I tell your grandmother to stop asking you to bead?'

She laughed, a swift, powerful feeling of relief swamping her at this change of subject and his suspicions allayed. He felt how much he always enjoyed her company.

'Yes, please.'

They walked slowly down the hill and arrived at Telok Ayer Street.

'Lian, do not neglect your English. Read books and some of the journals in the library.'

'Why on earth, Father? What use is it to a nonya housewife?'

Zhen had an idea which would save Lian from the fate of Lilin, the fate of living a useless life. It was probably controversial, but what was that to him. He and his apothecary would teach her about Chinese herbs and medicines. Dr. Cowper had asked him about them. He was an enlightened sort of Englishman, who wished to study the native plants and remedies. Once in a while such an Englishman came along. He wished to give them for free to the patients at the native hospital and in the Malay villages. If Lian could learn these things, she could write about them in English, a book, the first of its kind, perhaps, in English, which might be of immense benefit to science.

He stopped in front of the Tien Hock Keng temple with its heady odour of incense.

'Come inside. We will light some incense to ask all the gods to smile on us and I will explain.'

31

My eyes gaze at the returning swans
My fingers strum the five strings
I lift and lower my head in contentment
My mind, detached, saunters in the void

Jia Wen put the paper to the floor and put her hands to the zither. The tune she had learned was famous. It was the Guangling Melody of Ji Kang, the Taoist immortal, musician and poet, whose lines she had just read.

Zhen was fascinated and intrigued. To find such a woman in Singapore who could recite ancient poetry and play with such fluent beauty. Really he could not help himself. He came to Cheng's house solely to hear her.

The story was that of Zheng, son of a swordsmith in the Warring States period, who committed suicide after stabbing the King of Han in revenge for his father's death. The music, deliberate and slow, changes as Zheng's emotions turn from grief to hate, to vengeance then death.

Jia Wen played with all her art. She dared not look at Zhen, for she knew he was called that. Her maids were all Malay and could not speak Chinese but that was not needed to pick up all the gossip of the town. Her maid had told her he was a rich merchant, a widower. His wife had died many years ago and he had not remarried because he had a concubine. They called her the English concubine. The maid's eyes had opened wide and so had Jia Wen's. An Englishwoman was a concubine.

'Perhaps they are not like Dutch women,' she said and the maid nodded. 'Perhaps the Englishmen have harems too.'

They agreed that this was most likely. Jia Wen had not set foot into the town as yet. It half-terrified her and she watched it from her window. She had grown to womanhood in a quiet village and the immense crowds of Chinese all rushing about terrified her. She was not allowed, as yet, to leave the house, nor appear at the doors when the hawkers came. She understood them better than her maids and servants but she was not permitted to speak. She spent her days cooking for her father, practising the zither or reading Chinese poetry in the courtyard.

Zhen's mind wandered, the rice wine had made him tipsy. These evenings with Cheng and his daughter were currently the most peaceful of his existence. Cheng had got the liquor farm of course. He had bid more than three thousand dollars above what Hong had paid the previous year. And the violence had intensified. Smuggling was running amok. Cheng had visited Tay in Johor and they agreed to supply more *chintengs* to police it, but Hong's organisation was good. His house had been raided but no opium was discovered. *Chintengs* had scoured the rivers of the Straits for illegal farming and smuggling but so far there had been little progress.

Zhen had called Hong to him and asked him straight out what he knew about the smuggling. Nothing, he had respectfully replied, other than that Tay was a smuggler and so was Cheng. He was waiting, Zhen knew, biding his time until he could become the leader for he knew Zhen's role was temporary.

So Zhen continued as head of the kongsi. All the officers had appealed to him to stay for clan violence erupted almost every day. He had issued an edict for calm and it had been heeded for a while but, inevitably, it sprang up again.

Jia Wen plucked the final note and he smiled at her. She rose and bowed to her father and his guest and left the room.

Cheng poured more wine. 'I fear you must stay as leader until the leases come up next year.'

Zhen grimaced. 'Lao Cheng, please.'

'No, no. I must insist. Listen, I have formed a good relationship with Tay. I am paying for some of his chintengs and have offered to finance a patrol of the Straits. Four or five boats on regular patrol to watch for smugglers. The Temenggong and the Governor are pleased.'

'Good,' Zhen said.

'It serves as much my purposes as Tay's. I can also watch for liquor smuggling from Johor into Singapore. Hong wasn't happy about my getting the liquor farm.'

'The Governor was. Doubled his revenue.'

The two men smiled.

'The Malacca farm is owned by Tay's son-in-law so together they control that side of the Straits. I own Riau and it is only Hong who throws the log in the river. If I can outbid him next time, we will have the great syndicate. The Tay-Cheng syndicate. We will have a pact not to smuggle and the profits will be huge. Think of it, no need for the cost of chintengs and patrols, just pure business.'

Zhen nodded. It was a good plan. One year, then certainly Cheng would be in a powerful position to take over the kongsi. And what did it matter? He had no idea how to mend the bridges with Xia Lou.

'I would like to propose my daughter in marriage to you.'

Zhen was not entirely surprised but the abruptness of the proposal was startling.

'I like you very much,' Cheng went on. 'I would be honoured to have such a son-in-law, overjoyed to have such grandsons as you would make.'

Zhen felt a great warmth for Cheng, who had taken Tan's place in his heart. He had had no relations at all with his own father and these two men meant a lot to him. He knew that from almost every facet, Jia Wen was the perfect woman for him. She was young, beautiful and clever. She spoke his language, shared his culture. Their marriage would be passionate and harmonious in a way that his with Noan had not. Cheng was right to wish her married to him. And he would be foolish to refuse.

But marriage would mean an admission. The heart-wrenching agreement that his relationship with Xia Lou was over. She would never come back if he was married.

Cheng waited. He knew all about the business with the concubine. What he saw in this white woman, Cheng had no idea. She was old and, though still lovely, he supposed, she was surely no match for his daughter. Still he was wise enough to know the affairs of the heart were mysterious. This long silence meant he was reflecting on such a possibility. He had not refused and this was enough for the moment.

'Do not answer me now,' he said. 'There is no rush.'

Zhen was immensely grateful. He bowed to Cheng. 'Thank you.'

Zhen walked home slowly through the quiet streets of Chinatown. He knew Wang or one of his men was in the shadows. Thunder rolled far away and the wind suddenly freshened.

One month had passed since he had seen her beside the beach at Katong. He remembered another time, when they had met in secret there and made Lily together. He looked up at the stars. She had sent Alex and Adam to Scotland and returned to Batavia to have his child. And she had been brave. She had come back to Singapore and been with him, acknowledged Lily as his child. He loved her for all that.

Three years, not all easy, but they hadn't cared. He shook his head, regret washing over him. How had it all become so bad, so fast? He walked to Boat Quay and stared over the water. Some ball was taking place in the Court House; the English music wafted over to him. He remembered the English Commander. Was she going to him? It made his head burst.

If he remarried he would never see her again. Her ship would be here in a few weeks. He felt a wave of frustration wash over him and wanted to roar and roar until he was exhausted. Instead he turned and went back to Market Street.

32

Lian turned in Alex's arms, resting her lips on his chest. It was midnight. Alex had waited patiently for two hours hidden in the stifling closet, dozing. Ah Soon and Lian had gone to visit her grandmother at River Valley Road for a family occasion and all the eyes that followed them had gone too. She had returned and Ah Soon had gone to the opium den.

He ran his fingers down her back, through the silky tangle of her hair and over the soft skin of her buttocks. There was no limit to what he wanted to do with Lian, time and again. She snuggled against him. They were a perfect fit.

'Alex, I have something to say.'

'Mmm,' he kissed her forehead sleepily. When they had rested a while they would start again.

'I have missed my period. I think I'm pregnant.' She looked up at him. Sleepiness vanished and he took her face in his hands, then put his palm to her belly.

'Oh Lian, I love you.' He enclosed her gently into his arms.

'I'm scared.'

'No, no. It is natural. You should be pregnant. Your family will be thrilled and treat you like gold and by the time the baby is born you will be with me.'

'You will be married to Amber. In all this we have forgotten that one fact.' She sat up. Her skin lay white against the red embroidered pillows. He touched her belly again and placed his lips there, where his child lay, this piece of himself growing inside the woman he loved with all of his heart.

'I care nothing for Amber.'

'Yet you must make love to her.'

He looked up and smiled. 'Is that what you are worried about? Jealousy.'

'Of course I'm jealous, you fool. I have no wish to think of you making love to Amber for heaven's sake.' She got up and put on her gown, poured a glass of water from the table and drank it down, thirsty. He watched her from the bed.

'There is no other way. You know it. But so what? I don't care about her.'

'Can men just do it? No need for any affection? Just a lovely body and away you go?'

'Doesn't even have to be lovely,' Alex said and she laughed despite herself, then frowned.

In all these last heady weeks she had not once really thought about Amber. 'How is she?'

He rose, surprised, and drank too. He pulled the pisspot from under the bed and let slip a stream.

'How is she? I don't know. She had a little turn and I sorted it out. We're engaged. I hardly see her except for family occasions. She behaves herself.'

'She loves you. She has loved you since I've known her.'

Alex shrugged and went back to the bed. He lay gazing at the ornate wooden carvings, frowning at the upside-down bats, the fruit and the writhing dragons. 'That's not my fault. We can't help who we love.'

Lian looked over at him, handsome and perfectly formed, bathed in the low glow of the lamp. They were beautiful together. He felt like a part of her. She knew suddenly that this was a moment stolen from life. It was contained and held separate from reality. It was pure love and it was golden. No matter what came to them, he would never love anyone else this way. And neither would she.

'No,' she said. 'For good or evil. We can't help who we love.'

He smiled and extended his hand to her and she went to him.

* * *

'Well, well, daughter. You are with child.'

Zhen smiled at Lian. She bowed to him.

'Yes, Father,' she said. 'I am with child.'

He frowned. Something in the way she said it was chilling. He dismissed it. She did not love Ah Soon so perhaps she did not love this child now. But she would, surely. Ah Soon had gone back to the opium dens. Perhaps that was it. Again, he felt a silent regret for his daughter. The bed she shared with Ah Soon would be cold, for opium robbed a man of his manhood.

'Miss Charlotte departs today, Father.'

He looked up at her and she held his gaze. He had written to her, two letters. He had tried to explain, without actually explaining, what he could not explain. She had not replied. He had accepted her departure because he didn't know how to prevent it. Over here, on this side of the river, he was all-powerful. But over there in the European town, with her, he had no power at all.

Lian watched him. He seemed not to care a thing about the

leaving of the woman he had so faithfully loved for three years. Can people change so thoroughly? Can love just fade? She felt a tremor of fear and put her hand to her belly. Would Alex's love just fade? He sailed on the tide with Amber by his side and she must bear the unbearable until she saw him again.

He remained silent and she knew he would make no answer. Something in his demeanour gave her pause and she, too, said nothing more.

This was one of his pleasures, the preparation of tea, and she enjoyed watching him. Today he had taken out the brown pottery teapot with the monkey lid, which he never used. Since she had become a woman, she had looked more carefully at her father. He was a man of immense good looks, taller than any other Chinese man in the town, stronger, more powerful. But more than his physical appearance, which was considerable, he had a stature which she had not seen before. He commanded respect. And he had, she now recognised, a largesse of mind. It allowed him to encompass the possibility of her own schooling, of loving a foreign woman, of loving a half-blood child.

It was a ritual, the tea, and he carefully poured the boiling water on the leaves, wafting the aroma over them. He was present here, in this kitchen, but his mind was away, in a time long ago with this same teapot and she was sitting near him, pregnant with her second child, swollen and tired. He had made her this tea with this teapot.

He stared at it and put a finger to the lid. Then they had climbed the stairs and made love, careful of the child which lay inside her. It had been a moment of grace. To give her pleasure in such a circumstance, knowing she would leave on the next tide and they might never see each other again. He felt the intensity of this memory and sat down.

Lian sipped the tea. The atmosphere in the kitchen had thickened as if the air had absorbed some matter she could not understand.

33

It was a brutal sight. The room was splashed red and the body continued to ooze blood into the pool which lay around it. The knife which had been plunged into the man at least a dozen times was still in his chest. The body was covered in nicks and cuts too, especially around the upper thighs. Every cupboard and drawer stood open, clothes strewn everywhere.

Inspector Graves stood in the midst of the chaos. The man on the floor was stark naked and bound by his hands to the leg of the upturned chair. Graves blinked and went down on one knee. The man appeared to have a string attached to his scrotum. He got up and threw a look of disgust at the corpse.

The peon at the door was the one who had summoned him from Telok Ayer Station to the house on Hong Kong Street. He was still unfamiliar with this part of the Chinese town. Graves's Malay was poor despite being in Penang for a year.

'Who is this?' he said.

'House of Sang Qian.'

'What do you know of him?'

The peon said something he did not catch. He was on such shaky ground, linguistically speaking, and this was such a brutal crime that he ushered the peon out of the room and shut the door.

'Stay and guard this door. No-one goes in.'

The peon stared at him. Graves positioned the man in front of the door and put out his hand. 'Stay.'

He went down the stairs. All the servants in the house had gathered in the hall, gazing upwards. He pushed through and went out into the street. The peon had told him that screams had been heard from this house, a servant had rushed out and told him someone was being murdered. The peon did not tell his superior that he had been rudely interrupted in the middle of a lucrative negotiation with the gambling house which would ensure his cooperation and silence.

Graves looked up at the building. Quite a mean little place, squashed between two taller shophouses which he knew were brothels. Actually the whole street was brothels, taverns and illegal gambling houses. Ragged coolies begged, others slumped in the verandahs half dead. A dog gave a yelp as it was kicked. The place was a sinkhole. All the dregs of Asia poured in here. Added to the thousands of sailors that it burst with when ships came in, it was, in his opinion, unpoliceable and he wished fervently that he was back in Penang.

The language barrier was just insuperable. Until they had Chinese policemen there was nothing to be done and the Commissioner would not have Chinese policemen because they were all the foot soldiers of the triads. He needed the Chinese interpreter from the main police house over the river.

'Mr. Graves,' a cultured voice said behind him, and he turned.

It was that towkay, the one who spoke good English. He breathed a sigh of relief.

'Mr. Zhen, it is good to see you.'

Zhen bowed then looked up at the house of his friend. He knew something had happened here. As the peon took off for the police station, the samsengs had rushed to him.

'This is the house of my friend, Sang Qian.'

Graves adopted a serious demeanour but he was surprised. This man was friends with a fellow who had a string round his scrotum. Really the place and all the people were unredeemable. And he had heard that this fellow had an English woman as his mistress. Filthy. He allowed none of these thoughts to enter his voice.

'I am very sorry. Your friend is dead.'

Zhen went forward and into the hall. He raced to the first floor and was met by the terrified face of the Malay peon. He pushed him aside. Behind him he could hear Graves rushing up.

He opened the door and drew a great breath. Tears sprang to his eyes as he looked down on the poor, terrible sight of Qian, his life-long friend, lying in his blood. He went forward and snatched the knife out of his chest and threw it aside. He sank to the floor, pulled Qian to him, cradling him in his arms, his chest heaving and let out a groan of anguish.

Graves arrived at the door. 'You can't do that.'

Zhen ignored him. Graves, despite his disgust, made the quick realisation that this man was an important merchant and needed careful handling. The commissioner had made it clear that the officers were to understand very clearly who the elite natives of the colony were and treat them accordingly.

'Sir,' he said more gently. 'This is a crime scene.'

Zhen pulled a sheet from the bed and covered Qian's nakedness. He lay his friend's head gently on the floor and rose, his tunic covered in blood. He brought his emotions under control.

'Mr. Graves, I know who has done this and I will bring this man to justice.'

'Who is it?'

'I will make a statement to Mr. Macleod. The Chinese interpreter can interview the servants and the street. There will be no doubt.'

Zhen went out and addressed the servants. 'Cooperate with the policeman who will come. Was this Hafiz?'

They all nodded. Yes, they shouted. He ran away with a sack of belongings. He went towards the seafront.

Zhen turned to Graves. 'It is Hafiz, Qian's friend.'

Graves raised an eyebrow. Friend indeed.

'He has gone to the seafront at Telok Ayer.'

Graves shut the door of the room. 'Guard,' he said to the peon.

'The body,' Zhen said.

'Must stay here for the moment. You have destroyed the veracity of the crime scene but I will endeavour to describe it as I saw it.'

'Look,' Zhen said. 'You stay here. I will send my men to get Hafiz.'

Graves frowned. Locals were not supposed to … He gave up on that thought. Here such thinking was quite impossible. This man had his own security force. All the Chinese did and he might as well use it.

'Very well. Thank you.'

Zhen bowed and went out onto the street. A samseng had sought Wang and he ran forward, seeing the blood. His face expressed his horror and Zhen sighed. 'No. Not me. Go at once and get that Hafiz, the peacock has killed Qian. Telok Ayer. Probably a boat.'

Wang bowed.

'Don't fail and don't kill him. I want him hanged by the British.'

Wang saluted, his heart filled with the joy of this task for his Lord. Zhen watched him go. The grief for Qian began to overwhelm him he and felt his face would crumple and his strength fail. He stood, unmoving, head bowed, waiting for this moment to pass.

He went into the Heaven's Gate brothel, up the stairs to Min's room. He shut himself inside and lay on her bed and gave vent to his grief. Was there nothing but pain? The deaths of Lily and Qian, the loss of Xia Lou. He had not allowed himself to mourn her parting and now he could no longer hold this inside himself. He sobbed quietly.

Min came in and shut the door quickly. She went to him and took him in her arms. He clung to her. Min's tears flowed and she gripped him.

With Qian gone she wanted to give up this life. Two more girls had taken opium and killed themselves. She had cared for one very much. Tiny Xiao Li reminded her of her own sister. The sister she had last seen when she had been sold away from her family at fourteen and never seen again.

Xiao Li herself had been only seven years old when she had been sold as a bondservant by her father, a man with too many daughters and an addiction to gambling. She had gone to the woman who gathered these young children and trained them for future lives; some to be concubines of old men, some to be prostitutes, some maids to rich wives, some turned into nuns to worship at the ancestral tablets of wealthy childless women. Either way, they could all end up, on a whim, in the brothel, sold on because of displeasure or jealousy.

Xiao Li, not deemed good-looking enough to turn into a concubine, had been sold as the young maid in a rich man's house in Canton. She grew up there in conditions of great hardship, treated meanly and cruelly by all the women and all the children of the house. When she turned twelve, she was raped by one of the sons. It was a story so commonplace as to invite hardly a thought. She was beaten for tempting him. She continued to be raped by this man until she fell pregnant at thirteen, at which point she was sold to one of the most degrading brothels in Canton. The child was taken from her and she never saw it again. To escape this life she ran away and lived by stealing for a while. With another girl she went to Hong Kong and they both agreed to come to Singapore where, they were told, maids were in short supply.

Xiao Li was split up from her friend who was sent away to another place and arrived in Singapore where she was put in a brothel, five years ago. Min had met her then and they had formed a bond. Now there was talk of moving her, selling her on again because, at nineteen, she was still worth a good price. Down though, down to the coolie brothel in Cochin China. Min had desperately tried to dissuade Qian from this course of action but he had become deaf to all considerations other than money. So Xiao Li had taken all the opium pills she could get and swallowed them one by one.

She felt the tension go from Zhen's body and he rose, out of her arms and went to the bowl of water and splashed his face, washing away Qian's blood and his tears.

'I want to quit this life,' she said. 'Will you release me?'

Zhen looked at her in the mirror, took up a towel and wiped his face and hands.

'What will you do?'

'I have enough money for a small house in Kampong Glam. There is a man there, an Arab man. He's a carpenter who makes beautiful furniture. He's a widower and he wants to marry me.'

Zhen stared at Min and shook his head. 'Well, well, you are

the dark horse. When did this happen?'

'A year or so ago. He knows what I do. He doesn't care. I will take up Islam. It feels clean and I need to have a clean life.'

Zhen went to the window and looked down at the street. The police interpreter was talking to the servants on the step of the house. He was Malay but spoke good Chinese. He was unique in the town and was worked off his feet for he had duties in the magistrate's court and the gaol. Graves was nowhere to be seen. Qian was lying, covered in blood, in that house.

'I'll manage the brothels until after the funeral. Until Ah Soon can take charge. You can leave then.'

She came and took his queue in her hands, stroking it. She put it over her shoulder and her head on his back and ran her arms round his waist, holding him.

'I miss her.'

She hugged him tight.

34

Charlotte looked at Amber. She was as eager-faced as she herself had been as a young girl arriving with Tigran. A face filled with excitement but anxiety too at what lay ahead.

Alex was reluctant, she sensed it. This was not the marriage he had anticipated perhaps, if he thought about such things. He had been pleasant at mealtimes though he had eaten little. Amber had been seasick for the first two days and had kept to her cabin. She and Alex spent time with Captain Hall, whom she had misjudged. He had made her a handsome profit and been prompt in his duties. He told an excellent tale in that dry accent of his, and had a store of fabulous stories from the New Land, and the evenings were enjoyable. Charlotte had felt seasick and nauseous but had taken the ginger and fought it off. She knew it was the pregnancy. Her waist had thickened but not enough to show. In Batavia she knew she had a decision to make. There were women there who knew how to get rid of unwanted pregnancies.

When Amber had recovered enough to join them, Alex had been polite but distant. She had found him, sometimes, in the evening, leaning off the stern, gazing into the churning white water of the wake. She recognised the symptoms for she had done this exact same thing and felt this way. He was lovesick.

Did he love Lian? She had hardly heeded Zhen's words in a dark rush of anger at him and the subsequent misery of his loss. She had read his letters which explained nothing, spoke of nothing which truly mattered. He had duties and obligations. He would be done with them soon and wanted to come back to her. He longed for her. He had even written down a poem which he said he had sent to her years ago. A poem by a long-dead Chinese poet.

A gale goes ruffling down the stream
The giants of the forest crack;
My thoughts are bitter – black as death –
For she, my summer, comes not back.
A hundred years like water glide,
Riches and rank are ashen cold,
Daily the dream of peace recedes:
By whom shall Sorrow be consoled?
The soldier, dauntless, draws his sword,
And there are tears and endless pain;
The winds arise, leaves flutter down,
And through the old thatch drips the rain.

It had touched her, wormed its way into her soul, as only he could do with these beautiful old Chinese poems. But she knew she could not go back to him. She wanted a different life. She knew that now. She no longer wished to be the English concubine. As for Alex and this love, that would fade. They had never even been together, there was little for him to dwell on, feed on, to nurture the memory of her. It would disappear.

The house revealed itself as the horses pulled round the bend. Charlotte's smile faded. What was once snow white with glinting glass, a vast sweeping edifice with its fine Dutch gables. What had once been this, was now grey and streaked with green mould. Weeds sprouted from the roof and along the parapets. The gardens before the entrance were rank. The roof of the west wing seemed to have collapsed. The coach drew to a halt and Charlotte climbed down, aghast at this wreckage. Amber and Alex followed her and they all stood and gazed at the ruin before their eyes.

Servants appeared in clothes as poor as the house. They began to unload the luggage and Charlotte walked towards the great door with its VOC crest, with the greatest trepidation at what she might find inside.

Then Takouhi appeared. She too, was a shock. She had aged. She leant on a stick and her once beautiful skin was wrinkled, her hair grey. All Charlotte could think of was neglect. How she had neglected them all.

She walked into Takouhi's embrace. She felt thin and weak but her voice was strong.

'Welcome, sister.'

'Oh Takouhi, I'm so sorry to have stayed away so long.'

Takouhi took her hand and held out the other to the two young people waiting to one side. 'Alex, Alex. Amber, so big, so big.' She turned. 'Come, come.'

Over the next days, Charlotte discovered that, though the house had been neglected in great part because Takouhi did not use most of it, the estate itself was profitable and well run. She took the old carriage and the little horse and took Alex over it pointing out its kampongs, its rice fields, its orchards, its herds of cows and goats. Brieswijk was self-sufficient in everything except cooking and lamp oil and produced a surplus, which was sold at market.

She took Alex to Tigran's grave and told him something of

this man he believed was his father, determined he would feel the greatness of the family he belonged to. Together with Amber they went to the old chapel, itself somewhat neglected. Alex's mood seemed to improve. 'I shall take care of it all, Mother, when I am its master.'

'Yes, Alex. You will. I think to give you Buitenzorg also, for the tea plantations will pay for the repairs to the house. Tea is somewhat depressed at the moment but Captain Hall says that soon the railway will open up in America from the Pacific to the Atlantic and trade in that direction will boom. Not only tea, but pepper, wood, every product of the Indies can be carried directly to the United States of America's west coast and be transported across the whole country in no time at all.'

He smiled at her and she took his hand.

'As for the rest, I think I must sell the sugar lands to pay all kinds of debts. In any case they are difficult to run and I would rather concentrate our business here around Batavia. Matthias has the trading house more or less under control. As for the fleet, what do you think?'

'Captain Hall says the fleet needs to be pared down and modernised. He wants steam but with coal stations so far apart, the ships carry more coal to travel forward than they do cargo. I think we should wait for the moment.'

Charlotte nodded. They had spent hours over the account books. He had grasped the business with both hands and shown great acumen. He felt driven, as he had never before. Filled with ambition.

'I shall arrange for an auction of the sugar lands at Semarang. Would you like to go? I need to prepare your wedding and it is best if you are out of the way.'

'I want to be married as quickly as possible,' he said.

She was astounded. His attitude to Amber was one of complete indifference.

'I don't want to go to Semarang until I am married. Must it be a great affair, Mother? Can it be small?'

'Well, we have a position in society. Somewhat neglected I grant you, but nevertheless, such a marriage is an opportunity for you to meet the government and all the merchants of the city and to introduce Amber to her new social acquaintances. She must have friends you know. And of the Manouk House it is expected.'

Alex ran his fingers through his hair. 'Yes, a reception. A great reception. But a wedding, that can be small. Right here in this chapel. Can it not? The reception can take place later.'

Charlotte frowned. It was, of course, perfectly possible to do that. But why this haste? 'Why so fast, Alex? You do not seem so very keen on Amber."

Alex rounded on her. 'I am very keen, Mother. Very keen to start married life and grow into a love for her. And it is rather frustrating to be around a beautiful woman and not, well, you know.'

Charlotte was taken aback. This was rather frank.

'I am ambitious for Brieswijk, for my life here. I want a family and am keen to start one as soon as possible. I believe Amber wishes to be married as quickly as possible too.'

That evening, suddenly, a different Alex had emerged. He was charming and attentive to Amber. They walked in the park and Takouhi and Charlotte watched them as the light faded from the sky.

'He care her,' Takouhi said. 'Young love. Good.'

'Yes,' Charlotte said hesitantly. Takouhi's English had become rusty through disuse. She switched to Malay.

In the distance Alex took Amber into his arms and embraced her passionately. Takouhi smiled. 'The chapel needs a little fixing but no more than a week. We can have it ready and the priest from the Armenian church will come and marry them.'

'It seems to be what he wants.'

Takouhi looked at her old friend and sister-in-law. 'Is there anything you want to talk about?'

Charlotte took her hand. 'No. It is good that they are in a hurry.'

'Yes,' Takouhi said, and Charlotte knew she was thinking of George Coleman, her lover and father of her now long dead child.

'I'm sorry,' she said. 'I stayed away too long.'

'The Chinese man, Zhen. You loved him to distraction. You had his child. What happened?'

She had not written to Takouhi of Lily's death. 'She died.'

Takouhi gripped her hand. 'Oh, Charlotte, my dear.'

'And everything between us fell apart.'

'Yes, I know how that can happen.' When Takouhi and George's child, Meda, had fallen sick with fever, she had come instantly to Java, up to the high cool hills at Buitenzorg, to seek a cure. But Meda had died and George, angry and grieving, had gone away to Europe.

In the fading light, Alex took Amber again into his arms. She clung to him. He held her and willed himself to imagine another in his arms. She raised her head and desperately sought his kiss. He put his lips to hers but he felt absolutely nothing. An awful thought came to him. He might not even be able to do his husbandly duty on the wedding night. This was so terrifying that he concentrated hard and kissed her with ardour. She moaned against his lips and when he released her he saw her eyes filled with love for him.

Kissing was one thing, Alex thought, now somewhat worried.

35

Ironfist Wang waited patiently until his Master was free. The undertaker and the funeral organisers had departed and now the notices to the brothers were being made. It would go out to five hundred men who would line the street, following the catafalque. Wang loved a good funeral. Nothing was more inspiring, nothing more designed to show the power of the dragon in Singapore. The Lord could summon thousands of men in an instant. But five hundred were all that had been allowed by the government.

He probed a tooth with his tongue. He didn't mind a sword in his guts but he hated the apothecary who dug around in his teeth. He winced with the pain. He'd heard the ang moh had doctors for the teeth and lots of them had false teeth of gold set in some sort of rubber. Wang paid attention to this. He'd heard many false teeth were made from the teeth of corpses or donkeys, sometimes dogs, fashioned into human teeth. Wang shuddered but was not entirely revolted. The thought of pain-free teeth was tempting.

He rose as the English policeman came out of the leader's meeting room.

'Thank you, sir,' Graves said. 'The police work has been completed and, thanks to you, the culprit caught. The trial will take place when the Magistrate comes back from Penang.'

Zhen bowed. The peacock had been found a week after the murder, hiding out on Blakang Mati. He had surrendered because he was starving. As yet, no-one knew why he had killed Qian so brutally.

Zhen nodded at Wang who went through into his room. He held up the paper in his hand. 'Thank you for being so cooperative with this. With your permission, the procession will be long but I will ensure it is peaceful.'

'We are agreed on the number and on the route. No deviation please.'

Zhen held out his hand and Graves shook it. The man was, when you got to know him, really rather civilized. The business with the white woman seemed to have come to an end. Quite right. Graves departed and Zhen went to join Wang. He closed the door.

'Everything is in place for the funeral the day after tomorrow. You will have the men in place and ensure security. I don't want any trouble.'

Wang bowed. 'I have news.'

Zhen sat and waited.

'Informers tell me that Hong has organised a big delivery of chandu to Chioh Sua. Date is not yet sure but they will find out. The junk will come in to the west side of the island. The informer doesn't know where the chandu is made but thinks its maybe one of the rivers on the east coast. Says it gets stored on the island and from there is smuggled up the Straits of Johor to the river settlements.'

Zhen nodded. Chioh Sua was known in Malay as Pulau Ubin, an island off the north coast of Singapore. It had been used as quarries by the British for the granite but was now disused and the western end was wild and untouched.

'Good work. Pay them well.'

'If we catch the ship, the captain will be induced to tell us who has hired him.'

'Mmm. Better if we help the British catch this ship and its cargo. I don't want the kongsi involved if possible. We can supply information and locate the ship but they must supply soldiers and the steamship for the actual arrest. I want this to be a British coup and their courts involved. I want, if possible, to see Hong prosecuted and stripped of his farm and for the British to realise the extent of the smuggling.'

'Be careful, Shan Chu, Hong is a vindictive man. My informers in his camp tell me he already hates you because he sees that you support Cheng and Tay.'

Zhen dismissed this with a wave of his hand. 'Hong hates everyone.'

Wang stood shuffling his feet for a moment.

'What?' Zhen said half-smiling.

'Hong hears what we hear. That you will marry Cheng's daughter. In Hong's mind that is like treason. He is Hokkien, you are Hokkien. He hates Tay and now Cheng. They are Teochew. And such a union makes Cheng and you an even bigger threat to him.'

Zhen rose and Wang drew to attention.

'This is no-one's business. I will speak to the British policemen. You get hold of the date of the shipment.'

Zhen sent a message off with the boy to the police house on the other side of the river, requesting a meeting with Robert. This plan needed the agreement of the Commissioner of Police and at least the Resident Councillor. The governor was away in Penang. Zhen also wanted to include the Temenggong. If the information could be seen to come from him, it would improve relations between the young prince and the governor.

Zhen went to Ah Soon who, as the eldest son, must follow the catafalque. His reaction to his father's death had been drugged indifference. He needed to get Ah Soon off the amount of opium he was smoking, at least for a couple of days, long enough to carry out the rites demanded of him. After the funeral would come the business. The passing of the houses to Ah Soon; if the boy didn't want to be involved, they needed to be sold on. There would be plenty of willing buyers. Ah Soon might return to his studies, perhaps take up the law. He was wealthy enough to subsidise this and it would be an asset in the future and perhaps keep him off the opium.

He walked to Hong Kong Street to check on the funeral arrangements. The white banners announcing the death had been put up and blue lanterns hung before the house. Qian's body lay inside the house in its coffin, attended by the Buddhist and Taoist priests. Zhen could hear the chanting for his soul and the wailing of the official mourners. The house was redolent of incense and the burnt offerings.

Ah Soon had gone to the river with him and they had paid the river god for water to cleanse Qian's brutalised body. He had been dressed in the white garments he had worn on his wedding night and his coffin strewn with tea. Rice had been placed in his mouth to ward off hunger and a silver coin in his hand to bribe the judges of the underworld. A mirror to show Qian the way had been placed next to the body, the passport to identify him to the guardian of the underworld had been burnt and the ashes placed in the coffin then the corpse was packed around with hell money, talismans and personal items. Zhen himself had placed the blanket of gold over Qian's body. All this and more had been done according to ritual. Ah Soon was supposed to attend the body, mourning, night and day but when Zhen entered the house and paid his respects to his friend, he found the son missing.

As a pregnant woman, Lian was not permitted to attend the wake or the funeral for foetuses were believed to be particularly vulnerable to the spirits and death airs that accompany the dead.

He went to China Street but neither Ah Soon nor Lian was there. He then turned his steps to Circular Road. Lian had not been, initially, very enthusiastic about his idea for a book on Chinese medicine. But recently she had warmed to the idea and begun to spend several hours a day at his shop. She was there, behind the counter and his apothecary was explaining the mixtures of certain herbs. She was making notes and he stood outside, looking in at her for a few moments.

She walked around the counter and took up a handful of herbs and put them to her nose. She looked as slender as always. The baby had not begun to show for she was only two months along. He was going to be a grandfather again. He had several grandchildren. Two boys in Bangkok and one girl in Batavia but he did not know them. Daughters married away and their children became the children of their husband's family. But this one he would know and love, for Lian and Ah Soon would live in Singapore if he had anything to say about it.

She looked up and saw him and, for the first time in weeks, she smiled and his heart went to her. He liked to have women around him. And he liked to make love and that had not happened for many months. He missed it and his mind turned to Xia Lou. But she was not here and the inevitable happened. He dwelt on the supple and honey-coloured skin of Jia Wen and for the first time in a long while felt desire wrap its cloak around him. He shook it all away, pushed it aside. Such thoughts filled him with regret. He was not ready to give up Xia Lou yet.

* * *

Alex turned on his side. He had thought Amber might never go to sleep. She was insatiable, like a greedy girl who had discovered the delights of chocolate for the first time.

Their marriage had been a quiet affair carried out in the late afternoon when the air was cool. The Armenian priest had blessed them in the chapel where his mother had married his father. A small dinner had been prepared on the great terrace of the house. Then he had found himself alone with Amber. She was pretty, there was no doubt, and to any other man, it would be a fortunate night. She began to unbutton the fifty silk-covered buttons of the bodice of the white silk gown, run up in double-quick time by the tailors in the town.

He watched her and he saw the look of anxiety on her face. He knew he should go to her and kiss her, help her undress, caress her, put her at her ease and let her feel the growing excitement of her wedding night. But he could not. And as he sat in silence, she stopped undressing and sat on the chair.

'I don't want to act like a whore, Alex, but you must help me then.'

So he had risen, resigned to this act, and undressed her and kissed her and they had got into the big bed and, because she was nubile and soft and pretty and adored him and he was a man with natural appetites, he had consummated the marriage. He had hoped that would be enough for the night, but she, aroused, had kissed him again and again and finally, he had simply let his body take over his mind.

In a week or so he would depart for the auction at Semarang. That was a sufficient honeymoon. When he returned he would strictly control her access to him and his bedchamber.

Amber was breathing softly, fast asleep. Alex rose and went to the desk. From the drawer he took out the letter he had written to Ah Soon proposing employment at Brieswijk. He placed another piece of paper on the desk, took up his pen and began to write.

My love,

I am married and it is a desolation. I am desperate for you to come. Here is the letter for Ah Soon. Tell him he must reply agreeing to the terms. Then I will send him the money for the passage. Tell him to write instantly and post it on the next packet for Batavia.

Oh Lian, the voyage was a tyranny of pain, leaving you, pregnant with our child. Leaving you, a nightmare worse than anything I've ever experienced. They say love is a kind of madness and I know that is true. I am mad. I dream of your skin, your smile, your eyes. I dream of you and our baby. I love you and wait for you.

Alex

He put the letters inside the envelope and closed it with the red wax and the seal of his father. Today he had become the master of this great estate and he went out onto the verandah, the long verandah which ran the length of the back of the house. He looked out in the half moonlight down over the grounds to the distant gleam of the Kali Krukut, the river which ran through the property.

He would build her a beautiful house of teak, down there where the old tumbledown pavilions now stood. There on the banks of the river, so they would always hear the rushing of water when they made love. And, after a time, when their child had been born and this great house restored to its former glory, he would demand that Amber divorce him for adultery and abandonment for she would surely wish to do so and they would seek the same from Ah Soon. Then Lian would be his to marry and become the true mistress of Brieswijk.

No other thought concerning the upheaval and misery this was likely to cause entered his mind. His heart was wilfully engaged in his own desires and he returned to the bed. Amber moved next to him, half asleep, and put her hand to his back. He fell instantly into a deep sleep.

36

The embroidered cloth swayed as the men carried the heavy coffin through the streets. The lanterns went before, the soul tablet was carried by the priest in front of the coffin and behind came Ah Soon, dressed in a hood and clothes of sackcloth, his face smeared with ashes. The drums and pipes kept up a great noise to warn people of the passage of the dead and, behind the coffin, stretching into the distance in a sea of banners and flags, were the mourners summoned from the brotherhood.

Zhen had got Ah Soon to smoke less by dint of having him locked in his house and guarded by the samsengs. The town had turned out to watch this procession. Zhen walked with Wang behind Ah Soon, the lone figure before him. One sister, heavily pregnant and in Malacca, had not come, the other had died in childbirth, so he, alone, represented his father. He was supposed to moan and cry, beat his chest and act grief stricken but he did none of those things. He shivered, his feet plodding side to side in a daze. He was in a bad way and Zhen saw he might never be able to rid Ah Soon of this habit.

To each side of the route up South Bridge Road, police peons stood lookout, simply a token presence. Zhen saw Graves in the crowd. Many of the European residents of the town had come out to watch this colourful scene.

At the junction with Sago Street, the procession slowed and turned to go up the hill to the cemetery. A low murmur began somewhere at the back of the line. Zhen glanced back but could see nothing. The rocks were a total surprise, raining down on the coffin and the mourners. The brotherhood following the coffin fell out of step and men crowded in on one another. More rocks hailed down and Ah Soon was hit and fell. Wang stepped up to Zhen and they looked around.

The brawl began in a flash. A gang of a hundred men rushed out and began bashing the flag bearers and the samsengs. Blood spurted from one man's neck. A knife flew out of the crowd and thudded into the coffin. In an instant the coffin was abandoned and left lying on its side on the hillside. The bearers flew away or into the crowd which erupted in violent clashes.

Voices screamed and roared and a man stepped forward and raised a knife to Zhen. Wang turned and realising the danger stepped in front of Zhen. The knife struck him in the arm and he whirled in pain striking the attacker with a blow so strong the man went down, unconscious, to the ground. Wang drew his foot back and struck the man's head. Blood erupted in a fountain from the cracked skull. Another knife flew out and missed Zhen by inches, landing in the dirt.

Zhen picked up the knife and went to Ah Soon. He helped him up and looked around. The street was in chaos. He pulled Ah Soon to safety by the upturned coffin of his father. Then he went back to Wang. Graves raised his gun and shot several volleys into the air over the crowed. The peons massed with Graves in solidarity. As the shots rang out the riot ended as suddenly as it had started. The attackers melted away down Sago Street or Smith Street or into the woods.

Graves came up to Zhen. 'Are you all right?' he said. Blood was coursing from Wang's arm.

'I am all right,' Zhen said. He turned to Wang. 'Go, get treatment for your arm.'

Zhen signalled to a samseng. 'Help your master,' he ordered. Wang made noises of protest but Zhen stopped him with a glance. 'No. Go.'

Graves watched as this volley of Chinese flew back and forth. Finally the injured man moved away and Zhen turned to him.

'Thank you. Your quick action saved the day.'

'What has caused this?'

'Resentments.' Zhen shrugged. 'We Chinese can be quick to anger about our honour and it could be anything. A blood feud, a debt of money, a woman. Perhaps my friend had enemies. Disrupting his funeral is the ultimate insult to a Chinese.'

Graves contemplated Zhen. They were all so incomprehensible. He had no answer to what had just occurred other than what Zhen told him.

Zhen signalled men to go back to the coffin. It was righted and with great difficulty returned to the shoulders of the men.

'Allow me to bury my friend,' he said to Graves.

Graves stepped back and the peons returned to their positions flanking the procession. All the Europeans had fled. Zhen restored a dazed Ah Soon to his position but now he walked by his side and six samsengs surrounded them. The procession, returned to order, wound slowly up the hill.

Zhen was in no doubt what had happened. Hong had tried to kill him. An act of punishment was necessary and the surest punishment was to destroy his fortune.

* * *

Robert shook Zhen's hand warmly. He signalled to him to sit opposite him. He went to the cabinet and took out a bottle of whisky. 'May I offer you a dram?'

Zhen smiled. He knew what this meant. He and Robert had often drunk together on evenings spent at Bukit Jagoh or at North Bridge Road. In many respects, since Zhen had been with Charlotte, Robert had assumed the mantle of brother.

'A wee one.'

Robert laughed. He poured them both a drink and sat.

'I have never expressed,' Robert said, 'my sorrow about the death of Lily. I am truly sorry, Zhen, for your loss and my own, for she was my dear niece.'

'Life and death are a thread, the same line viewed from different sides.'

Robert nodded. Zhen was always quoting odd things and Robert, not a man of very philosophical mind, generally could not fathom any of it.

'You also have experienced sorrow.'

'Yes,' Robert said.

'I too am sorry for your loss. She has joined the river of life. And it has been returned to you in the birth of your son. It is a circle, an ever-rolling wheel.'

Again, Robert hardly knew what to reply. But he knew that these were words of sympathy and he was grateful.

'My wife, Teresa, you remember.'

Zhen nodded. He had rarely met this woman except on public occasions but he knew who she was.

'Well, she's taken my boy in for the moment. Since Amber went off and got married, well, a child needs a mother and he is half brother to Andrew, my son.'

'Indeed, a most sensible arrangement,' Zhen said and Robert

beamed, pleased.

'Your daughter has married,' Zhen said. He longed for news of Xia Lou and Ah Rex.

Something in his voice made Robert look at him carefully. Alex was his son, unacknowledged, but nevertheless, it must be hard.

'Alex is a strong man. Like you.'

Zhen met Robert's eyes. 'Thank you. I am grateful. It is sometimes …'

'Yes, yes.' Robert said. 'He has become the owner of Brieswijk. Charlotte has given him the estate and intends him to have the tea plantation too. So you see, he will be a great man and you may draw pleasure from that.'

Zhen smiled at Robert. It was a great kindness.

'As for my sister, well. I don't know what happened between you. It is presumptuous to mention it.'

'No, no. I would like news of her.'

'My dear Zhen. I am not a man of great understanding of the female mind. But from my poor grasp I think that the death of Lily and your separation worked on her until she could not bear it. She has talked to me of this not at all. I merely surmise.'

'I see.'

'But women need affection, do they not? The constant attentions of the men in their lives. It gives them security.' Robert shrugged. 'I don't know. What do I know?'

Zhen nodded. 'You're right. Through no fault of my own she felt neglected. And, as you say, the death of Lily.'

'Yes, yes. I think that the gossip, the constant pressure of eyes turned on her, the whisperings, you know, have taken their toll. I have endured similar mutterings myself. But men do not really care. We are even admired the more women we have. Perhaps you have discovered that yourself. But for a woman it is not pleasant to be the constant source of scandalous gossip. Women never let up, like a dog with a bone, they keep on at her.'

Zhen found nothing to answer Robert. For a man who was not especially perspicacious about women, if that was true, he had hit on the reason. She was sick and tired of being the English concubine. All these other things – their separation at the same time as the arrival of the English sailor who clearly loved her, the death of their child which felt like a punishment for their unorthodox lives, his neglect of her when she had most needed him – all these had conspired to build up a case for departure.

Robert waited but nothing further ensued on this topic and he changed it.

'Your daughter, too, has married.'

Zhen smiled. 'Yes, she is expecting her first child.'

'Many congratulations,' Robert said, and clapped his hand on Zhen's shoulder.

'It hardly seems but a few years since I made your acquaintance in the old police house by the river. You were shy and spoke not at all.'

Zhen smiled. He recalled everything of that night. His first encounter with a foreigner, his first visit to the European side of the river and, more than these extraordinary things, the sound of the swish of her skirt on the floor and the sight of her in the doorway, lovely, more lovely than anything he had every seen. That night had kindled his obsessive passion for her. He glanced at Robert.

'I remember it very well. You offered tea and sandwiches. I have never understood sandwiches.'

Robert laughed. 'No, nor I. Abominable things.'

The two men shared a laugh and then Zhen's face turned

serious. 'Robert, I have come to tell you of how your police may make a great arrest.'

37

'Oh, Aunt, I am so very happy.'

Amber looked ravishing. Her eyes shone and her skin glowed.

'I have never been so happy. To be here in this wonderful place. It's like paradise. And I have so many maids. You didn't tell me it was a palace. Why, Singapore is nothing compared to this.'

Charlotte smiled. 'Well, perhaps today we might leave paradise and ride into town and do some shopping and have a little lunch at the hotel.'

Amber took Charlotte's hands and kissed them.

'Yes, yes. And then bathe, do you think, Aunt? Aunt Takouhi says you all used to bathe in the river in sarongs, like the native women. How I should love to do that.'

'Perhaps we might. An afternoon picnic perhaps.'

Charlotte poured coffee and gazed out over the grounds. It had never felt so right to be back here. She put her hand to her waist. She still could not decide. She knew she had only a few weeks more.

'Alex will be back soon, won't he?'

'Do you miss him so much?'

'Oh I do miss him terribly. He is so wonderful.'

Charlotte contemplated her niece, now her daughter-in-law. It seemed that Alex had been true to his word. All this glow and joy was from bedroom discoveries. Charlotte was certain Amber would be pregnant very quickly and would be an excellent mother.

'He should return in four or five more days, depending on the seas.'

'Do you think he will bring me a present?'

Charlotte laughed. 'Perhaps.'

A small frown furrowed Amber's brow. 'Why have Alex's things been taken from our bedroom?'

Before he departed for Semarang, Alex had ordered his effects moved out of the wedding chamber which formed the corner of the building and into the rooms Tigran had often occupied over the central pillars of the verandah. These rooms were large and well-appointed, with a drawing room and private bathroom as well as the bedroom, decorated in a decidedly more masculine way. The maids were busy taking down the dusty drapes and cleaning it.

'Well, dear, it is the custom here. For the wedding night and for some little time after it is customary to occupy the wedding bedroom. After that a move is usually made to separate apartments. No-one of Alex's status would not have his own apartments. You may choose any rooms you like for yours of course. Your own drawing room too, so you may entertain your friends when you have made them. We shall make them over exactly as you wish.'

Amber frowned. 'My father shared a bedroom with Mother all the time. Did you not with your husband?'

'No. Tigran and I had separate apartments.'

'But,' Amber said, hesitantly, 'does that mean …'

'Yes?' Charlotte said knowing perfectly well what was on Amber's mind.

'Does that mean he will not …'

Charlotte put her hand to Amber's.

'It means he is the master here. That he will do as he wishes.'

Charlotte contemplated Amber. Was she ready to understand how most men lived in the Indies? There was never any question of keeping to one woman. The principal wife was mistress of her domain, but no rich *Indische* man would think twice about keeping several mistresses and often nyais who occupied rooms in the house or resided on the estate. What was scandalous in Singapore was perfectly normal here.

Tigran had kept only to her. They had been married when he was in his forties, she nineteen, and he had loved her so much he had not wanted another woman. But a man of Alex's age, barely nineteen, so young. And he did not love Amber passionately, if at all. It was better to let the girl lower her expectations.

'My dear,' she began as the butler appeared at her elbow with a tray. 'Marriage is an arrangement of inequality. The man always has the upper hand. You know that, you knew that before you agreed to marry Alex.'

She took the letters.

'Ah the post. Look, a letter from Sarah Blundell for you.'

Amber squealed, took the letter and ran to sit under the waringan tree. Charlotte watched her run off, kicking her heels like a little lamb. She would understand, eventually; little by little, Charlotte would explain this to her. She could not have Alex to herself, she had to share him. The sooner she understood that, the sooner she would find some measure of contentment. She recognised the hypocrisy of it all, even her own complicit hand in it. But in return Amber would have wealth, status and high social position, none of which would have accrued to her in marriage to a local Singapore merchant. Perhaps she ought to have explained all this to Amber before she married, but she had wanted this to be done, for Alex to agree to leave Singapore. Selfish. But one is selfish. Amber wanted Alex for her own reasons. Charlotte shrugged. Alex would be back soon and she would discuss all this with him frankly.

The other letter was from Robert and she opened it.

Sister,

News from Singapore is most exciting.

In a daring raid on pirates in the Straits of Johor, your brother has proved most heroic. Following information given to us, a party got together in the government steamer and waited, by dead of night, off a certain bay in the west of Ubin. When the junk appeared we pounced. The effect of surprise was so enormous that after a short skirmish we prevailed. It was all most admirably organised.

Charlotte smiled.

The governor has mentioned me to the government in India. I fancy there might be a medal in it for me. A great quantity of chandu was recovered which was intended to be smuggled into Johor. And now suspicions fall on the farmer Hong and if we can get the captain to talk he may well find himself in hot water.

I am well, I suppose. I have somewhat recovered. Little Robert does wonderfully well with Teresa, who, considering my treatment of her, acts as nobly as a queen and I draw comfort and remember Shilah in this child.

Amber does not write me at all. Selfish as all young married girls are I suppose. Father forgotten and only the husband in her eyes. Well, give her my love.

The letter went on in this vein for some time. News of a visit by this and that potentate, others of their acquaintance, until she came to the part which caused her to gasp.

Sister, the most shocking news is that Zhen's friend Qian was murdered most foully by his attacker in the strangest circumstances. Of that least said. You might not know that Zhen was attacked by a gang of thugs on the day of the funeral, but he is perfectly all right. He was instrumental in helping my force capture the smuggler's boat. Naturally he mourns the loss of his life-long friend in such tragic circumstances.

Should she write to him? His grief at the loss of his friend must be great. Then she recalled his actions at the death of his own daughter.

'Doubtless your grief will be of short duration,' she said to herself. She rose to get Amber and spend a pleasant morning in town.

38

The Buddhist and Taoist priests had gathered in a huddle of yellow and black, chanting furiously around the coffin of Ah Soon.

Zhen sat in the temple as the incense swirled smoke around them, shutting out the wailing of the paid mourners, the smoke from the paper offerings practically choking him, and closed his eyes.

The women, his mother-in-law, her sisters and cousins were gathered in a group, praying fervently.

Nothing, he knew, in all the beliefs and superstitions of the Chinese about death was more feared than this. First the father had died, murdered. Now the son had perished from an overdose of opium. Of all the spirits that might come back to haunt the living, those who died in this way, through unnatural causes, were the most dangerous.

Death was not final, in these beliefs, merely a transition to an alternative form of life. For seven weeks the soul would pass through seven courts of hell facing trials and judgments about its conduct in life. Then with the offerings of the living, the spirit would reach the Underworld, ruled over by Yanluowang. Here, with the help of the generous and ceaseless benevolence of the deceased's living relatives, they would enjoy their life much as they had on earth, with money, homes, food and opium.

But those who died of unnatural causes were trapped forever in limbo, unable to enter the Underworld until they themselves had lured another unfortunate soul in to replace them. They were feared for this reason.

Zhen was not permitted to leave. He was the deceased's father-in-law and the only living man in the family able to placate the spirits. It would be eternally his duty to keep Qian and Ah Soon from visiting the earth and stealing another soul.

Zhen was relieved when, finally, the coffin was taken from the temple on the hill and carried to the cemetery and interred near his father. More money and incense was burned, the black smoke carried far into the sky. The mourners shrieked, the priests chanted, and then it was done and the gravediggers began to fill in the grave.

Zhen made his way down the hill ignoring those who tried to speak to him. Wang watched discreetly.

His mother-in-law had spoken to him of Lian going back to River Valley Road. What better place to birth her child and raise it. But Zhen knew this was the worst possible outcome for Lian. He walked to the house in China Street and went into the hall.

'Lian,' he called. The house smelled of incense and he knew she had been asked to light it at Ah Soon's shrine. Her life, now, as his widow, was to placate him in death. If a son was born, then it would fall to him. He shook his head. These rites made his head ache.

Lian appeared and he put his arm around her. She had been crying and it was not for Ah Soon.

'The maid will bring your belongings. You are coming to Market Street to live with me until the baby is born.'

Lian threw her arms around her father. Her greatest fear was that she would be sent back to River Valley Road.

'After the baby is born then we shall see. I think to make over the medicine shop to you.'

'Oh, Father,' she said smiling. 'Wait please. I shall get a small bag.'

Zhen nodded. This was the right thing to do. After five minutes she returned holding a small carpet bag. She ran to get her hat.

They walked slowly and silently to Market Street and all Lian could think of was Alex. What would he do when he found out? Their plan was in tatters. As she was now a widow, Alex had no reason to ask her to come to Batavia.

Zhen took her up the stairs to the first floor. Here was her bedroom and a sitting room. Here she could be private and away from them all. Lian looked around and threw open the shutters.

'Thank you, Father.'

'I shall not always dine here,' he said. 'And it is not customary for men and women to eat together, but I have become somewhat English with the years with Xia Lou and here, in the privacy of this house, we shall do as we like. Will you eat with me tonight?'

She smiled. 'Yes, Father.'

When he left she watched him walk from the house towards Boat Quay. What was life to be for her now? Well at least it was not to be with her grandmother. She would wait to hear from Alex. In the meantime, she planned to convert to Christianity. Not the least because Christian widows could remarry. Tomorrow she would go and speak to Father Beurel at the Catholic church.

She touched her waist. Two months pregnant. Alex's child lay there quietly inside her and it was a comfort. 'Come to me,' she said and sent her words out across the sea.

Zhen walked to the godown. He saw Hong approach with two of his henchmen. Wang came to his side. Hong bowed and passed on. To say this man was a threat was an understatement.

He went over the accounts with his Eurasian bookkeeper and spoke to his brother-in-law, who had been at the funeral. They liked each other, these two, and together ate the meal from the tiffin carriers that his second wife had sent down.

Wang appeared.

'Come,' Zhen said. 'Join us. There's plenty and Ah Teo's wife is a good cook.'

'Thanks,' Wang said, 'but I've got toothache.'

Ah Teo and Zhen shared a look. The man's mouth was a nightmare.

'This mail has been sent to you from the Post Office. It is addressed to Ah Soon, but the man said you should take it.'

'Oh,' Zhen said and put down his chopsticks.

He went to his room and took up the letter opener. The letter was from Batavia. It must be from Alex. He sat and slit open the envelope and took out the papers.

There were two. One was an offer of employment for Ah Soon. Alex offered him to work in the office of Manouk & Sons trading house. The salary was generous. The passage for him and his wife would be paid.

Zhen contemplated this letter. Did Ah Soon know about this and would he have gone? He put the paper down and opened the second letter.

He read it through from beginning to end and then read it again. He sat back and looked at Ah Teo finishing his lunch. Wang was drinking tea and complaining about his teeth.

Zhen folded the letters and put them in his pocket. A noise began outside. Another skirmish. All this was to do with Hong.

The man was a menace. The confiscation of his stash of chandu had hit him hard but it was time for even more drastic measures.

He signalled to Wang.

'Go to Hong's house tonight when he's in bed and asleep. I have heard he likes to smoke a pipe or two so he will not wake. Kill the two thugs who guard him. They're responsible for more deaths than I can count. Tie the servants and lock them up. No dead servants or women. I don't want a reputation for cruelty, only swift justice. Understand?'

Wang nodded.

'Take their heads and put them in bed with him and leave the laws of the brotherhood by his bed. Be silent, be quick. In the morning I want him to wake up alone with a bed full of blood and two corpses at his bedside. Paste news of my just retribution all over Chinatown. Everyone must know what happens if they threaten my life or my authority.'

Wang nodded and smiled. This was the correct decision. If the Shan Chu did not act now, all his authority would evaporate. Even his sore teeth couldn't stop him enjoying this.

When Zhen returned to Market Street in late afternoon, the maid said Lian was bathing. All her things had been moved to this house. He dismissed her and went to Lian's room. On the bed was the carpet bag.

He opened it and took out the two letters from Batavia. He read them and his jaw tightened. This had been the plan all along. Alex was a clever boy, a boy with the same passions and obsessions as he himself. He had acted just the way Zhen had acted for love of Xia Lou, bold and reckless. He put them in his pocket alongside the others.

He went to his bathroom and bathed, washing away the incense and smoke, the heat and sweat of the day. At the dinner hour Lian appeared, fresh and clean. What a lovely girl she is, he thought, this daughter of mine. He felt a great sorrow swell inside himself.

When the dishes had been served he dismissed the servants. Lian was shy. It was unusual to eat with a man, even her own father, and she selected morsels from the plates silently. He waited until she had eaten her fill. He took some food and finished his rice. Then he lay down his chopsticks.

He took out the letters and laid them on the table.

She looked up and suddenly realised what they were. She rose and he lifted his hand.

'Sit down, Lian.'

She burst into tears and threw her hands to her face, filled with shame. Zhen began to speak and, as he did, she took her hands away from her face and shame was replaced with horror. She began to sob and looked down at her belly. She touched herself there and her hands began to shake uncontrollably. Zhen called the maid who arrived, terrified at the sight of her mistress.

'Go to bed, Lian. I am not angry.'

Lian stumbled upstairs and threw herself on the bed.

'Get out,' she screamed at the maid and the girl rushed from the room. Lian pulled her hair and began to wail.

When the house was silent, at midnight, she slipped out of the back door. She knew the samsengs watched this house but they were creatures of habit and mere men. Both of them were dozing. She walked quickly along Telok Ayer Bay looking neither right nor left. She passed the slumbering fishermen in their boats, their silhouettes caught by moonshine, their craft lulled by the soft waves lapping the shore, passed the towers of the mosque and the peaceful temple with its odours of incense. At the end of the street she turned and began to climb up the hill. Without a moment's hesitation she walked to the edge and out into the void.

39

Alex looked up as the servant brought the tray with the post. He sorted through it swiftly. Still nothing. Four weeks and still nothing. Tonight he would write again. Or perhaps he should just take the *Queen* and go back and get them. Yes, that would stop all this waiting. But the *Queen* was on voyage to the spice islands and wouldn't be back for two weeks. He thrummed his fingers on the table and felt his agitation.

He finished his coffee and walked down to the river. It took half an hour and he walked off his energy in the cool of the morning under the spacious arms of the rain trees. The auction had gone reasonably well. Several bidders had driven up the price. The debts had been paid and more than enough money was left to begin repairs on the house. And build the river house of teak. The massive teak logs had arrived and work had begun.

At least he had his own apartment now and could wake alone without Amber's cloying attentions. He lost himself for days in the work of the estate, riding out to survey the rice paddies and speak to the kampong people in his barely remembered rudimentary Javanese.

He had visited Amber more often than he had thought he would. It wasn't just to keep her satisfied, he needed to relieve the sexual tensions that threatened to overwhelm him when he thought of Lian. Last night Amber had told him she thought she was pregnant. She begged him to sleep with her but he had left. He didn't care if she was disappointed.

He heard her calling and ignored it. He strode out to the river and greeted the men. The carpenter and he went over the plan. It would be beautiful, four rooms, all in glowing teak wood and a great verandah overhanging the swift flowing waters of the Kali Krukut, the most beautiful river in Batavia. At the back the cookhouse and servants quarters separate, at a distance from the house.

Amber turned away, disappointed. Charlotte contemplated her. She had missed by two weeks. She was probably pregnant. Perhaps now it was time for her to explain. That Alexander was building this river house was a sign. He intended it for another woman at some stage. Alex spent a lot of time with Matthew and Pieter and knew how things worked for men in the Indies.

She put on the coat which covered her thickening waist. She knew now that she could not do anything but keep this child. He or she would be the last piece of Zhen she would ever have. In a few weeks she would announce it to Alex and the devil take the hindmost.

Takouhi had gone into town. She had decided, now that Charlotte was back with Alex, that she would go and live in her old house at Nordwijk. It had been tenanted a long time and needed refurbishment. It was smaller and closer to all the fashionable shops and hotels.

Charlotte heard a carriage drive up and went to the windows looking down to the drive. She had just begun to plan the great reception for Alex and Amber. Now before Amber began to show. This might be the man from the Harmonie Club. She intended to hold this great banquet and ball in town.

She went out onto the landing which gave down onto the blue and white Dutch tiles of the hall. A figure entered, dressed in a black silk coat, under the great shield of the VOC and the coat of arms of Van Riemsdijk, the owner and builder of this great house.

He looked up and she gazed into the eyes of Zhen. She couldn't believe it and staggered slightly. He stood, looking up at her, unmoving.

She did not want to go down, but she knew she had to. She buttoned the loose coat over her dress and walked down the stairs and his eyes never left her. As she came up to him he bowed. He looked thin, she thought.

'You, here.'

'Xia Lou. I have come to speak of serious things.'

'Come outside.'

She led Zhen out to the long verandah which occupied the entire back of the house and looked down from the knoll out and over the lawns and down to the river. From here she could not see Alex for the house he was building was at a bend in the river where the rocks stood up and the water was particularly fast and brilliant.

She turned her gaze on Zhen. He was looking at her and she suddenly blushed. How did he do it? But he did not smile.

'Would you like something?'

'Yes. Something. Some water perhaps. Soda water. Do you have it?'

'Yes.' She called a servant.

She sat and he sat, too, and looked over the estate.

'Beautiful. I never came here. Only up to the house in the hills.'

'Yes,' she said and a feeling of tenderness came over her. He had saved her from the opium, up there in the hills. She felt the flutter in her womb. If she had never been pregnant she would never have noticed it, but she knew it was his child, moving inside her. With Lily they had shared this moment, his hand on her belly, his lips too, overjoyed to be together. She gazed at him.

'Zhen, I want to say I'm truly sorry. How we left everything.'

He nodded. 'Yes, I too. But that is not why I'm here.'

Amber came out onto the terrace and approached them. 'Oh. Mr. Zhen. What a surprise. How nice.'

She threw a glance at her aunt. This man's presence was incomprehensible.

Zhen did not rise. Charlotte smiled. Chinese men did not rise for young women. She sensed him tense. 'Amber, dear. Leave us for the moment. I want to speak to Zhen alone.'

Amber bobbed a curtsy. 'Of course.' She turned to go, then hesitated. 'I hope Lian is well,' she said but as nothing was answered, she departed, out across the lawn and down to the river, seeking Alex.

'What is it?' Charlotte said. Something was very wrong.

The servant arrived with the water and she contemplated Zhen as it was decanted. 'Enough,' she said impatiently and the servant scurried away.

He drank. 'Ah Soon died of an overdose of opium.'

Charlotte put her hand to her mouth. 'Oh no. Poor boy. Poor Lian.'

'That is not why I'm here.'

Charlotte rose, agitated, sensing, in some ill-defined way, disaster. 'Why are you here? Just tell me.'

'Lian was pregnant. Two months or so. But the child was not Ah Soon's child. It was Alexander's.'

Charlotte reacted as if she'd been shot. She jumped back

and her hand flew to her throat. She shook her head. 'Don't be ridiculous. She was married to Ah Soon.'

'Yes, but somehow or other they contrived to come together … and more than once, I think. Lovers are most adept at deception.'

She blushed again knowing the import of his words. 'You cannot know that. How can you know that? She's pregnant. It must be Ah Soon's child.'

Zhen stood. 'No, Xia Lou. It was Alexander's. There were letters between them. Love letters. He was planning to bring Ah Soon and her here, to keep her here, for himself.'

Charlotte's eyes flew to the river and the invisible house. Was that possible?

'He would not have done that if she was not already his, if the child was not his.'

'No, no. Think what you're saying.'

'Yes. I told her.'

Charlotte stopped moving and she opened her eyes in shock. 'You told her?'

'I told her she was Alexander's sister.'

Charlotte felt her face being to crumple and she looked at him beseechingly. 'She … You said, she was …'

'She was pregnant. She is no longer.'

'Oh Zhen.'

She rose, the horror of what he was intimating striking her. He stepped forward and caught her in his arms. She began to wail. Amber, halfway to the river, turned. Zhen held her to him for a moment, then she pushed him away violently.

'Tell me,' she said.

'She is not dead,' he said. 'She jumped from the cliff but she is alive. The baby is dead and she had terrible injuries, but Dr. Cowper operated and we used our medicines and we saved her.

Together we saved her.'

'Oh Zhen,' she said and he wanted to hold her but she stood away from him and hugged her gown to her body. Amber watched from a distance. She had better stay away. Something emotional was going on. She turned and continued down to the river, fanning herself.

'Now you must tell Alex. He loves her, make no mistake. He loves Lian as I ...'

He could not continue. Charlotte shook her head.

'No, I can't tell him. He will hate me.'

'Enough. Enough. It should all have been done years ago when we had the chance. This is your fault. Not mine. Yours. I wanted to tell him when he was a boy, when I had a chance of being his father.'

Charlotte stared at him and suddenly shook her head violently.

'No, no. He wouldn't have believed you. He would have hated you.'

'You don't know that. You never gave it a chance. We could have told him when he came back from Scotland. Then when he was grown and before they had met once more. I warned you. But you are stubborn and it has led to this dreadful ...'

Suddenly Zhen could not go on with this interminable argument.

'You have to tell him about Lian. You have to tell him who he is, why she jumped off a cliff.'

Charlotte slumped into a chair. 'I thought ... I thought ...' She looked up at him. 'I haven't the courage.'

'Then I'll tell him. It must all come out. No more lies.' He turned and looked down the grounds. Amber suddenly reappeared and by her side was Alex.

Charlotte saw them too and began to shake.

Zhen strode away. She couldn't take her eyes off him, his tall figure moving swiftly over the grass. In a moment he would be there and everything would be irrevocably broken. She rose and ran inside the house, too cowardly to watch.

She stayed in her room and sat, just sat. She heard a great shout of anguish and she knew. She put her face in her hands and cried. Then she rose in a frenzy of concern and looked down to them.

Amber was nowhere to be seen. Alex was on his knees, collapsed. Zhen's hand was on his shoulder. It was like a tableau, silent and still, but she knew it heralded the storm.

40

'He has gone to the hills,' she said, 'up to Buitenzorg. Flown away. Couldn't bear to be around me.'

Zhen sat opposite her. Charlotte sat quietly. Her fingers held a square white box. He glanced at it and frowned. 'He took it badly but he has to find a way to understand it.'

They were on the verandah of her house. He was staying with the Kapitan Cina of Batavia, whose son was married to his eldest daughter. When he had told Alex, the boy had rushed away from him, run with all his heart down to the river. Charlotte could not speak to Zhen and he had departed.

Now two days later Zhen had returned, desperate to help her and make one last request. She looked at him. 'He no longer wishes to stay at Brieswijk. Sell it, he said. Sell everything and go to hell.'

'He had to know.'

'Amber is distraught. I told her because he would not. He left without a word to her.'

She stopped touching the box and drew the shawl more closely around her shoulders.

'It has been hard. I'm sorry, Xia Lou. But at least there are no more secrets between any of us.'

Charlotte gazed down to the river. 'The young girl?'

'I don't want her. That is the truth. But if you will never want to come to me again ...' He spread his hands.

She nodded. Her face showed him nothing. Strangely she was the one who showed nothing, as if they had changed places.

'Ever the pragmatist. It's an admirable Chinese trait.'

Zhen's rose and stood in front of her. Her took her by the shoulders and gently pulled her to her feet. He locked his eyes to hers.

'I have been constant. I have been the constant heart. You are always filled with fear. We can be together again. I offered once before to marry you and you refused for fear of Alex. But that is done with now. They must make their own road now they know the truth. But you and I, we can marry and help Alex and Lian get over ...'

Charlotte pulled herself away from his hands. She took the white box and placed it in his pocket. He looked down.

'Alex is lost to me and you.'

'Come back,' he said. 'For me alone.'

He took the box and opened it. Inside lay the necklace he had given her twenty years ago. A perfect pearl under a latticed silver mount shaped like the upturned eaves of a Chinese temple on an entwined rope of red silk threads.

She gazed away from him into the gently waving branches of the tamarind grove.

'I will marry Edward,' she said calmly. 'He has asked me.'

There was no sound and after a moment she turned. He was not there. She sat heavily on a chair and hung her head.

Amber came onto the terrace, her face contorted with grief. 'He hates me too. He hates you and now he hates me.'

Charlotte straightened her back and looked at Amber. 'This is not about you, child. It goes far back.'

Amber came forward in a swift movement, drew back her hand and slapped Charlotte's face. 'You are evil,' she said. 'You put us together knowing he would never love me. Knowing he loved his own sister.'

She ran away into the house.

Charlotte watched her. She was a child in love. Sixteen, pregnant and heartbroken. How could she explain all this to Amber? It was her fault. They were all right. Her stubbornness and her fear had caused this.

She grew suddenly deathly tired. At her age this pregnancy was taking its toll. She remembered Shilah. Perhaps she would die giving birth to this child. Perhaps that would be right. She smiled. Come what may. She no longer cared.

A long shudder passed through her body as if the hand of death had truly been placed on her shoulder and she cried out.

'Zhen,' she said.

Why had she let him go? She didn't want to die. He was right. They could be together. The pain stabbed her so suddenly it took her breath away and she stood, her hand to her back. A second knife thrust to her guts and she leant against the table and cried out.

She looked down. A bright red stain spread slowly on her dress and she collapsed to the floor.

41

Charlotte touched the two statues on the plinth.

'This is really a very good likeness of you and Mariam.' Takouhi smiled.

'I feel rather foolish, coming to church and gazing on my image. Still they aren't *inside* the church anyway. That feels like blasphemy.'

'You and Mariam have donated a great deal of money to the church and to the poor and destitute Armenians through the Haykian foundation. The Armenian community naturally wanted to thank you.'

'And I thank them. Come, let's go back to Nordwijk. To the Salon des Glaces. The newspaper reports a shipment of ice. And Pascal's advertises un grand deluge de chaussures.'

The carriage took off at a clip up Koningsplein West.

'You will be all right here?'

Takouhi held her hat and gazed about her.

'I shall do very well. I have friends all around me. My old house is now like new. To tell the truth, at my age I prefer it to that huge house.'

'Yes, you're quite right. My agent has let Brieswijk to a very grand man. Albertus Jacobus Duymaer van Twist who is to be Chief Counsellor to the Raad van Indie. He will come with Mevrouw van Twist and half of his dozen little van Twists. Perhaps he has allowed himself to be deprived of the great and sophisticated pleasures of Amsterdam because he has heard that, here in Batavia, the strictures on keeping only to his lady wife alone, are not so onerous as in Holland.'

'Men have been coming here for that for centuries. And Madame van Twist will forget all about the little nyais when she realises that, as inferior in all the land only to the Governor General's wife, she can play the lady of the manor in grand style.'

The two women smiled. Takouhi put her arm in Charlotte's.

'Still nothing about Alex?'

'No. Nothing. Disappeared. The servants at Buitenzorg say he never went there.'

'When he has done with grief and anger, he will come back.'

Charlotte nodded. 'Perhaps. I have accepted my guilt. I only wish I could apologise to him.'

At the Salon des Glaces, they waited. All the seats were taken, the place overflowing. When ice arrived in town, it was always bursting with women and children. The owner, Georges Pouligner, came rushing forward, bowing.

'Mesdames, soyez les bienvenues.' He signalled to a waiter and in an instant a table and two chairs had been placed in the shade of the large fig tree which stood before the house. A snow-white cloth flew over it and silver cutlery and a vase of flowers quickly adorned it.

Takouhi and Charlotte sat.

'Vanille,' he said, 'ou chocolat. Sorbets de fruits, aussi.' They placed their orders and he bustled away.

'He is keen to pack us in whilst the ice lasts.' Takouhi smiled.

'We are very well placed here to observe the rest of the town.

It is my new pastime.'

'How does Amber?'

'Not well. She cries a lot. But at least she will talk to me now and I've tried to explain my actions.'

'Give her time. Four months is not so long to get over such things. Especially with a baby growing inside her.'

'Yes. We will go back to Singapore when the affairs of Buitenzorg are completed. That has taken longer than Brieswijk, but the agent says he has a buyer and at a good price. I shall set half the money aside for Adam's heritage. He will certainly never come out here. It's pulpits, not plantations, that interest him.'

Charlotte glanced at Takouhi. 'Do you mind? Losing all this which was Tigran's heritage.'

'Oh, you know. I went up there a year ago. It's beautiful but it reminds me too of my own father and his cruelty to my mother and me. It was him, not Tigran, who made it. I can do very well without it. It might as well go to someone who will care for it.'

'Yes. Matthew seems to have the trading house in hand. I have made it all over to him and Nicolaus's family. As for the fleet, well, many of the ships are coming to the end of their life. My fleet manager can sell them, one by one, for coastal vessels.'

Takouhi nodded. 'It is good to get things settled. And Brieswijk will stay in the family for Amber's children. And perhaps Alex may return.'

The two women gazed at each other.

'What of this Edward you spoke of and his suit?'

'Oh, dear Edward. But that was so impossible. I thought I could go back and recapture something with him. Some sort of spurious respectability. But it would be a disaster for him and for me. We are too changed. I have written to tell him and make my apologies. I believe I led him on for the most selfish reasons.'

Charlotte touched the huge bulge of her belly.

'And of course this was an unsurmountable obstacle.'

Takouhi nodded a greeting to an acquaintance, an admirer, who bowed to her.

'You had a scare. But all is well now. Must you go back to Singapore, though? So much pain over there. I could never go back.'

'For a time I must. Amber wants to live with her father. Teresa has returned to him, did you know? They are all a little family again.'

Takouhi smiled. 'No! After all that divorce business. Well, perhaps it's for the best.'

'Robert can't live without a woman taking care of him. He always truly cared for Teresa and, despite everything, she is mad about him. I foresee more children. Amber will be well placed there to have her baby and raise it in the bosom of the da Souza family.'

The ices arrived with a flourish carried by M. Pouligner himself.

'Then I must rent out the North Bridge house and, at some point, book a passage on the P&O. A visit back to Scotland is called for. Jeanne has not been well.'

The women put spoons into the ices and savoured the cool sweet taste.

'Will you come back?'

Charlotte met Takouhi's eyes. 'I don't know,' she said and put her hand into her sister-in-law's.

Takouhi gripped it then released it. 'And what of the man, the Chinese man you have rejected so many times.'

Charlotte shrugged. 'He is doubtless married now. I think I should leave him alone.'

Takouhi's eyes fell to Charlotte's bulging belly. 'The child will be born in Singapore unless you mean to have it on the high seas. It is his child. Do you mean to repeat the same old story?'

Charlotte put her hand on her belly as the baby moved inside her. She was big with this child now but she did not mind.

'I thought I'd lost it and found that thought was intolerable. If I never come back, I will still have Zhen with me. It's a boy, I'm certain of it.'

'You haven't answered my question.'

'Because I can't.'

42

Zhen put down the newspaper. There were two items of interest in it today. The first was the fact that Hong Boon Tek had been found guilty of murder. The captain and other witnesses had testified that Hong had ordered two of his men to murder a Malay headman and his family two years previously for stealing his own illegal chandu. Those men, had, since then, been murdered themselves. The article went on about the revenge killings and the appalling state of the Chinese town.

Wang had had no small hand in this, pressuring the Hongmen brothers to give Hong up to the British. The captain of the captured junk had been quick to reveal these murders for a leniency in his own punishment. These men were as ruthless as Hong and could always sense when to desert the sinking ship. For his pains Wang had been murdered one evening on the outskirts of the town, his throat cut but no-one had been convicted of that crime.

Hong would go to Calcutta to be hanged. The lease for the opium farm had passed to Cheng as the only other bidder and he had earned the undying love of the governor by offering to continue at the present price until the leases came up again next year. The great opium syndicate of Tay-Cheng had begun and offered unrivalled prospects of peace and profit.

The second item was the shipping news. The *Queen of the South*, Capt. Hall, from Batavia, had arrived in the roads with a cargo of timber, nutmeg, mace, rattans, sarong cloth, Japanese silk and porcelains and would be held on commission at the godown of Robertson and Kerr.

He could not be sure that she was on it. Robert had merely told him that his daughter was returning home. The ship had arrived in the twilight and disembarked quickly. Had she returned too?

Cheng strolled into the godown.

'You're sure you won't stay on?' he said, 'as leader?'

Zhen shook his head. 'No, we have discussed this. Your status in the town has rapidly become very great. The Temenggong says you are "our friend, beloved of us". The coup of continuing the lease price with the government has endeared you to the governor. Your gift of two thousand dollars to the Poor Fund has endeared you to the church and your offer to fund regular patrols of the junks to prevent smuggling has endeared you to the police. You have done very well. The English establishment adores you. I wouldn't be surprised if, in six months' time, they offered you a position on the Grand Jury. Better learn English.'

'I couldn't have done this without you.'

'I know.'

Cheng laughed.

'Which is why, when you become Shan Chu, I would like your word that you will help me find my Scottish son. He has disappeared but there are Chinese everywhere in the East and one day I will find him if enough eyes are watching.'

'You have my word. I thought we might share a meal today. Jia Wen has brought us lunch.'

Zhen smiled and rose.

On the other side of the river Charlotte gazed down on Boat Quay from the open windows of the upper hall of the court house. She saw Amber move slowly across Thomson Bridge and disappear.

She returned her gaze to the godown as Zhen emerged from the darkness in the company of an older man. He stood in the brilliant light of the day, strong and handsome. He was always heart-stoppingly handsome. She put her hand to her belly. A little foot came to greet her hand.

The men greeted a woman, a beautiful, honey-skinned young woman dressed the way the Javanese did, in the tight bodice and sarong. She was slim and fine boned and even from here Charlotte could see she was pregnant. Perhaps four months. The bump was obvious and the woman stood, the way pregnant women do, her back slightly sway and one hand protectively to the side of her belly. She smiled widely at the two men. She indicated the tiffin carriers in the hands of her two servants. Zhen lifted the lid on one and peeked inside the top level. He smiled and bowed to her. Charlotte let out a gasp.

She knew the wives brought lunches to the men in the godowns. She had seen this scene enacted a thousand times.

She turned away. So now she had only to decide when to leave. She was seven months pregnant. It would not be comfortable to travel with such a belly on the open seas, even on such new steamer passenger ships as were offered by the P&O. The overland part of the journey across the desert would be arduous. She should wait and see Amber settled, have her child.

But she couldn't do it. All the hardship in the world was not equal to the pain of being in the same town with him. Any revelations about this child would be embarrassing and pointless. He had begun a new family, one which would belong to him entirely.

She turned as Robert entered. His eyes flew open and his jaw dropped.

'My God, sister,' he said, staring at her belly. 'Is there any child of yours which will not be a total surprise.'

'Sorry, Rob,' she said, 'I do rather make a habit of it.'

He looked at her and put his head on one side.

'It's Zhen's?'

'Never mind that. Let's go. I need some lunch and then I want you to send a boy to get me a first-class ticket on the next liner leaving Singapore for London.'

'Like this. Blown up like a balloon. You intend to travel like this. And alone.'

'I came alone and I can leave alone. There shall be plenty of passengers on board willing to be my companions. And I shall not mind if there are not.'

Robert shook his head.

'How are little Robert and Andrew?'

Robert immediately forgot his sister's problems.

'Marvellous, marvellous. And Teresa is marvellous too. What a woman.'

Charlotte smiled and took Robert's arm.

* * *

Amber waited across the street from the medicine shop, watching. This was a quiet street of cloth merchants, pepper and gambier shops, spice emporia, trade goods which arrived from India and Persia and China, silks and porcelains, tin trays and manufactures from England, fine wines and perfumes from France.

An old Baba woman and her middle-aged daughter emerged

and Amber crossed the street and went inside.

A Chinese medicine shop has an odour peculiar to itself of herbs and mushrooms and wood all boiled together. It was strange but reassuring like the kitchen of her mother when she tried a new recipe.

It was empty and cool. The young clerk looked up and bowed. It was somewhat unusual to see an English lady in the shop but not rare. And she was pregnant. He moved around the counter and put a stool at her disposal.

'Thank you,' she said.

Unfortunately he could not speak English. He put up his finger, asking her to wait and went quickly upstairs to the office of the mistress. Dr. Kow Pah was leaning towards the mistress, their heads close together over some papers. He knocked and bowed.

Lian looked up from her desk. Dr. Cowper moved away to the sofa, looking embarrassed. Lian smiled at him.

'What is it?'

'An ang moh, downstairs,' he said. Lian glanced at John.

'Not ang moh, remember, *Englishman.*'

'Oh sorry. Not Englishman. *Englishwoman.*'

'I'm coming.'

The young man ran downstairs.

'I'll be a moment,' she said to John.

He came up to her and took her hand and put it to his lips. She kissed his cheek. She owed this man everything. Her life, first and foremost. His brilliance as a surgeon had saved her leg which had been broken in three places. He had repaired it and though she would always limp she had full use of it. He had repaired the gash in her skull too and, together with her father, they had found medicines and formulas to keep all the fevers at bay. She had been saved from instant death by a series of small shrubs that had broken her fall. John had done the rest.

But that was not why she loved him. She loved him because he had restored her mind through hours of care and love to a place where she was able to put aside, for the most part, the feelings of guilt and anguish.

'Say yes.'

'No, not until my baptism. And not until you have asked my father formally. I know he is happy about this and you're his friend but you're still an ang moh.'

'*Englishman*, remember,' he said and she laughed.

'I want everything by the book. Ask my father formally.'

'All right. But it doesn't have to be a religious ceremony. A civil marriage can be performed by Blackwood or even the governor.'

'I should like to be married in your church and in your faith. It's important to you and it is important to me too.'

He kissed her lightly on the lips and she pressed against him.

'My faith, as you put it, is not in the least important to me. I should just as well like a civil marriage. I would very much like not to wait too much longer, my darling.'

Lian kissed him again. She too wanted their married life to begin, but a swirl of doubts, like flocks of sparrows, occasionally assailed her.

'You are not certain I can have children, John. If that is the case, are you absolutely sure?'

He put his hand to her cheek.

'Absolutely sure.'

She put her lips to his and he took her in his arms, kissing her with a wildness belied by his seemingly gentlemanly nature. Under his English calm, he was a passionate man and she wanted his wildness and passion. It struck a chord in her nature and she loved him for being wild for her, knowing all her dreadful transgressions. His love absolved her and she kissed him back, abandoning herself to his kiss. She would be happy with him, of that she was absolutely certain. He picked up his hat and ran lightly down the stairs.

She followed him more slowly, careful of her leg, and instantly recognised the woman waiting for her.

'Amber,' she said quietly and went into the shop.

Amber turned. Lian's eyes went to her belly. Alex's baby. She was not sure she would ever quite get over Alex. She still loved him so much. The fact that it was morally wrong to love your half-brother in such a way did not mean such feelings disappeared. Certainly not in the short months since she had recovered her health. But this love was now tempered with reason and quiet resolve. Amber moved forward and Lian took her hands.

'Oh thank you for coming. Come upstairs.'

She led Amber to her sitting room and Amber saw how she limped and frowned a little. She looked around at the paper-strewn desk and the boxes of herbs and pills.

'You live here?'

'Yes. Father gave me this building and the shop to run. I am writing a medical treatise in English on Chinese medicine.'

'Gosh, Lian. You work?'

'Yes, amazing isn't it.'

'Gosh, your father is the most unorthodox man.'

Lian smiled. 'Yes.'

Amber sat on the sofa and Lian drew up a chair.

'Are you well, Amber? The baby.'

Amber looked down and patted her belly. 'Yes, all right. Been a bit hard, actually.'

'I'm sorry. I have no words.'

Amber looked up at Lian and tears sat in the corner of

her eyes.

'Are you angry with me, Amber?'

'Was. Really was. But what's the use. You nearly died.'

'I nearly died. Father and Dr. Cowper saved me.'

'You lost the baby.'

Lian felt the furrow of pain between her brows, then breathed deeply. 'Just as well, don't you think?'

Amber nodded. 'He went away. He couldn't stand us.' A silence fell into which floated the sounds of birdsong from the cages on the balcony next door.

'Will he come back,' Amber said, her eyes sad, 'do you think?'

'Perhaps, in a few years. He'll want to see his child.'

'I miss him, Lian,' Amber said and burst into tears.

Lian went to her friend and sat next to her and the two girls hugged. I miss him too, Lian wanted to say, but knew she could not.

'I know it's morally reprehensible to say it after all we've been through, but this baby of yours, well, it's my niece or nephew.'

Amber sat up and dried her eyes. 'Gosh, I never thought about that.'

'Can I love it, Amber? Will you let me love Alex's child?'

'You're my oldest friend, you know. It's not our fault. Aunt Charlotte told me that. It's her fault. Your father begged and begged to tell Alex but she never would. None of this would have happened if she'd told Alex who he was.'

'Poor Charlotte. She was so good to me, you know. Tried so hard for me. I can't blame her. We all do things we regret.'

Amber sighed. 'Yes. We do. Of course you can love this baby. Why should it not have as much as it can get? Its father might not be around.'

'Oh, thank you, Amber.'

The two girls hugged again.

'You know,' Amber said, 'I'm frightfully thirsty.'

'Want some tea? Chinese tea.'

Amber made a face. 'Gosh, Lian, how foul. Are you mad?'

'English then. Come on, in the kitchen.'

Amber rose. 'Did you hear Sarah Blundell married some massively fat and wealthy old Anglo Indian towkay? Marry for love indeed, little hypocrite.'

Lian laughed. In the kitchen she added some sticks to the fire and put water on for the tea. She busied herself with cups. Amber sat and rubbed her belly.

'I'm glad to be home. Aunt Charlotte's going back to Scotland.'

'Is she? That's sad.'

'Not so much sad as mad. Sailing on ships at her age when she's so pregnant is jolly silly.'

Lian turned and faced her friend.

43

'The booking is made,' Robert said. 'First class all the way. Steamer to Bombay via Galle, then on to Suez, train overland and pick up the steamer in Alexandria. Goes to Marseilles, train to Paris then Calais and packet to Dover. Thirty-six days, give or take. The ship departs in three days.'

'Rob, amazing isn't it. Remember our voyage out? Took six months under sail on the high seas. How did we manage it?'

'Ignorance and nothing else to be done. But Kitt, I am worried. This is such a rush. You've hardly been here a week and now you intend to depart. Thirty-nine days when you are now over seven months pregnant. At Dover I'm told the rail line is not complete and in imperfect condition so you may have to take a coach. And even then you will have the long train journey to Aberdeen. It is a voyage of some enormity in your condition. Anything could happen. And nothing in place up there for the birth. Reconsider, please. Wait and have the baby here and then we can organise nursemaids and such and you can travel in perfect safety.'

Teresa rose and came to Charlotte's side.

'Yes, dear Charlotte, please reconsider. This journey is unwise at this time.'

'All will be well. Don't worry.'

'Mr. and Mrs. Macpherson are travelling to Edinburgh on the same voyage. I've asked them to look out for you.'

'You see, I shall be perfectly fine. And doubtless there are many others. We shall all be a jolly crew.'

Teresa shook her head angrily and frowned at Robert. He responded. 'Sister, nevertheless, this is foolhardy. Without a doctor on board, I am worried.'

Charlotte smiled.

'Look at you two. How lucky is little Robert to have you, Teresa, so forgiving and loving. Robert, you are a lucky man.'

She rose. Teresa threw a look of anguish at Robert.

'Kitt, I feel this journey is most unwise.'

He had tried to inject a tone of manly authority in his voice but he knew he had failed. Charlotte left the room.

Teresa rose and put her hand on Robert's.

'Something is terribly wrong. It's like she doesn't care if she survives or not. I am very worried.'

Robert patted Teresa's hand but he, too, now considered his sister to be taking steps which would endanger her life and the child's.

'You must stop this, Rob,' Teresa said.

'My dear, she has never listened to me in her life. Why would she start now?'

Teresa walked to the window, agitated, her handkerchief twisting in her hand.

'Robert, is there no-one who can speak to her? Surely there is someone.' She reeled suddenly and looked at him intensely. 'Whose baby is this? In all this with little Robert and Amber returning, I never thought to ask.'

'Well,' Robert said, looking at his feet.

'You're a fool, Robert Macleod. And so am I. Of course, it is the Chinese man's child. She's never loved anyone else, the same way as I have never loved anyone but you. He must know. If he has an ounce of decency he will stop this.'

She went into the hall. She took up her bonnet. Robert opened his mouth but no sound came out. He felt drained and longed to return to murder and thievery.

Teresa had seen this man many times. Her sister-in-law had been, truly still was, notorious. She had not cared, for Charlotte had always, through all the trouble with Robert, been kind to her. She had never spoken to this Chinese man, but now she did not consider this at all. She called for the carriage and told the syce to drop her at the wooden bridge.

She crossed it with purpose and sought the godown she knew he owned. On the quayside she saw Lian, Amber's friend, the daughter of Zhen, the Chinese man. And Lian saw her.

'Teresa, hello.'

'Lian, my dear. Are you all right?'

The suicide attempt of this girl had been a great shock. It seemed to be connected to her marriage to the Chinese man but other than that Teresa knew nothing. But, over the last few years, Teresa realised that certain miseries were known only to oneself.

'Now, yes. Thank you.'

'Look,' Teresa said, 'I need to speak to your father. About Charlotte.'

'Yes, I've come to speak to him too.'

Teresa, surprised, nevertheless forged on. 'She intends to depart for England in the most inauspicious circumstances.'

'You mean she is pregnant.'

Teresa stared at Lian. 'Yes, she is very pregnant and if she takes this voyage it will be the death of her and the child. I'm certain of it.'

'My father doesn't know.'

'Doesn't know?'

'That she is pregnant. I'm quite sure of it.'

Teresa looked towards the godown. 'Come on,' she said.

She hesitated before the door. She had never in her life set foot in a Chinese establishment of this sort. Lian took her arm.

'Father,' she called.

* * *

The suitcase was almost finished. The maid had done an excellent job with the trunk. She folded her nightgown and felt a pain in her side. She sat on the bed. These pains had increased over the last few days. She tried to think. She was almost seven and a half months pregnant. If she went into labour now, the child might survive but how could she know? She longed so to leave. She felt driven by this one imperative, unable to think of anything else.

She heard the bell downstairs. Robert coming to try to persuade her to stay, she presumed. She was so tired of them all. She rose from the bed and checked the tickets. The steamer to Galle took four days, was that right? Then on to Bombay. She felt a great fatigue and put the tickets away.

I'll look at them later, she thought.

A knock came at the door. The Malay maid entered. 'A visitor to see you, puan, in the drawing room.'

'No,' she said. 'No visitors.'

The door flew wide.

'Xia Lou,' he said.

He gazed at her. She was immensely pregnant. It was true. Lian and Teresa, Robert's wife, had beseeched him to come. 'Go,' he said to the maid, and shut the door. 'What are you thinking?

You intend to travel in this condition?'

'Go away,' she said.

'No,' he said. 'Here we are again. This is my child.'

'So what,' she said and shook her head. It felt like it might fly off her shoulders.

'Why will you never tell me? First Alex and now this.'

She shrugged.

'Do you have news of Alex?'

'No, but I will. It's only a matter of time. Eyes and ears are all over the East. He's strong. He'll be all right.'

'Do you think so? Really, Zhen? How can he forgive me?'

'Time. Time will do it. And he may wish to see his son one day, eh?'

Charlotte nodded. Then she looked at him sharply. 'You might have taken some precautions,' she said. 'It was that afternoon. Why must you always be so damned imperious? You just do whatever you want.'

She ran out of that thought. It hardly seemed to matter. She moved away from him. He followed her with his eyes.

'You like what I do very well,' he said and she shook her head, exasperated. 'You did not marry Commander Whatshisname?'

She turned and cast him a look of annoyance, indicating her belly. 'Hardly, with your child growing inside me.'

'So it was a lie. In Batavia. You had no intention of marrying the man. You knew you were pregnant and told me a lie.'

Charlotte flushed and turned away from him.

'You could have got rid of it, married him. But you didn't.'

Charlotte sighed and shrugged again.

Zhen walked towards her, stood close behind her. 'Xia Lou, it's time to put a stop to all this.'

She turned, startled to find him so close, her belly touching him. He looked down and put his hands on either side of this bump, holding her gently to him. She pulled away. 'Stop it. Yes, time to stop it. I'm leaving. I want you to have this new life. A new wife, a child.'

'What are you talking about?'

'I saw her. The beautiful young one. Pregnant. On the quayside.'

Zhen nodded. 'Ah, yes, the beautiful one. Pregnant. But not by me.'

Charlotte stared at him. 'Not you.'

'No. She is the daughter of Cheng Sam Teo and married to the Temenggong's youngest brother, Hussein. He's twenty and splendidly handsome and besotted with her. They are immensely happy, or so I hear. A most auspicious marriage. Certainly for Cheng.'

Charlotte moved to a chair and sat. Her belly felt heavy as lead. 'I'm so fat,' she wailed, hardly recognising the relief at this news.

He shook his head. He knelt before her and put his lips against her belly, then ran his hands around it, feeling the child within. 'You are pregnant. That is what happens.'

She gazed on his head and put her hand to his queue. 'Zhen, I ...'

He rose and put his lips to hers in a long soft kiss.

She closed her eyes and fell into it, this kiss. Like their first kiss, so exquisite, so melting. Then her eyes flew open. 'You aren't married.'

He smiled. 'Of course I'm not married.'

'But concubines, do you have any?'

'Just one very reluctant one, whom I love.'

She knew it was all true. Tears sprang to her eyes. 'Whom

you love.'

'Yes,' he said and put his lips against her ear. 'I love you,' he whispered.

She laughed and wiped the tears away. He'd said it, those tiny words which she had thought never to hear him utter.

'We made love when I was very pregnant.'

'Yes,' he said. 'It was delicious. I remember.'

'I feel incredibly aroused all the time,' she said. 'When I'm not absolutely exhausted, of course.'

'Do you?'

'Yes.' She put her lips up to his, wanting his kiss again, but he stood and backed away from her.

'Most unfortunate.'

She struggled to stand and he put out his hand. She grasped it and came to her feet. 'Why?'

'Because I realise that I can't touch you again until we have done the only thing left for us to do.'

She raised an eyebrow. She felt better. Much better. She put her hand onto her belly. The child had woken up and was clearly feeling full of vitality.

'Which is?'

'To get married. For heaven's sake, woman, I'm growing old. Just say yes.'

She smiled. She had contemplated a life without him and even the idea of her own death. What fears did this step hold any more?

'Yes.'

He grinned and took a white box from his pocket. The necklace emerged in his hand.

She went to him and he bent and put his lips to hers, softer than silk. She sighed and put her arms around his neck, touching the thickness of his queue, burying herself in his kiss. Nothing had changed, she could kiss him for hours.

The child gave a great kick and he laughed.

'It's a boy. I'm certain of it.'

She released him. 'Does it matter?'

'No. It doesn't matter. I will love any child of ours. You know that.'

She smiled at him and put her hand to his cheek. 'I know. But you Chinese. You're all mad for boys.'

He moved behind her and fastened the clasp. The red threads settled onto her neck and the pearl lay cool against her skin. He put his lips against them, the silken threads. This love for her. It was a constant and intriguing mystery.

'You know,' he murmured. 'There is a legend.'

The Straits Quartet

by Dawn Farnham

Singapore's most passionate series of historical romance

Drawing on real-life historical personalities from 19th-century Singapore, author Dawn Farnham brings to life the heady atmosphere of Old Singapore where piracy, crime, triads and tigers are commonplace. This intense and passionate romance follows the struggle of two lovers: Charlotte Macleod, sister of Singapore's Head of Police, and Zhen, triad member and once the lowliest of coolies who attempts to beat the odds to become a wealthy Chinese merchant.

Opium, murder, incest, suicide, passion and love ... an intoxicating combination in the sin city of the south seas.

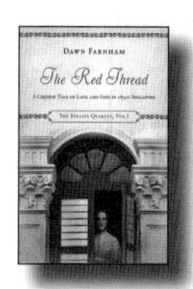

| THE RED THREAD | THE SHALLOW SEAS | THE HILLS OF SINGAPORE | THE ENGLISH CONCUBINE |

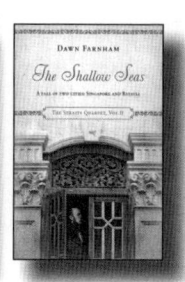

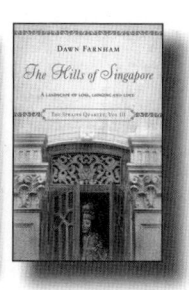

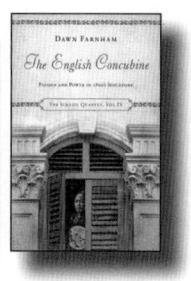

A Crowd of Twisted Things

by Dawn Farnham

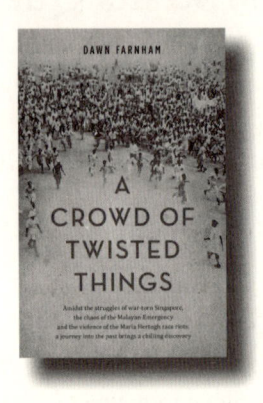

In December 1950, the worst riots Singapore had ever seen shut down the town for days, killing 18 people and wounding 173. Racial and religious tension had been simmering for months over the custody battle for wartime waif Maria Hertogh between her Malay-Muslim foster mother and her Dutch-Catholic biological parents.

In May 1950, Eurasian Annie Collins, following this case and filled with hope, returns to Singapore seeking her own lost baby. As the time bomb ticks and Annie unravels the threads of her quest into increasingly dangerous territory, she finds strange recollections intruding, ones that have nothing to do with her own memories of her wartime experiences: disturbing visions and dreams which force her to doubt not just her past life, but her whole idea of who she truly is and even to question the search itself. Twisted memories, twisted minds, twisted lives, twisted beliefs, the twists of fate and their tangled consequences.

A Crowd of Twisted Things is at once a lament for the loss and damage of war, an unravelling mystery and a journey into suppressed memory and the nature of self-delusion.